Addicted to Glove

Kelly Reynolds

Contents

Author's Note

Welcome back to Rose City, Oregon, home of the Roasters! Dani and Brooks' story marks the fourth installment—and third novel—in this smalltown baseball romance series about big girls and boys with bigger . . . *baseballs*. **That being said, every book can be read as a standalone**.

Please be advised that this book is an open-door romance, meaning there is on-page, explicit sexual content (between consenting adults) including oral sex, vaginal sex, spanking, lots of dirty talk, and one very sensual leg shaving session. And just in case, you prefer to skip—*or skip to*—the **NSFW content, check out chapters 3, 13, 14, 22, 23, 27, and 30**.

There is also recreational use of alcohol, multiple scenes in a doctor's office and/or hospital room, plus discussions about biphobia, pregnancy, and parental neglect. Mature readers only.

This book is meant to be enjoyed alongside a bowl of ice cream . . . pickles and potato chips, optional.

*For the women who dream of motherhood **and** the women who'd rather raise hell than children—*

your choice is valid, your story matters, and you are whole either way.

Roasters Lineup

#12   Roman Garcia   1B
#16   Wesley Nuñez   CF
#2   Johnathan Tucker   2B
#4   Soren Sinclair   3B
#18   Matty Miller   SS
#9   Peter Diaz   LF
#6   Bennett King   C
#16   Nathaniel Wu   RF
#0   Jared Pink   P

Dani

Opening Day

The only thing better than pound cake at two a.m. was getting pounded at two a.m.

Unfortunately, the only one getting pounded tonight was my roommate's girlfriend. The two of them had been going at it for over an hour.

I nearly tumbled from my perch on the kitchen counter when the cuckoo clock in the dining nook chimed—the one Pink had insisted on bringing back from Germany last month, despite the astronomical shipping cost.

Make that two hours.

I scooped up another bite of cake, topping it off with some Cherry Garcia, a handful of Flamin' Hot Cheetos, and finally, the pièce de résistance, one of Pink's homemade bread and butter pickles. The guy might have painfully loud, wall-banging sex, but at least he knew his way around the kitchen.

And garden, for that matter. Our fridge was stocked with more homegrown produce than most farmers' markets thanks to his green thumb—er, *Pink* thumb. Who would have guessed that living with a pro-baseball player would yield so many benefits?

Just not *those* kinds of benefits.

A series of moans and groans echoed down the stairs, keeping pace with the headboard thwacking the wall. For fuck's sake, I knew that athletes—especially those nearly ten years my junior—had incredible stamina, but they had to come up for air at some point, right? Or, at the very least, replenish their . . . fluids.

Bleh.

I suppressed the urge to gag. It was probably best not to focus on my friend-turned-roommate's fluids while eating. He had already tainted donuts for me when I'd walked in on him and Nessa acting out some phallic ring toss fantasy in our living room on Valentine's Day.

There was no way he was taking Ben and Jerry from me, too. Especially not when I needed them most.

Growing up, ice cream had always been a luxury, one reserved for every other birthday—to "keep me humble"—or when my mom had brought home more tips than usual. It had been all she could afford, and I'd accepted that. But I'd also more than made up for it as an adult.

These days, I kept at least one pint stocked in the freezer at all times. It was a hard and fast rule of mine, a reminder of just how far I had come since leaving our one-bedroom apartment in South Baltimore fifteen years ago. Just yesterday, I had re-stocked my supply, opting for Cherry Garcia and something called Spuds and Fudge.

Nothing exorcised my personal demons quite like a bowl of Vermont's finest—it was my therapy in a cardboard cup. That or a long run. I could outrun half of the guys on the team, and I had the gold medal from this past fall's Rosé Run to prove it.

Pink was still salty about that one.

I rested my head back against the upper cabinets and focused on the swirl of cherry, chocolate, and pickle brine coalescing in the bottom of my bowl, like a chocolate milk and pickleback hybrid. Minus the alcohol, of course.

Fuck, I was gonna miss vodka.

"Hey."

I looked up just as Nessa padded down the final few steps, clad only in a T-shirt, panties, and that "I just get railed" smile.

"Couldn't sleep?" she asked.

"It's a little hard to, what with all the . . . banging."

A pink hue colored her cheeks. It wasn't a blush born from embarrassment, but rather satisfaction—earned and shameless—the kind of glow that came from good sex and zero regrets.

And why shouldn't she be proud? Nessa, a born and bred Rose City native, had bagged *the* Jared Pink, Cy Young Award nominee and, as of last year, a World Series champion. On top of that, business was booming at her romance bookstore, Smutty Buddies, though that had less to do with who her boyfriend was and more to do with her being a boss ass bitch.

Then again, it didn't hurt that several of the guys on the team had started their own book club and were known to stop by the shop at any given moment. The Rose City Roasters had officially made it to Booktok.

Nessa and I had become fast friends even before she and Pink had started dating. No surprise there, though. Two tattooed, bisexual girls who used sarcasm as a defense mechanism? We'd basically been cut from the same dysfunctional cloth.

"Right," she said, biting her bottom lip like she was almost sorry. *Almost.* "Guess we weren't exactly subtle."

I gave her a look.

"Subtle? Ness, the drywall moved."

She laughed, soft and low, rubbing the back of her neck like she was trying not to look too pleased with herself. There was no hiding the pride in her eyes . . . or the glint of something else—concern, maybe—once she took in the nearly empty bowl in my lap and the way I was clinging to my spoon like it might help me fend off reality.

"Did I interrupt a . . . party?" she asked gently, nodding toward my briny ice cream soup.

"More like a . . . meltdown," I muttered.

Nessa arched her brow and leaned against the counter, close enough that I could smell her signature vanilla lotion beneath the remnants of sleep and sex. "Everything okay?"

And just like that, the mood shifted. The casual banter between us dissipated, leaving behind an aftertaste that was neither sweet nor pickle-y. This was it, the moment I had been dreading all day. But there was no point denying the obvious any longer. It was time to put on my big-girl panties—preferably the purple cotton ones with skulls—and get this over with.

The test was still in the pocket of my *Scooby-Doo* pajama pants, tucked beside a crumpled tissue and antacid. I pulled out the offensive piece of plastic and tossed it onto the counter, watching it slide across the white quartz until it skidded to a stop next to the still-open pickle jar.

Ness looked down at it, then up at me, then back down, as if the word blinking up at us like a small, digital billboard might change any second. Maybe if we stared at it long enough, it would.

"That's a pregnancy test."

Wordlessly, I reached into my other pocket and pulled out the others—all three of them.

Her jaw dropped a little. "That's a whole *lot* of pregnancy tests."

"Well, I'm a whole lot pregnant."

She let out a weird little puff of laughter that was one part disbelief and two parts trying not to ask too many questions at once.

At least now we were on the same page.

"When did you— How did you— Who did you?"

I choked back a laugh. "You're lucky we speak the same language."

That language being *Da Fuck?!?*

"And to answer your questions," I said calmly, finally accepting my fate. "I just found out today. As for how, assuming my guesstimation is correct, that would be up against the wall outside your brother's bar. Is that specific enough for you?"

The furrowing of her brows told me she was too busy doing the mental math to register my snarky response. "And *who*?"

That was the million-dollar, hormone-fueled question—a curious case for Velma, Shaggy, and the rest of the Mystery Gang. The case of a *bump* in the road.

Only, this mystery wasn't so mysterious after all. There had only been one man in my bed for months now, and judging by the sudden widening of Nessa's grayish green eyes, she knew as well as I did who was to blame for my . . . situation.

"*Who*, Dani?"

I swirled my spoon through the sweet sludge in the bottom of my bowl, avoiding her glare.

"Don't you dare hide behind Ben and Jerry." She reached over, snatched the dish out of my hands, and plopped it on the counter with a dramatic thunk. "Talk."

I sighed, long and slow. "It's Brooks."

Nessa blinked. "Brooks Bailey-Ward?"

"The one and only."

But that wasn't true. Brooks Bailey-Ward—*my* Brooks Bailey-Ward, though I had never, and would never, refer to him as such in public—was in fact, the *third* in a line of professional-baseball stars-turned-coaches.

And I might be carrying the fourth.

Fuck, that was a sobering thought.

"Holy. Fucking. Shit."

"Shh," I scolded, eyeing the stairs at her back. "Keep it down."

Pink did *not* need to know about this—not yet at least. Hell, I was still trying to wrap my head around the idea of being a parent without feeling like I might throw up or shit myself—or worse, some combination of the two—at any given second, so the thought of telling my roommate—my *best friend*—that I was three months pregnant with his boss's spawn did not sit well with me.

Also, there were certain things you just didn't discuss with friends, and one of those was the R-rated play-by-play of how their boss had knocked you up.

Hard pass.

"I can't believe it." Nessa's hands flew up to her mouth. "You're having a baby with Coach Daddy."

"Please, never call him that again."

"Oh, I will one-hundred percent be calling him that again. Between the muscles, full body tats, and slutty little glasses, the man looks like he could be on the cover of a romance novel." Her eyes lit up. "Or a calendar. Oh, Dani, can you *please* organize some kind of Roasters calendar?"

I dropped my head forward. "One crisis at a time, please."

Nonetheless, I made a mental note to reach out to the head of our community relations department. If the bachelor auction during last fall's Buns and Roses Festival had proven anything, it was that the girls, gays, and theys all wanted a piece of the Rose City Roasters.

Nessa paced across the tiles, one hand raking through her mussed sex hair, the other waving at the pregnancy tests like they were cursed relics. "How long?"

"Geez, I don't know. It might take a few months to organize the photo shoot, but we could definitely get the calendars out by Thanksgiving—"

"No." Nessa leaned on the counter across from me, her teasing expression slipping into something gentler. "How long has it been since you guys started things up again?"

Silence stretched between us. The rain outside ticked against the kitchen windows like a metronome counting down to impact. Nessa and Pink were the only ones who knew about my fling with Brooks—the first time around, that was. Like most of my relationships, ours had been short, hot, and complicated beyond repair. As had our breakup, if you could even call it that.

What had started one hell of a fuck fest had quickly spiraled into the most awkward night of my life, one that had ended with Nessa and Brooks bumping into each other in our upstairs hallway.

Naked.

There'd been no coming back after that—nothing soured a secret relationship faster than the truth.

"It's not like that," I said.

Nessa gave me a pointed look. "Please don't tell me you've been secretly hooking up with Coach Daddy this whole time."

"Not the *whole* time," I replied, holding up my hands in mock surrender. "We had a nice little stretch of mutual avoidance. Very healthy. Very mature."

She gaped at me. "And then?"

I gave her a slow, knowing smile.

"Then came New Year's Eve."

Dani

Three Months Ago

*A*nother year, another vodka lemonade.

We were closing in on midnight, and thank fuck for that because I was freezing my ass off. It was my own fault for choosing a skirt over my go-to pair of high-waisted, acid-wash jeans that looked like they had been pulled straight from a 90s Abercrombie ad. In actuality, I had "forgotten" to return them to my ex after she'd dumped me for her coworker.

That's what happens when you cheat on me.

She couldn't keep it in her pants . . . so I'd taken them.

Sure, it was probably too cold for a skirt, but it was also New Year's Eve. I owed it to my hot ass self to show a little leg. Especially since my latest thigh tattoo—a fine-line tarot card design I had gifted myself for my birthday—had just finished healing.

An empress for an empress.

I had picked up the skirt on a whim during the team's last road series to Nashville. It was short, black, and cut with a deep slit on the left side that would have made my mother cringe—just the way I liked it. It was snug but not suffocating, showing off the tattoos that curled up my legs like wild ivy, and it paired perfectly with my deep burgundy tube top that left little to the imagination and even less room for a bra. Not that I would have worn one anyway. I was a card-carrying member of the itty-bitty titty committee, so the girls were doing just fine on their own.

Platform combat boots completed the look, because five-foot-three or not, heels had never been my style. I liked knowing I could stomp someone if I needed to—metaphorically or otherwise.

If I was going to ring in another year full of questionable decisions, I might as well do it while looking like a bad ass bitch.

"Thirty minutes to go," Nero shouted from behind the bar. "If you want a fresh drink before midnight, grab it now. Don't be the dick who waits until 11:59."

Hoots and hollers sounded over the music.

Thorn Tavern was glowing. Not in a flashy, gimmicky kind of way meant for attracting social media influencers, but rather in the warm, familiar glow of a place that had been well-loved for generations.

Nero wouldn't have it any other way.

It was a neighborhood bar through and through—always had been, even well before the Roasters had moved into Rose City, Oregon. He had made some cosmetic changes since inheriting it from his mom, but something told me he would sooner burn the place to the ground than see it turned into an Instagrammable watering hole. Hell, he'd nearly blown a gasket last week when Pink's sister, Bella, had recommended he stock kombucha.

"This is a bar, not a farmer's market," he had told her, this coming from the man who infused his vodkas with yuzu and orange peels.

Thorn Tavern had become the Roasters' favorite postgame spot, which meant men and women alike came from far and wide to enjoy a game—along with the game-day drink specials—and hopefully, if they were lucky, take home a hot baseballer.

In my experience, a quick and dirty fuck—even with a professional athlete—was easy to come by. The tavern's famous

"Totchos," on the other hand, were one of a kind. I had had *naughty* dreams about those ooey-gooey, bacon-covered potatoes on more than one occasion. Positively sinful.

Speaking of sinful things that were no good for me . . .

I checked my phone for the umpteenth time and then cursed myself for doing so. *Don't go there.* New Year's Eve was all about starting over, after all. A fresh start. Yet here I was, decked out in sequins and dripping in sex appeal, and all I could think about was a certain bearded and bespectacled behemoth—more specifically, about how that beard felt between my thighs.

"Nope," I said, popping the "p" with my copper-painted lips.

"No, you don't want Champagne?"

I looked up from my phone just as Nessa settled back into the empty chair to my left, armed with two Champagne flutes. Her silver-gray jumpsuit hugged every delicious curve of her size-twenty body. Seriously, if Pink didn't wife her up someday soon, I would happily volunteer.

"Earth to Dani," she said when I didn't answer. "Champagne?"

I waved her off, gesturing to the glass in my hand. "I've already had more than I probably should."

"And I haven't had enough, so gimme!" June demanded. "We've got thirty minutes until the new year. That's plenty of time to squeeze in at least one more bad decision. Two, if I'm lucky."

Nessa, June, and I had taken over the corner booth next to the jukebox. Pink was currently at the bar with Nero, probably arguing over pour size, a losing battle if I ever saw one. Clarke was holding court in one of the large, leather reading chairs beside the fireplace, half on Soren's lap, half in her umpteenth glass of punch. Her party hat was on sideways—not that she or Soren seemed to care. He was too mesmerized by her exposed cleavage, and she was too focused on trash-talking our shortstop's new girlfriend. A match made in heaven.

"I'm just saying," Clarke slurred lightly, "Matty deserves better."

"Blondie, you only met her once," Soren soothed, stroking her bare shoulders with love and admiration, like she was the most precious gem in the world. To Soren, she was.

"Once was enough. The woman has her nose so high in the air she could . . . drown in a rainstorm."

I snorted around my sip of vodka lemonade. Clarke and I had been working together for nearly a year and yet somehow, she still managed to surprise me with her Southernisms. They certainly made the workday more interesting—because yes, believe it or not, even being the social media director for a pro-baseball team had dullish moments.

Nessa leaned into my side, close enough for her minty-fresh breath to fan my cheek. "Who is she talking about again?"

"Matty's new girlfriend," I answered. "Lila something. Apparently, she talks about herself in the third person."

Nessa grimaced. "That's not *that* bad."

"*And* she's a wine snob," Clarke added.

We all collectively groaned—even Soren. There was a special circle in hell reserved solely for wine snobs, just between the losers who didn't return their shopping carts and men who never washed their assholes.

"Yikes," June said through gritted teeth. "A double whammy."

"Poor Matty," Nessa lamented.

"Poor *Lila*." I polished off my drink. "Mo is going to eat her alive."

Mo was Matty's nine-month-old basset hound and the most territorial bitch I had ever met. This Lila didn't stand a chance.

I sat back, tuning out the girlfriend slander and instead, turning my attention to the string lights draped overhead, reflecting off the glassware polished to a shine. The whole tavern smelled like campfire, wood varnish, and whiskey-soaked memories. It was exactly what you wanted from a neighborhood bar, the kind of place where people *actually* knew your name and where they came to remember, forget, or fall in love—and sometimes all three in one night.

That was Rose City, a town that made space for strangers and residents alike, exactly as they were—messy, loud, broken, brilliant. They all had a home here.

And I did, too.

I was still trying to wrap my head around it—or maybe that was the vodka talking—but at some point over the past few months, I had stopped thinking of Rose City as just another stopover in my career and had started treating it as a potential forever. Me, a thirty-two-year-old orphan who had spent the first half of her life dreaming of a world beyond her rowhouse stoop and the second half bouncing from one city to the next, searching for somewhere, anywhere to belong. Who would have guessed I would find it three-thousand miles away in a town so small, it didn't even have a mayor?

The clock ticked down, inching closer to midnight. Partygoers flocked to scoop up snacks and drink refills. In between the chaos, I couldn't help but notice a blond man leaning against the bar top, watching me like he thought he was being subtle.

Spoiler alert: he wasn't. I had clocked him thirty minutes ago, as had the rest of my friends.

"You should go talk to him," Clarke suggested, appearing at my side like a chaotic party goblin. "Don't you want somebody to kiss at midnight?"

I arched a brow. "Aww, babe, are you offering?"

She never had a chance to respond. A large, hairy arm circled her waist, dragging her away. "Sorry, Dani," Soren said, his voice thick with lust. "I've already got big plans for her lips tonight."

Clarke giggled, settling back onto Soren's lap. "I'm serious. He's cute and well-dressed *and* really knows how to rock a . . ." She turned toward June. "What do you call it?"

"Porn 'stache."

The table burst into a fit of giggles while Clarke blushed at the mention of anything remotely risqué.

Pink tilted his glass in my direction. "I'm with Clarke Kent. He doesn't look like a total douchebag. In fact, he reminds me of somebody."

"Freddie Mercury?" I offered. "Temu edition."

He leaned in conspiratorially and winked. "Just imagine what he can do with that mustache."

"Jesus," I muttered, but I couldn't help the laugh that slipped out. "I appreciate the thought, but hey, I'm not the only single one at this table. Maybe June wants him."

She shook her head. "Nah, I'm officially declaring myself emotionally unavailable to male energy for tonight." Her eyes bounced between Soren and Pink. "No offense, guys."

"None taken," they answered simultaneously.

"You don't have to marry the guy," Clarke said, not letting up. She had officially crossed from tipsy and cute to drunk and bold. "But some harmless flirtation couldn't hurt. Or a kiss at midnight. When was the last time you really kissed somebody?"

Nessa arched a brow at me over her drink, making my stomach lurch. We were skirting dangerously close to the edge of that memory. To *him*. But Clarke didn't know that.

In fact, the only people in the world who knew anything about my last kiss were Pink and Nessa, and that was only because Nessa had bumped into him in our upstairs hallway.

Naked.

Him, not Nessa.

The events that followed were permanently etched in my brain like the ink on my skin. Nessa had screamed, Pink had rushed in, and that was how my best friend *and* roommate had found out that I was screwing his boss, Brooks Bailey-Ward.

Coach Daddy.

He may have been Coach Ward to Soren, Pink, and the rest of the Roaster family, but the fans had affectionately—sometimes *too* affectionately—had referred to him as Coach Daddy since he'd signed with the Roasters. With good reason, too—he was a daddy, in all senses of the word.

He was probably at home right now. Warm house, dim lights, his daughter, Carolina, tucked in upstairs with her mermaid nightlight and a mountain of Squishmallows. I imagined him reading to her, voice low and steady, that soft scratch of stubble on his jaw as he turned the page. I could practically smell the cedarwood on his hoodie.

God, I was pathetic.

"You're zoning out," Nessa said, leaning into me like a nosy little devil on my shoulder.

"I'm good," I told her, a little too fast.

"You're lying."

She wasn't wrong.

I pulled out my phone and reread his last few messages.

Brooks

> Carolina and I watched Princess Diaries. You were right. She loved it.

A smile tugged at my lips when he followed up almost immediately with another text.

Brooks

> I did, too.

That had been three weeks ago.

I stared at the screen for a long moment, thumbs hovering. This was a mistake. It was nearly midnight. He was a single dad; he was probably in bed by now.

And still, I hit send.

Me

> Happy almost New Year.

There. It was too late now. I stared at the speech bubble, heart thudding wildly.

Me

> Nessa and Pink dragged me out to the tavern to celebrate. Lucky me. Do you have Carolina tonight?

Nessa was watching me like a hawk now, which made it even worse. Thankfully, she didn't press me on it.

Seconds turned into minutes. The music swelled around us until finally, we reached the final countdown to midnight. I tried to sink into the noise, into the safety of my friends and the chaos of a bar gearing up for a new year, but my brain was somewhere else entirely—looping back to Brooks's well-worn, navy hoodie that always smelled like *him* and the way he carried his daughter in one arm while holding a coffee in the other like some goddamn domestic fever dream.

Competent men were my kink.

And just when I had given up hope, my phone buzzed across the table.

I didn't check it. Not right away. Not with Nessa still eyeing me sideways, like she could smell the emotional recklessness on me. Hell, she probably could.

"I'm gonna use the bathroom," I said, sliding out of the booth.

"But it's almost midnight," Clarke sputtered. "Don't you want—"

"Clarke, I love you, and I promise, first thing in the morning, you can continue your matchmaking efforts. But right now, all I really want is to pee in peace."

I barely spared my friends a glance before darting through the crowd, my heart pounding harder than it should've been. I wasn't even sure why I'd texted him. Maybe I was a glutton for punishment. Or maybe I just needed to touch the wound, make sure it still hurt.

I never made it to the bathroom. Instead, I ducked under somebody's arm and found an empty spot at the end of the bar. Being short and petite definitely had its perks.

"Ten . . . nine . . . eight . . ."

Around me, strangers threw arms around each other. Champagne flutes were raised, the air vibrating with possibilities—or the illusion of them, at least.

"Seven . . . six . . ."

I glanced down at my phone, my finger poised over his name, unread message still glowing.

"Five . . . four . . ."

Maybe it was nothing.

"Three!"

Maybe I was hoping it wasn't.

"Two! One!"

Maybe I needed to get some fresh air.

The room erupted into cheers. Couples crashed together in a series of wet, messy kisses, strangers clapped, someone—Temu Freddy Mercury—howled at the ceiling like a wolf, and I smiled through every second of it, faking it like the pro that I was.

I pushed through the crowd and out the front door, the cold air hitting me like a slap.

And that was when I saw him, hands tucked into his joggers, wearing *that* hoodie and his signature, black-rimmed glasses.

Nerdy and dirty, just the way I liked them.

The world faded behind me, the noise muffled by the glass door I'd just walked through.

"Hey," he said softly.

I blinked. "What are you doing here?"

"You texted."

"I know, but I didn't think . . ."

I trailed off when he stepped forward, closing the distance between us. And just like that, I wasn't cold anymore. In fact, I was burning up.

"Happy New Year, Dani."

Brooks

Three Months Ago

This was a mistake.

I knew it from the second I pulled out of the driveway, when I rolled through not one, but two stop signs during the fifteen-minute drive over to the bar, and then again when I parked across the street and just sat there, staring through the windshield like some creep with poor judgment and even worse impulse control.

That was what Dani Bernal did to me.

I hadn't heard from her in nearly a month, not since my pathetic attempt at sparking conversation about Anne Hathaway movies, like some high-school boy. She had no idea how many times I had drafted a text to her over the past few weeks, all of which I had promptly deleted.

Type, pause, insert emoji, rethink emoji, backspace, backspace, backspace.

Every fucking time.

But when *she* texted *me*? The second her name lit up my phone, all reasoning went out the window.

One minute, I was watching *Below Deck: Mediterranean*—my latest guilty pleasure, "brain rot" show—and eating vegan chicken tenders, and the next, I was speeding down the hill.

All because she texted.

It was official: I had it bad. For a woman twelve years younger than I was, no less.

Fuck, maybe I am a creep.

There was no other way to explain loitering outside the only bar in Rose City on New Year's Eve—my least favorite holiday—like a fucking idiot, freezing my fucking balls off, all because I hadn't thought things through long enough to grab a real fucking coat.

I should've waited in the fucking car.

But when the door to the bar opened and I saw her, my entire body went up in flames. She stared at me like she had seen a ghost. Gorgeous green eyes blinking rapidly, pouty lips agape. Blood rushed straight to my cock when I remembered the delicious things she could do with those lips.

Cheers and music filtered through the bar windows. "Sounds like one hell of a party."

She straightened. "What are you doing here?"

"You texted me."

"Well, yeah, but I didn't think you would just—"

She waved her arms wildly, gesturing toward my body. I bit back a smile when she zeroed in on my crotch.

"And yet, here I am," I said, stepping closer to her.

She looked good. *Too good.*

Her jet-black hair had grown out since we had last seen each other, enough for the teal-colored ends to tickle the roses inked on her neck, just below her ear. Dani changed her hair more often than most people changed their bedsheets, which honestly said more about the general population's lack of hygiene, but that wasn't the point.

The woman was allergic to blending in. It was impossible *not* to notice her.

I rubbed the back of my neck, trying—and failing—not to focus on her perfect tits pressing against the fabric of her top. There was no way she was wearing a bra. Talk about freeing the fucking nipple.

And that skirt. *Goddamn.* That thing should be illegal.

It rode up high enough to show off every inch of her shapely, tattooed thighs—the same thighs I had spent endless hours buried between—and clung to her hips like it had been painted on.

But underneath it all—the makeup, the boots, the armor—she was still *my* Dani.

Only she wasn't *mine*, never had been.

I willed myself to drag my eyes back up her body before I did something stupid. Like press her against the nearest wall and make her forget every second we'd spent apart. There was a chance I still might.

"To be fair, I didn't expect you to actually read it." Her eyes lit up with amusement and, dare I say, a hint of mischief when she took in my disheveled appearance. "Wait, were you in bed when I texted?"

I paused. "No."

"You were, weren't you?"

"No."

"Probably watching one of those trash shows you love, like *Real Housewives of New York.*"

It was a little unsettling how well she knew me. Our relationship, if you could even call it that, had only lasted a few months, and most of that time had been spent fucking our way through every room of my house—plus a few in hers, too.

But somewhere between all those hours of mind-blowing sex, Dani and I had shared more than just bodies.

She knew I had a soft spot for "trashy" reality shows, mainly because they made my own life feel less chaotic, and I knew about her thing for quirky, colorful socks. To be fair, I also had a thing for *her* in quirky, colorful socks. I had jerked off—more than once—to visions of her in a pair of black and purple striped thigh-highs and nothing else.

We had done our best to avoid talking about anything more personal than that, though she never failed to ask about Carolina, even now. Still, I couldn't ignore the nagging feeling that there was something darker, something painful lurking behind those gorgeous, green eyes and . . . goth Tinkerbell exterior.

But tonight wasn't the night for unpacking generational trauma—hers or mine.

"First of all," I said, nailing her with a pointed look, "it was *Below Deck: Mediterranean.* More importantly, you know that I'm a Salt Lake City fan."

She laughed, just barely, and it hit me like a punch to the gut. "Does that mean you don't have Carolina tonight?"

"We spent Christmas together, so she's with her mom."

My cock twitched when she nibbled her lower lip. *Dangerous territory.* That lip had been the beginning of the end for me more times than I cared to count.

"You could've at least brought a coat," she said, voice quiet now.

"And you could've warned me you were dressed like that."

I let my gaze drop just long enough to make her squirm. There it was again—that vulnerability that tugged at my chest and made me want to wrap my body around her like a shield and protect her from everything.

"Why did you come, Brooks?"

Finally, a question I knew the answer to.

"Because I missed you, kitten."

There. I said it. The thing that had been weighing down my mind and heart since the second we'd called things off back in October. There was no point in pretending otherwise, not when my voice was tinged with yearning and my erection was tenting my pants.

The gravel crunched beneath my feet as I stepped toward her. "Because I can't stop thinking about you. About us."

She clung to the lapels of her coat, twisting the fabric between her fingers. Her eyes widened, as she was no doubt surprised by my raw honesty. That made two of us.

To say that I had never been much of a people person would be an understatement. I didn't speak unless spoken to, didn't share personal information unless it was pried out of me. Hell, I much preferred the company of my six-year-old daughter and her stuffed animals over people my own age most days of the week. But with Dani, the words came whether I wanted them to or not.

The silence between us stretched, thick and charged. I could feel it, the way she was trying to talk herself out of this. Out of *me*.

So, I said what I needed to say.

"Because I didn't want to start the new year wondering what would have happened if I'd come."

She exhaled, shaky. "Brooks."

My hand found her waist, fingers pressing into the curves I had spent hours committing to memory. Her breath hitched, but she didn't pull away. If anything, she leaned in, like her heart had already made the decision her brain hadn't caught up to yet.

"Did you kiss anybody at midnight?" I asked, voice rough.

"No," she replied, barely above a whisper.

"Good answer, kitten."

Thank fuck for that because the very thought of her kissing someone else—smiling against someone else's lips while the clock struck twelve—was enough to make me see red. I was barely hanging on as it was.

With two fingers under her chin, I tilted her face up to mine. She came willingly, eyes locked on me. I was used to her looking up at me—she was nearly a foot shorter than my 6'2" frame—but this time, it felt like she wanted to.

"Five . . . four . . ."

Her hands fisted in the front of my shirt.

"Three . . ."

I lowered my head.

"Two . . ."

She surged up before I could finish, smashing our lips together like the world was about to end.

And hell, maybe it had. Maybe the clock had struck midnight and this was some alternate . . . multiverse version of us, one that didn't pull away and ruin a good thing just because we feared how much it might matter. Or maybe I had just watched one too many Marvel superhero movies.

Her lips moved against mine with a feverish kind of urgency. I kissed her back like a starving man, because that was exactly what I was. She tasted like whiskey and winter air, and beneath it all, the same sweetness that had always fucking wrecked me.

I gripped her hips, pulling her flush against me. She gasped when she felt the weight of my cock straining against my sweats, and I took the opportunity to deepen our kiss, sweeping my tongue into her mouth like I owned it.

We both knew that wasn't the case, though. If anything, *she* owned *me.*

A broken cry fell from her lips, and I swallowed it whole. She pressed closer, tugging at my hoodie like she wanted to tear it off and crawl inside my skin.

Works for me.

"This is a bad idea," she breathed.

"The worst," I agreed, trailing kisses down the side of her neck. "Still want you, though."

Her hands fell away from my body, and for a second, I thought she might give into reason and stop. Thankfully, lust won out over logic. She circled her arms around my neck and hoisted herself up, wrapping her legs around my waist.

"*Fuck,*" I growled into her mouth. "I'm parked across the street."

"Don't stop."

"Dani—"

My knees nearly buckled when she tugged my lower lip between her teeth and bit down. Just enough pressure to light me up, to make my hands tighten on her ass and hitch her farther up my body.

She released me slowly, lips brushing mine, and gave me a look that told me she knew *exactly* what she was doing.

"I need you, Brooks," she whispered, hot breath fanning my face.

"Then you'll get me," I rasped.

That one little bite had unraveled something in me—something I had spent months desperately trying to keep buried because "it was easier that way," or so I had told myself.

Fucking idiot.

A burst of laughter spilled from the bar, followed by a high-pitched squeal. It broke through the haze just long enough to remind me we were still in public and I was still the head coach of the reigning World Series champions.

We were too exposed out here. All it would take was one rabid fan, one grainy photo for this—whatever *this* was—to spiral into an endless stream of degrading memes and headlines. And once the rumor mill started turning, it didn't stop. It was a relentless cycle, always hungry, never fair. Especially to women.

Because the truth was the fallout wouldn't hit *me* the hardest. It hardly ever did with men. I would probably get a slap on the wrist, maybe a few sharp questions at a press conference, but Dani was a different story. She would be dragged through the mud, dissected by strangers who'd call her unprofessional, a gold digger, or worse. The world wasn't kind to women, especially not the ones who dared to want something for themselves or, heaven forbid, their bodies.

She deserved better than to be reduced to a scandal. Which was why we needed to make this party a bit more private.

I tore my mouth from hers. "Hang on."

Neither of us said another word as I raced across the lot with her in my arms. Her hot pussy rocked against me with every step I took, and the friction nearly undid me.

We rounded the side of the bar in record time, past the glow of the security light and around the far end of the dumpster. Not exactly romantic, but it would have to do.

Besides, this wasn't about romance; we were scratching an itch, nothing more. And that was the story I was sticking with.

I spun us until her spine met the bricks, probably a little rougher than necessary, but she didn't seem to mind. She gasped into my mouth, fingers digging into the back of my neck like she needed something to hold onto or she'd fall apart right there. She was all heat and softness and need, and I didn't even pretend to fight it this time.

"Still good?" I growled against her lips.

She nodded, eyes dark and wild. "Still want you," she answered, echoing my words.

That was all the permission I needed.

I ducked my head, kissing her again. Harder this time, slower. Like I meant to brand it into both of us, like I could press everything I felt into her—every sleepless night, every minute I'd spent convincing myself this wasn't worth the risk.

Her hands slipped under my shirt. I let out a muffled curse when her icy palms connected with my back. She giggled into my mouth, and the sound shot straight to my dick.

"Fuck, kitten." I kissed a path across her collarbone, teeth scraping the black and grey flowers inked on her skin. "You have no idea what you do to me."

"Show me," she said breathlessly, tilting her chin to give me more room to play.

Fucking hell.

My hands were everywhere in seconds—under her coat, sliding up her sides, fingering the edge of her top. With one clean move, I tugged it down to her waist, baring her small, perky tits to the cold.

"Fuck, I missed you," I murmured, thumbing her nipples into hard points.

"Me or my tits?"

"Do I have to pick?"

I leaned down, sucking one nipple into my mouth, and then the other. Her hips rolled against mine, and I let out a low groan when I found her wet and wanting beneath her skirt.

She gasped, a sharp, broken sound.

"You have to be quiet, kitten." I teased her weeping cunt, swirling two of my fingers through her slit. "You don't want anybody to see, do you?"

Her breath hitched when I pushed my finger inside her, curling it just right, hitting the spot I knew drove her insane.

"You don't want them to know how wet this pussy is for me."

She shivered when I added a second finger.

God, I hadn't touched her in months, but my body hadn't forgotten a damn thing. She was tight and trembling. I wanted to stay here, just like this, with her pussy gripping my fingers like a vice and her teeth sunk into my shoulder to keep from screaming.

"Fuck," I groaned against her throat. "You feel goddamn perfect."

She didn't answer, not with words at least. She just rolled her hips against my hand, chasing more. Little did she know, I would lay down my heart to give her everything. I watched her face, how it crumpled with pleasure, her lashes fluttering, lips parted and breathy. It hit me hard how much I'd missed this. Missed her. Not just the way her body responded to mine, not just the way she said my name when she came, but *this*.

The vulnerability, the surrender.

It was a rare gift—especially from a formidable woman like Dani Bernal—one that needed to be cherished.

My cock throbbed, still pressed against her core, hard as stone. Every muscle in my body was strung tight, but I didn't rush this. I wanted to watch her come apart first. *I needed it.*

Her hands grabbed at me—hoodie, shirt, anything she could hold on to—as she writhed against my hand.

"That's it," I whispered, lips brushing the shell of her ear. I thrust a third finger inside her channel, stretching her wide. "Ride my fingers, kitten. Take what you need."

She cried out as she came, and this time, I couldn't bring myself to care if someone heard us. Not when she was creaming my fingers, drenching me with her cum.

When she finally finished convulsing around me, I pulled my fingers free from her pussy, dragged them up her body, and painted her neck with her release.

She tipped her head back in offering, and I took it, my tongue following the slick path I'd left, up her neck, across her jaw, tasting every drop until finally, I claimed her mouth. She moaned into the kiss, our tongues dueling for control. It was dirty and delicious, the best goddamn meal I had ever tasted.

My body lurched when she reached a hand between us to palm my cock. "Jesus, Dani—"

"*Please*," she cried.

"Please what?"

"Please stop teasing me."

"Who's teasing?" I said, voice cracking. "You've been in my head for weeks, kitten. Every goddamn night."

Her hand cupped the back of my neck, dragging me back to her mouth.

"Then stop thinking," she whispered. "And fuck me."

I didn't hesitate.

I dragged her panties down just enough, freed my cock with a clumsy, desperate hand, and buried myself to the hilt inside of her. She choked back a groan, burying her face against my hoodie so as not to scream.

"Fuck, Brooks—"

"Say it again."

"*Brooks*," she breathed, again and again like a prayer. Or maybe a curse. I had been under her spell since the day we'd met.

Her pussy was like liquid lava, still hot and fluttering from her orgasm. It was almost too much. Almost.

My fingers dug into the backs of her thighs as I lifted her up and down my cock and pounded into her. She tightened her legs around my waist, hanging onto me like a lifeline. There wasn't a doubt in my mind that we would both have a few scrapes and bruises tomorrow, but I didn't care. On the contrary, I would wear her marks with pride.

At least then, I would know this was real.

I felt my climax building, but I wanted to get her there one more time. I shifted my hold on her, moving a hand around her hips until my thumb brushed her clit. She tightened around me, a fresh rush of arousal coating my cock.

Fuck, I wanted to bathe in her juices.

Preferably with her laid out on my bed, legs splayed wide open, completely bare except for the boots that were currently digging into my ass.

She gasped as my fingers circled her clit again. She was right there; we both were. Just a little harder and—

"Oh god, don't stop!"

Perfect.

Her second orgasm tore through her like wildfire, sharp and sudden. That was the last straw. I lost it with a groan, hips jerking as I emptied inside her.

A small, nagging voice in the back of my head told me we probably should have had the safe sex talk before I was filling her up with my cum. But I hadn't been with anybody but her for nearly a year, and she was on the shot or had been when we'd first hooked up earlier that summer.

So much for being a responsible adult.

Tomorrow, I would go back to being the straight-laced, single father who spent his days coaching baseball and his nights watching *Bluey*. Tonight, I was too caught up in the feeling of Dani's strangled breath fanning my cheek.

We stayed like that, forehead to forehead, gasping for air, as the weight of the world slowly crept back in. The evening chill brushed against our damp skin, but I barely felt it.

I held her for as long as she let me, until eventually, she lowered her unsteady legs to the ground and pulled her clothes back into place. She adjusted her skirt in silence, and I tucked myself back into my sweats, heart still thundering, trying to make sense of what had just happened.

That hadn't just been about sex. Not to me, at least. Not when she'd looked at me like that, *said* my name like it meant something. But she was already pulling away, rebuilding whatever wall I had just cracked.

I'd seen her do this before—retreat into herself, piece by piece. The first time I'd kissed her, she'd smiled afterward like it was any other day, like the universe hadn't shifted the moment her lips had met mine. Same thing the first night we'd slept together. She had slipped out of my bed before morning without a word or kiss goodbye.

I reached for her hand, brushing her knuckles with mine.

"Dani—"

She stepped back, evading my touch. "Can we just skip past this next part?" she asked quietly.

I blinked.

"Neither of our situations have changed," she added. "We still work together. You still have Carolina."

My jaw tensed at the mention of my daughter. It wasn't what she'd said—it was how she'd said it. Like Carolina was a barrier separating me from any semblance of a personal life. To be fair, she wasn't entirely wrong.

Carolina came first—always had, always would—and Dani respected that. It was hard enough growing up with divorced parents; doing it in the public eye with a dad who was on the road for four months of the year was something else entirely.

I owed her the relationship with her father that I'd never had.

"Brooks." She took a breath, but it caught in her throat. "*Please.* Don't make this harder than it has to be."

I wanted to argue. To tell her it didn't have to be one or the other—that just because Carolina was everything didn't mean there was no room for *anything* else. For *her*.

But the way Dani looked at me just then—guarded, stand-offish, her decision already made—I knew it wouldn't matter. At some point in the last few minutes, she had rebuilt her walls, and I was no longer welcome inside the fortress.

So instead, I nodded. Slow and numb, like my body was moving half a beat behind everything else.

Dani gave me a ghost of a smile, one that didn't reach her eyes, and turned away.

I watched her walk back toward her car. The silence between us stretched longer with every step she took. A leftover firework cracked somewhere in the distance, too late to matter.

And I just stood there like a fucking moron, watching, wondering, asking myself how something that had never officially started could already feel so over?

Dani

Roasters 1–0

The twenty-sided die rolled across the table before coming to a lopsided stop on sixteen. "Does that mean my levitation spell worked?"

I looked up from my character sheet to find four sets of eyes gaping back at me like I had grown a second head. Technically, I was growing another head, but that was beside the point.

"Wait, wait, wait." June blinked rapidly, like she was trying to reset her brain. "Rewind and play back the tape, please."

Jo muffled a laugh. "The tape, *mami*? You're really showing your age."

"Shut up," she said, swatting at his shoulder. Not that he could feel it through his thick wool sweater. "You're the oldest one at this table."

He clutched his imaginary pearls. "By seven months. And those months gave me wisdom, thank you."

No one laughed, though.

The banter dried up as everyone turned their attention toward me. The weight of it settled over the table like a dense fog.

Clarke was the one to finally break the silence. "You're pregnant."

Oof, that was going to take some getting used to. I had just wrapped my head around the idea of being pregnant. Saying it aloud or hearing it said to me—*about* me—was a completely different story.

I pivoted in my seat to face my friend, and that was when I saw it: the tiny flicker of hurt in her eyes. And damn, if that didn't burn more than the acid reflux I had been experiencing lately.

Just another fun side effect of pregnancy.

Clarke was a lot more than just a colleague. We had worked together every day for over a year now. I had been the one to hire her for the social media team when she'd been fresh out of a toxic relationship, desperate for a new start. Since then, we had become a two-woman army—cloaked in matching Roasters' jerseys, living off stadium pretzels and sarcasm, and texting during meetings like middle school tweens.

And still, I hadn't told her about Brooks.

I shifted in my seat, suddenly wishing I could shrink inside my hoodie. "Yeah, I am."

She didn't say anything right away. Just nodded like she was adding it up in her head—my recent mood swings, the bouts of nausea during the first away series that I had played off as food poisoning, my sudden obsession with Flamin' Hot Cheetos and ice cream. And Flamin' Hot Cheetos *dunked* in ice cream.

I swallowed hard. "I wasn't trying to hide it from you. Any of you. I just— I needed time to figure out how I felt about it before I said the words out loud."

Clarke gave me a tight-lipped smile.

I deserved that. I hadn't planned on dropping the whole "Oops, I had a secret relationship with the sexy as fuck baseball coach and now I'm carrying his spawn" bombshell during our bimonthly Dungeons & Dragons session, and yet somewhere between the charcuterie spread and Jo's guava pastries, it had just spilled out of me.

To say my announcement had surprised my friends would be an understatement. Nessa was the only one who didn't look like she needed a cold compress.

"Sooo," June said, sitting up straighter on her floor pillow. Typically, we met at the tavern for D&D, but tonight, we had opted for a cozier spread at Smutty Buddies. "Now that everyone is caught up on who you did last summer, do you want to discuss next steps?"

"Slaying the orc queen, obviously," Nessa answered quickly, even though she knew good and well that June wasn't talking about the game.

We all knew exactly what June was *really* saying. I still had options. It was early enough to end this pregnancy if I wanted to. There was no shame in that, not in this group, and definitely not in my own mind.

"I've decided to keep it," I told them.

Judging by their expressions, none of my friends had pegged me as the baby type. To be fair, I hadn't either.

I liked my space and control. I never cooed at passing strollers or daydreamed about names for my future children. The very thought of giving birth scared the ever-loving shit out of me, and I was starting to realize that I had an unsettling, deep-seated fear that my little parasite might grow up to become a serial killer.

Blame it on my love of true crime podcasts.

I had never done anything conventional, so motherhood had always seemed like a farfetched concept.

But as complicated and terrifying as it felt, there was something in me that had settled around the idea of having this baby. Like the part of me that had always braced for abandonment for as long as I could remember had finally found something—or in this case, someone—to stick around for. And that quiet certainty, however new, was enough to move forward.

"I know it sounds crazy," I told them, voice thick with emotion. "And it probably is because I have no idea what I'm doing, but that's never stopped me before. Besides, it's not like I can do worse than my mom."

Nessa sat forward, resting her hands on her tattooed thighs. "Badass."

"Yeah," June added. "*That* alone is how I know you're going to be a great mom."

I'm glad somebody thinks so.

Because the truth was, I was more scared of being a mom than I was of having a baby. And yeah, I knew those two things were supposed to be one and the same, but they didn't feel that way to me.

Having a baby was physical. It was swollen ankles and hemorrhoids and, according to the pregnancy book I had downloaded to my Kindle, dry nipples, all of which led up to that moment in the hospital when someone put a tiny, squirming person in your arms. Terrifying, yes, but there was a beginning and an end to it.

Being a mom, though . . . that was something else entirely.

That was waking up day after day, trying to be someone new. Reliable. Selfless. Someone who could put another person first without resenting them, a feat my own mother had never fully grasped.

But what scared me the most wasn't the pressure to be a good mother—it was the fear that somewhere along the way, I would stop recognizing myself. That I would vanish into the job.

And being a mother was a job—fuck anybody who said otherwise.

"By the way," June said, shaking me out of my existential spiral. "I still can't believe that you were secretly juggling that man's rosin bags for months."

"June!" Clarke cried.

Nessa buried a laugh behind her hands.

"Oh, come on," June protested. "I feel like I deserve a little credit for that top-notch baseball innuendo."

I massaged my temples, half-laughing despite the situation. This was why our "Bitchcraft" group got on so well. One second, we were battling an orc queen and foraging for magical fungi with levitation powers, and the next we were breaking down my emotional news like it was an episode of *Love Island*.

Damn, Brooks would love that reference.

There wasn't a doubt in my mind that any one of these foxy, queer weirdos—aside from Clarke, the "token straight friend" of the friend group—would offer me a place to stay or an alibi, if needed.

"Speaking of Coach Daddy," Nessa said between sips from her *Enemies-to-lovers is a valid life choice* mug. "Does he know yet?"

I hesitated.

Jo gave Nessa a look like *not now*, but she held up her hands in surrender. "Just asking."

"Not yet," I admitted.

The words hung in the air for a beat too long, until Nessa reached over and popped another apple slice drenched in brie into her mouth.

"Well," she said, "Coach Daddy or no Coach Daddy—"

"Please don't call him that."

"—just know that this kid is going to have a full library by the time they're born. I'm talking classics, queer fairy tales, picture books about feminist icons. And yes, I will be curating it personally."

"Of course you will," I replied, my heart squeezing in the best way.

She winked at me. "No child of yours is going to grow up without knowing the importance of consent, dragons, and a well-written epilogue."

Jo grinned. "And this *guncle* comes with a killer *pastelón* recipe that he would love to pass on to the next generation."

I smiled and blinked away an unshed tear. *For fuck's sake.* I had cried more in the past few weeks than in the last five years—pregnancy wasn't for the weak.

June, who had been nibbling the edge of a cracker like it was a delicate art form, piped up to say, "And when this tiny goblin starts walking, Auntie June will make sure they're doing toddler yoga and have a strong plank game by age three."

Everyone laughed, but she added, a little softer, "Also, if you ever need a break or, like, two hours to nap, I would be happy to babysit."

"Seriously?"

She smirked. "Dani, you're giving up sushi and booze for nine months. It's the least I can do."

Damn. Sushi, too? Apparently, I hadn't reached that chapter of the book yet.

All eyes turned to Clarke, expectant.

"Well," she started, crossing one leg over the other. She smoothed out her floral skirt and gave me a look that was equal parts sass and sincerity. "I wish you would've told me sooner, but now that I know, I will march into every baby store in Oregon and veto any beige onesie they try to sell you."

Jo snorted. "You hate beige that much?"

"It's not a color. It's a cop-out," she said with dramatic flair.

Clarke finally smiled, small but genuine. I nodded, and something unspoken passed between us, solid and forgiving.

"If it helps," June said. "Babies are basically just loud potatoes for the first few months anyway."

A sharp laugh busted out of me. They didn't know what they were doing either, none of us did, but they were mine. Messy, ridiculous, and ride or die to the end.

"You're all disasters," I said.

June grinned. "Disasters who will help you keep the tiny potato alive."

Nessa clapped her hands once. "Okay, feelings acknowledged, love affirmed. *Now* can we kill the orc queen?"

I nodded. "First, we kill the orc queen," I told her. "Then, we figure out how I tell Brooks he's going to be a daddy . . . again."

Brooks

I heard the crunch of gravel before I saw the car. I should have known better than to start making dinner before my ex-wife dropped off our daughter. Unlike most people, Allie had a knack for being early to everything.

It was one of the few things that we had always had in common. That and a love for Thai food, hence the vegan coconut curry soup currently simmering on the stove.

I switched off the burner and moved the stockpot to the back of the stove, away from tiny hands. Carolina was six going on precocious, and her latest passion was cooking. Baking, actually. Her mom had introduced her to *The Great British Baking Show* during the holidays, and now she was obsessed.

Damn, my little girl was growing up fast. One second, she'd been playing make-believe with Barbie, and the next we were whipping up meringue in her KitchenAid mixer. Her "Roasters' red" mixer, of course, because Carolina was nothing if not her daddy's biggest fan.

I snagged my hoodie off the sectional and headed out the door. Allie's hatchback eased around the bend the moment I stepped outside.

My lips twitched when Carolina's tiny fingers pressed against the back-seat window, reaching out for me. Carolina *hated* the car. She always had. Even as a baby, she could never sleep through a drive. It was one of the main reasons Allie had stopped bringing her to my games when she'd been little.

But she was old enough to know better now. Which was why she waited until her mom unbuckled her from her booster seat before leaping out onto the pavement, a glass jar clutched to her chest like she was smuggling something precious.

Her sneakers thudded against the concrete. "Daddy!" she cried out. "It's bubbling today."

I caught her up in a half-hug with one arm, careful not to jostle whatever culinary experiment she was so proudly carrying.

"What is?" I asked.

She held the jar up between us. It was full of what looked like gooey, beige paste, with some suspicious fizz at the top.

"My sourdough starter."

She said it as though that cleared everything up. The only thing missing was a perfunctory eye roll. Hopefully, if I had it my way, we were still a few years away from that.

"Oh, this is the thing you bake bread with."

"Yes," she said, practically vibrating in my arms. "We have to name it."

I squinted at the jar. "It's bread mix."

She gasped like I'd said something sacrilegious.

"It's *alive*, Daddy."

Allie walked up just then, laughing under her breath. She looked like she always did when she dropped Carolina off—comfortable, casual, like she was fresh from the beach, when in actuality she lived forty minutes across the river in Washington.

She wore an old denim jacket I vaguely remembered from back when we'd still been married, the sleeves pushed up to her elbows. Half of her box braids had been piled into a bun atop her head, while the rest hung past her shoulders.

She looked older, sure—we both did—but it suited her. It was hard to believe that this was the same woman who, at one point in time, would spend hours straightening her hair, worrying about what she wore, buying heels she never walked in. That version of Allie had been beautiful too, but it was the kind of beauty that took effort. This version—natural hair, running shoes, and a faded Roasters hoodie underneath the jacket—was the kind that stuck.

The kind that made me remember how much growing up we both had done over the past decade. And how some of that had happened apart.

"That starter has been in my fridge all week," she said, nodding her head toward the jar. "It needs feeding every twelve hours."

"And a name, too, apparently," I grumbled under my breath.

"I suggested Bread Sheeran, but she wasn't amused."

I choked back a laugh. Allie gave me a look that said, "Can you believe the things we do for this tiny human we created?"

"Go hug your mom, cutie."

Carolina didn't need telling twice. She wrapped her arms tight around Allie's waist, pressing her face into her mom's middle like she was trying to memorize her shape.

I watched them from my spot on the porch, my lips kicking up in a sideways smile. Carolina might have had Allie's mouth—and the wicked sarcasm that came with it—and her thick, brown-almost-black curls, but those long, gangly limbs and constant need to be in motion were all me. Just last week, she had bounced herself into a near coma on the trampoline in my backyard, and I had the photos to prove it.

Sometimes it startled me, seeing us both so clearly in her.

The way she got quiet when she was frustrated—me. The way she happy-danced when she tasted something delicious—Allie. She was a living, breathing, fully baked (pun intended) amalgamation of our best and worst qualities.

Allie smoothed a hand over the back of Carolina's head, kissing the top with the same kind of quiet ritual she always used when saying goodbye.

I knew the feeling well.

Each drop-off and pickup came with its own small weight, a lingering reminder of the life we had built together and then promptly divided down the middle. But we made it work better than most, so I couldn't complain.

"Have fun with Daddy," Allie said, pressing one last kiss to Carolina's forehead. "Mitchell and I will pick you up on Tuesday."

"Okay!"

"I love you."

"Love you, too, Mommy."

Carolina darted past both of us and into the house, carrying her sourdough starter like a peace offering.

"Stove is hot, cutie," I called after her. "Hands off."

I left the door open behind her, allowing the scent of warm pine and rain-soaked pavement to drift inside.

The house was my own personal fortress, tucked back behind a winding gravel road, half an hour from the stadium, and surrounded by forest on three sides. Secluded, peaceful. Truthfully, it was the way I preferred it—I had never been much of a city boy.

Out here, the sound of the world felt muted. Fewer cars, fewer crowds, nothing but crows and the occasional low groan of branches shifting in the wind. Oh, and my friendly neighborhood rabbit, whom I had taken to calling Randolph. He was a cute fucker, though I was still salty about the havoc he had wreaked on my garden beds last year.

After years of living out of hotel rooms, and then in a high-rise, being in a place where I could hear the rain hit the roof and not a damn thing else felt like a kind of luxury I hadn't earned but desperately needed. Four bedrooms was probably too much for one man, but when Carolina was here—running barefoot across the hardwoods, pretending the trees were dragons or that the driveway was a moat full of crocodiles, because if you asked her, her daddy lived in a castle—it felt less like a fortress of solitude and more like home.

"What are we cooking up tonight?" Allie asked. "Smells delicious."

"Coconut curry soup. You're welcome to join us."

Her lips scrunched up as she weighed her options. "I really should head back before the rain picks up." She quickly added, "*But* if you feel like you *have* to send Carolina home with leftovers on Tuesday, you won't hear me complaining."

I nodded.

She continued lingering on the steps. There was something else she wanted to talk about. She had that look—subtle, patient, like she was choosing her words before she said them.

"What's up, Allie?"

"We were talking about her birthday party this morning," she said.

The season had just started last week. Carolina had been born at the end of May, so we were still a few months out from any party plans.

"It's a little early, isn't it?"

"Yes, but I wanted to put it on your radar now because she wants to have it *here* this year."

That landed harder than it should have.

We both knew that this was about a lot more than a birthday party. What Allie wasn't saying, what she was too nice to say, was that I had missed enough already. Too many firsts, too many birthdays blurred together in FaceTime calls from hotel bathrooms and stadium tunnels with the sounds of batting practice in the background.

I'd missed her second birthday because of a wrist fracture during a grueling one-hundred-degree game in Arizona. Had missed her fourth when a rain delay had turned into a double-header.

Worst of all, I had missed her *birth*—the whole fucking thing—because I'd been squatting behind the plate in Kansas City, two thousand miles away, trying to close out a no hitter. I remembered the call coming in during the seventh inning. I hadn't seen it until after the Champagne had already been popped, and by then, I'd had two things to celebrate.

In all my years of ball, nothing could have prepared me for that moment, for the mix of joy and guilt.

Allie had understood; she'd always known this was a part of the game—pun intended. But that didn't make it okay.

I must have watched the footage she'd sent me a thousand times, memorized every moment. Her voice in the hospital room, Carolina's newborn cries, my name whispered like a question. I had always told myself I was doing it for her—for both of them—chasing the contracts, keeping the endorsements coming in, building a future for us.

But Carolina didn't care about any game stats or World Series rings, even if she did like the way they "sparkled." No, all she wanted was for her daddy to blow up a few balloons and cut her goddamn birthday cake.

So that was exactly what I was going to do.

"I can make that work."

She arched her brow. "Are you sure? Because it's just as easy for us to have it at our place, and I don't want you to commit to it if you don't think you can—"

"I can," I snapped, much more harshly than she deserved. "Sorry, what I meant to say is that I would love to have her party here, and since I know about it so far in advance, there's no reason I can't make that happen."

Allie studied me for a second, then smiled. It wasn't the old smile—the one I had fallen in love with years ago—but it was one I was more familiar with these days. Something steadier.

Teamwork.

"She wants to do a baking theme," Allie relayed. "I'm talking about a dozen first graders, covered in frosting, rainbow sprinkles everywhere. Think you can handle it?"

I scoffed. "Please"

"Is that a yes?"

"Allie, I manage a locker room full of grown men who eat sunflower seeds out of each other's cleats and whip each other with towels. I think I can handle a few sugar-hyped first graders."

"Famous last words." She grinned, tossing her keys from one hand to the other. "Just wait until one of them cries because their cupcake collapsed. Or someone licks the communal spatula."

"Sounds like the 2016 postseason bullpen."

She laughed, the sound short and warm, and I caught the edge of it in my chest.

"Alright, coach," she said. "You're on the hook now. We can discuss the details later."

I leaned my hip against the porch rail and looked at her. "Thanks for this, Allie."

She tilted her head. "The party?"

"Yeah. And just . . . for letting her choose this."

Letting me do this.

Allie shrugged like it wasn't a big deal, even though we both knew it was. "It's what she wants. She's old enough to know now."

That landed too. She *was* old enough now. To notice who showed up, to remember who didn't.

"I won't let her down," I vowed, quieter this time.

"I know," she said, softer still. "I wouldn't have said anything if I didn't think you were ready. She notices the effort. We both do."

There was a beat of quiet, the kind that might have lingered too long if Carolina's voice hadn't floated out from beyond the doorway just then.

"Daddy, I'm hungry! And we need to name my starter."

I looked at Allie. "Do we really need to name the dough?"

She held her hands out defensively in front of her. "Hey, I was voted out of the naming committee days ago. She's all yours now, so start thinking . . . yeasty."

"What the fuck does that even mean?"

She winked and started back for the car. "Night, coach."

I stood there for another minute or two even after her car rolled away, just listening. The hum of the forest, the distant knock of cabinet doors opening and closing, the giddy voice of a six-year-old ready to conquer the culinary world. And some-where, in the middle of it, a jar of living dough demanding a name.

I stepped inside and closed the door behind me.

This was the life I used to be afraid of missing, and now nothing could tear me away. No missed flights, no excuses.

I took a breath, rolled up my sleeves, and braced myself.

"Alright, chef," I called out toward the kitchen. "Let's name this blob."

Dani

"I'm just saying," Clarke said, flipping her pen between her fingers like she was about to chuck it at me. "If we don't add Mic'd Mondays back into the weekly rotation, the fans might fly off the handle."

"The fans are chaotic gremlins," I told her. "If it were up to them, we would livestream Pink taking a shit."

She paused. "Do you think he would?"

"Don't even joke about that."

I leaned back in my chair and stared at the giant wall calendar we had spent the morning filling in with color-coded sticky notes, half-baked ideas, and at least one slightly pornographic sketch of River, the team's hipster barista mascot.

"Although, now that you mention it, let's talk to J.P. in digital media about having him do a series of gardening videos for YouTube."

She twirled her pen excitedly, as though it were a magic wand. "*And* we can use the rooftop garden for it, emphasize the sustainability of the stadium's facilities, and tie it into—"

"—the farm-to-table events," I finished for her, already scribbling out a reminder for myself. "I love it."

The Roasters' stadium was one of the few in Major League Baseball that had integrated an edible garden into its design. Nearly eight thousand square feet of the roof over the press box had been converted to an organically maintained rooftop farm that grew seasonal herbs and vegetables year-round.

In fact, there were already plans to add a greenhouse in the next couple of years and begin growing our own coffee beans. We already had an in-house coffee roastery, which meant fans could take home a fresh bag of Rose City Roast on game days, subscribe to the monthly coffee club, and attend latte art classes with guaranteed "guest barista" appearances by some of the players.

"Speaking of, we also need to lock in a date for the Farmers Market Feast."

Just one more thing to add to my seemingly never-ending to-do list.

The last couple of weeks had flown by, and it was like all I could do was hang on for the ride. I hadn't felt this kind of bone-deep exhaustion since my first year of grad school, when I'd been running on cold coffee and cortisol, praying that my Wi-Fi would hold out until I'd submitted a paper at 11:59 p.m.

What could I say? Last-minute deadlines made me horny.

There had always been something oddly addictive about them—the chaos of a looming deadline, that strange mix of adrenaline and dread humming just beneath my skin.

Pregnancy, as it turned out, wasn't all that different.

I was closing in on my second trimester, and everything had already started shifting—physically, mentally, and emotionally. My favorite jeans no longer buttoned without the help of some higher power, and my skin, which had been reliably low maintenance my entire adult life, had turned against me overnight.

And then there were the dreams.

Absolutely. Fucking. Unhinged.

Just last night, I'd dreamed I gave birth to a baguette and cried because the crust was too hard. Needless to say, Pink had been horrified when he'd come downstairs for breakfast and found me sobbing into my toast.

But the work didn't stop. I was still booking photoshoots, still hoofing it up and down the stadium to engage with fans and sponsors, still smiling at my friends and coworkers, who had no idea that beneath the ripped-to-shit denim and pleather jacket, I was quietly building a human being from scratch.

"I'm okay with adding Mic'd Monday into the mix." I held up my hand to cut off her response. "But if Diaz goes on another ten-minute rant about how characters never finish their food in shows or movies, then I hurl myself over the side of the stadium."

"Fair enough," she said without missing a beat. The entire team, plus most of the staff, was used to my dark sense of humor. "Just be sure to do it on the third-base side. There's better lighting, and I already know which lens I'd use for the slow-motion fall."

I shook my head. "Remind me to never give you a performance review."

The two of us were camped out in what we fondly referred to as the "fishbowl"—a small office space in the corner of right field with floor-to-ceiling windows overlooking the diamond. It had taken us a year, but we had finally upgraded from a couple of old clubhouse chairs that smelled vaguely like sunflower seeds, and a mini fridge full of energy drinks to a plush sectional and fully stocked kitchenette.

Was it glamorous? No. Functional? Barely.

But it was absolutely ours, down to the life-size cardboard cutout of David Bowie from *Labyrinth*. He never failed to make us smile.

I flipped through our content calendar, tapping my pen against my cheek. "Next week we're also dropping the 'Which Roaster Are You?' filter on Instagram, so plan on adding some of those to the social media queue."

"Done."

"Oh, and between you and me, I'm rigging it so that nobody gets Roman."

That was what he got for missing the team's mandated weekly social media training. *Fuck with me, I fuck with your ego.*

"You're a monster."

I shrugged. "I prefer the term *visionary.*"

It felt good to be back in the office, especially after a week-long road series in Tallahassee and Atlanta. *Fucking humidity.* I had never been so excited to come back to the rainy Pacific Northwest.

This was the fun part for me—the calendar coordination, the brainstorming sessions, the quiet chaos of trying to wrangle professional athletes into acting like adults on camera. *Easier said than done.* What I did not appreciate was the nausea that had been slowly creeping up on me since that emotional piece of toast this morning.

Clarke looked up from her laptop, narrowing her eyes like she could read my whole internal monologue.

"You okay?"

"I'm fine," I told her, even though there was a good chance I might throw up on my planner any second.

She twisted her lips, unimpressed with my answer. I should have known better than to lie to her, of all people. There were three things that set Clarke apart from the crowd, all of which made her the ideal coworker.

First, as a former socialite, she had extensive media training herself—poise, charm, and the kind of camera-ready resting face that could make a senator sweat.

Second, she knew how to coax just about anything out of anyone, and she did so with a smile on her face and honey in her voice. There wasn't a player on the team who hadn't been taken with her charm. Platonically speaking, of course. Soren would never give her up without a fight.

Third, she always had a fully stocked mini pharmacy in her purse—antacids, Advil, floss picks, even backup tampons in three different sizes. The woman was a walking CVS, and more than once, she had saved my ass.

And stomach. And vagina.

"Nausea?" Clarke asked.

I nodded.

She reached into her Mary Poppins bag and produced two separate packages. "Ginger chew or lollipop?"

"What, no Saltine crackers?"

"Those are in my other purse."

I waved her off. "I think I just need to take a break for a few minutes."

She closed her laptop. "That works for me. Soren wanted to meet me for lunch anyway, before he meets with Coach Daddy."

The bile in my throat flared instantly, and this time it had nothing to do with the hormonal havoc going on in my lower abdomen.

I sat up straighter and leveled her with a look. "Oh my god. Not *you*, too."

"Sorry, but it's a catchy nickname," she defended, trying to suppress a giggle. "Once you say it out loud, it sticks."

I buried my face behind my hands. "I hate it here."

"And yet, here you are," she said sweetly, reaching for her latte. "By the by, since we're already on the subject—"

I groaned, loud and long, tilting my head back toward the ceiling like I was summoning divine intervention.

"—have you told him yet?" she continued, ignoring my dramatics. "Or do we need to discreetly plant a positive pregnancy test on his desk next to the scouting reports?"

"You wouldn't dare."

The twinkle in her eyes told me she very well might, given the chance. So much for that sweet, Southern-belle demeanor.

"We could do it tastefully," she hedged. "Maybe tuck it into a Roasters-branded onesie."

I pinched the bridge of my nose. "I'm just waiting for the right time."

"And will that be before or after game seven of the World Series?" she asked flatly.

"I don't know," I snapped, then immediately regretted it. "Sorry, I just— It's not exactly something you mention in between takes of a TikTok video. I mean, what am I supposed to say? 'Great game, coach! By the way, I'm carrying your fetus.'"

Clarke's expression softened, just a little. Enough to remind me she was pushing because she cared.

"Well, hells bells. First of all, *incredible* line delivery, though I think we can do better than that."

I swallowed past the nausea and tried to catch my breath.

She reached out and squeezed my hand. "I know it's scary, hon. I do, but I think it's just going to get harder the longer you wait."

That's what she said.

Fuck, I had been living with Pink for too long.

"I know."

Clarke was quiet for a moment. Then carefully asked, "Do you think he'll freak out?"

"Honestly? I don't know. Brooks is already a great dad, but this wasn't exactly part of the plan."

"Yours or his?"

"Either."

She nodded. "Still, he deserves to know, regardless of what happens between the two of you."

I winced. "That's part of the problem."

She gave me a knowing look. "Because you like him."

"I never said that."

"You didn't have to."

I stared at the ceiling, unsure whether I wanted to laugh, cry, or crawl under the couch and live there permanently. Whatever was between Brooks and me, it wasn't nothing. But it also wasn't *something*. Not yet. And maybe that was what scared me most.

"Why don't you lie down for a few minutes while I grab lunch, and I'll bring you back some soup?"

"And crackers?"

"Of course."

"And maybe a pint of ice cream?"

She snorted. "We'll see."

A few minutes later, I had a folded shirt draped over my eyes like a makeshift sleep mask and one hand resting on my stomach, attempting to will my nausea into submission. The sectional wasn't exactly designed for actual sleep, but it was horizontal, and at this point, that was good enough for me.

The lights were low, Clarke was probably off having midday sex with Soren, and for the first time in a long time, nobody needed me for some random caption or cheesy hashtag.

It wasn't perfect, but it was close.

That was, until I felt the cushion next to me shift under the weight of another body.

I tensed, half-expecting Clarke with another ginger chew or, worse, a player needing content approval. But then I heard the unmistakable sound of Velcro sneakers and the soft exhale of someone much too young to be an adult.

I lifted the shirt just enough to peek.

Brooks's daughter, Carolina, sat cross-legged at the far end of the couch. Her sneakers were scuffed, her pigtails slightly uneven, and she was holding a spiral notebook in one hand and a purple marker in the other.

She smiled, perfectly at ease. "Hi."

"Hi," I said, propping myself up on one elbow. "What are you doing?"

"Working on names for my sourdough starter," she replied, flipping to a fresh page in her notebook like that answered everything. "Ellie left me alone for too long, and I got bored, so I decided to explore."

"Ellie?"

"My nanny."

I sat up fully now, stomach flipping for a whole new reason. "You *ditched* your nanny?"

She grinned, pleased with herself.

I swung my legs off the couch and stood, steadying myself. The nausea hadn't disappeared, but Carolina had distracted me enough that I didn't feel like actively dying anymore.

She closed her notebook and looked up at me. "Are you going to walk me back?"

"Yes, ma'am."

"But I don't want to go." Her attention flicked to something behind me. "You and Clarke have better snacks."

She wasn't wrong. We *did* have excellent taste in snacks.

Probably because neither of us ate vegan, like Brooks. Apparently, we both had the palate of a six-year-old girl, and our snack drawer was proof enough—fruit snacks, peanut butter crackers, and enough candy to sedate a polar bear.

I held my hand out to her. "Tell you what. I'll let you take two snacks back with you if you promise not to wander off like this again. Deal?"

"Four snacks."

"Two."

"Three snacks."

"Two." Her brows pinched together. "*And* I help you come up with a name for your sourdough."

She smiled and placed her hand in mine. "Deal."

By the time we reached the lower level, Carolina had already polished off a bag of crackers and shot down at least a dozen name suggestions.

"What about Doughly Parton?"

"No."

"Little Bread Riding Hood?"

"No."

A light bulb went off. "Crumbelina?"

She giggled and the adorable sound echoed down the hall.

"You are one tough cookie, Chef Carolina."

We walked side by side, her warm, light-brown hand swinging in mine with casual trust, like it was the most natural thing in the world. It caught me off guard—how easy it felt, how right.

I had held a lot of hands in my life, but this one made my chest ache in a way I wasn't prepared for.

Like maybe I was already starting to understand what it meant to be someone's mom.

Just as we rounded the corner toward the coaching offices, a door slammed open hard enough to rattle the wall. Less than a second later, Brooks came barreling out, looking like he'd gone from zero to full panic in sixty seconds flat. Eyes wide, phone in one hand, his jaw tight enough to crack.

The second he saw Carolina beside me, he froze.

Relief washed over his face like a wave—sharp tension dissolving in real time—and he ran a hand down his beard before lowering the phone and exhaling hard.

"There you are," he said, coming toward us. "Jesus, cutie. You can't just wander off like that. I was about to send the entire security staff out after you."

Carolina blinked up at him, unbothered. "I wasn't lost. I was with Dani."

"Yeah, I can see that," he muttered, then looked at me.

"To be clear," I said, offering a small smile, "she came for the snacks."

"That sounds about right." He crouched down to Carolina's level and smoothed his hand over her hair. "You okay?"

"I'm fine. We were just making a list of names for my sourdough."

Brooks looked up at me, half-exasperated, half-amused. "She told you about that?"

"She showed me the list. I'm invested now."

He stood back up, and for the briefest second, I forgot how to breathe.

His fitted, black Roasters hoodie did nothing to hide the sculpted muscles underneath. He had pushed his sleeves up to his forearms, exposing his tattoos. The salt-and-pepper beard only made his jaw look sharper, more defined, and his square-frame glasses—fuck, those glasses—should not have looked that good on a man who coached for a living.

He met my eyes with something like gratitude and exhaustion in equal measure. "I owe you."

Oh, I can think of something you can give me.

Fucking hormones.

I coughed. "That won't be necessary." Turning to Carolina, I added, "Next time, give someone a heads-up before you disappear like a tiny bread-making ghost."

"Okay," she said solemnly.

I thought about telling him then.

The words hovered on the edge of my tongue, ready to tumble out any second. But Carolina was still clutching her cracker wrapper, and Brooks had that weary, dad-on-the-brink expression like he hadn't sat down in hours—he probably hadn't.

This wasn't the moment. It wasn't even close.

Instead, I cleared my throat and took a step back. "I'll let you two get back to your sourdough saga."

"Bye, Dani."

I waved my goodbye.

Brooks gave me a nod, eyes warm but unreadable. "Thanks again, kit—"

His eyes narrowed. Mine widened.

I turned, walking away faster than I meant to, already regretting the words I hadn't said. But just before I rounded the corner, I glanced back over my shoulder.

Brooks was still standing there.

And he was still watching me.

Brooks

Roasters 5–4

T he TV screens behind me glowed with looping video clips. Pitch sequences, batting angles, field coverage charts—flashes of motion and heat maps that only made sense to guys who lived and breathed this game. Luckily, every person in this room did.

We were deep in pregame mode, the kind where nobody really blinked and nobody checked their phones. They knew better than that.

Well—*most* of them did.

Roman had once tried to hide his cell inside his glove during a meeting, like I wouldn't notice him tapping out a text with his pinky through the laces. I'd confiscated it and made him watch film with the rookies for a week straight. He hadn't slipped up since.

They were a good bunch of guys, my best crop of players yet. Probably because all of them had been hand selected by me. It wasn't every day that you were offered the opportunity to put together a franchise from the ground up, and when the Roasters' front office had given me the green light, I hadn't wasted it.

After signing my contract, I had spent months with my head buried in scouting reports, watching grainy footage from minor league parks in the middle of nowhere. I'd sat in half-empty bleachers at college fields, flown overseas to scout arms in the

Dominican Republic, and spent a week in Japan watching my right-fielder take fly balls until midnight.

I hadn't been after stars. I'd wanted grit. Guys who could take a hit and still show up the next day hungry. And somehow, I'd found them.

I clicked the remote in my hand and the screen shifted to a split screen of our batting order against the opposing team's pitching rotation.

"We all know that there's nothing worse than losing to a team you know you should beat," I said, my voice calm but clipped. "Which is why we're stacking today's lineup with hitters. This list swings early and swings hard."

The team's ASL interpreter mirrored my words so our catcher, Bennett, could follow along. Bennett wore cochlear implants, but signing was still the clearest and most efficient way to communicate with him, especially in a clubhouse full of noise, chaos, and guys who forgot to enunciate.

"And you know what that means."

"Work the count," came a few voices.

"Exactly. Force the long innings. They don't like playing behind, and their bullpen falls apart after the sixth. If we can wear down the starter by mid-fourth, we control the rest of the game."

I moved to the side of the monitor, nodding toward a looped clip of an outside pitch their leadoff hitter chased three times last series. "Same goes for pitchers. Don't be predictable. Mix your tempo, use the corners. Make them earn it."

Roman snorted from the second row. "No pressure."

Fucking loudmouth. You could hear our first baseman coming from a mile away, and it had nothing to do with his massive . . . feet. Then again, like most world-class shit-talkers, the guy also had one hell of a work ethic. He was secretly one of the hardest workers on the team. The kind of guy you'd want next to you in a bar fight or, better yet, a brawl at home plate.

"Garcia," I said without looking at him, "try fielding something clean today and we'll call it even."

That earned me a couple of laughs. The kind that told me the tension was still there, but it was cracking a little.

We had a tough series ahead of us. The Vancouver Tridents had been knocked out of the playoffs last season earlier than expected, so we all knew they were hungry for another shot. We were, too. That World Series title wasn't going to defend itself.

I turned the screen off with the remote. "Sinclair, you're up."

Soren "Sin" Sinclair, the team's duly elected team captain, was on his feet before I finished saying his name. He gave me a nod as I stepped back, and then he turned to face his teammates.

The room went dead silent.

Not because Soren demanded it, but because that was what happened when Soren talked. People listened.

He didn't pace, didn't raise his voice. He just looked at his teammates like he saw every one of them for exactly who they were.

"This is our house," he said.

A couple of heads nodded. Damn, he was going to make one hell of a coach one day.

"We've worked our asses off to get here. We've trained for hours, rain or shine, played through injuries, sacrificed time with friends and family, and it's all led to here. Whatever they bring tonight, is nothing we can't handle."

He glanced toward tonight's starting pitcher, Jared Pink, and gave him the smallest grin. The two had become somewhat of an unlikely dynamic duo during our first season, and even though they fucked with each other at every turn, I knew it was done with love and admiration.

"Pink's throwing gas," Soren continued. "We've got heavy hitters stacked all the way down the lineup. And our fielders? Best in the fucking league."

That got a few shoulder bumps and low mutters of agreement.

"But none of that matters if we don't play like a unit. Not just nine guys on a field—*one* team. Start strong. Stay locked in. And no matter what happens out there, don't stop swinging."

He set his sights on Matty Miller, our starting shortstop. "Unless you're swinging at balls four feet outside the zone."

The room cracked up. Matty flipped him off half-heartedly, grinning through it.

I still hadn't quite figured Matty out just yet. He was all Southern charm on the surface—always smiling, always polite, the kind of guy who brought his own tea and sugar packets on road trips because nobody made sweet tea the way he liked it, and whose All-American boy looks drove the fans wild—but something about him felt just out of reach. Like there was a closed door in that laid-back exterior he didn't plan on opening for anyone. Not even his coach.

"Play hard," Soren continued. "Play clean. Play for the guy sitting next to you. Let's go win this thing the way we know how."

Then he paused, looking around the room with that calm, level stare of his.

"And don't forget, the faster we finish this, the faster we get to postgame tacos."

Roman pumped a fist in the air. "*Let's fucking go.*"

I shook my head. The room erupted in applause, chairs scraping back as the guys stood, hooting and clapping each other on the back. There was no denying that this group was food motivated. And hell, I couldn't blame them.

Tacos were delicious as fuck.

I let the pandemonium ride for a few more seconds, then clapped my hands twice. "All right, that's enough taco talk. Get loose, get your heads on straight. BP starts in twenty."

"Coach," Tucker said as he passed me. "I'm gonna hit one into the upper deck for you tonight."

"Appreciate that. Try not to strike out twice before you get there."

He laughed, tossed his warm-up hoodie onto the bench, and jogged off.

One by one, the guys filtered out of the meeting room, jogging out toward the field with that pregame swagger that always made me feel part-proud, part-anxious. I checked my watch.

10:25.

If I was going to make it in time, I had to go *now*.

Athletes lived and died by their pregame routines and superstitions, and coaches were no exception. For some guys, it was a specific brand of sunflower seeds—my assistant coach scoffed at anything other than Vlasic Dill Pickle. For others, it was a lucky headband or pair of sweat-soaked socks—our centerfielder, Wesley Nuñez, received at least two complaints per week.

I had a different kind of lucky charm, though—a pint-sized sexpot in denim who just so happened to have a thing for soy chai lattes.

I cut through the weight room, past the tunnel to the field and toward the main concourse, taking the steps two at a time. I didn't need a calendar invite to know that Dani would be there. Same as she was every home game, just before the players hit the field for warmups.

We hadn't talked in a few days. Not since Carolina's disappearing act last week, which, yeah, *might* have taken ten years off my life. Dani had handled it like a pro, though—calm, cool, and collected. In fact, Carolina hadn't stopped talking about her all weekend, or the list of sourdough starter names they had come up with together.

Since then, my interactions with Dani had been few and far between. No sarcasm or flirtatious smirks. No smartass jabs about my whey protein bars tasting like chalk.

It was official; she was dodging me.

And that bugged the hell out of me. Worse, the fact that it bugged me, bugged me even more.

She didn't even know what she did to me—storming around the stadium with her latte in one hand and phone in the other, barking orders at men twice her size like she'd been born to run the show.

Because she had.

And maybe, that was why we hadn't won a game at home this season without me first catching a glimpse of her.

Coincidence? Maybe. But I wasn't about to risk it.

10:30 a.m. meant coffee o'clock.

So, here I was, walking way too fast for a guy *not* trying to "accidentally" run into someone.

I slowed my pace when the on-site roastery came into view, casually adjusting the fit of my cap and glasses, pretending like I hadn't just damn near jogged to get there.

To nobody's surprise, Dani was already at the counter, waiting for her drink. She had traded out her usual pair of jeans and boots for black leggings—that did incredible things for her ass—and Chuck Taylors to match. Her windbreaker was half-zipped, and her black and blue hair had been piled into two matching buns on the top of her head that reminded me of cinnamon rolls. Or maybe I was just hungry.

Hungry for a taste of Dani Bernal, that was.

I didn't say anything, just watched her for a second. She hadn't seen me yet, and for some reason, that made my chest ache more than I wanted to admit.

The barista looked up, eyes flicking from Dani to me. "Your usual, coach?"

I nodded. "Thanks."

Dani's shoulders hunched. She turned to face me slowly, like something out of *The Exorcist*. She gave a polite nod, not quite meeting my eyes. Not cold, just . . . careful. Like she didn't know where we stood anymore, and frankly I couldn't blame her.

"Fancy meeting you here."

I shrugged. "I needed something to settle my stomach."

"And you decided on—"

Her eyes narrowed when the barista slid my drink across the counter, then lit up in that way that made my stomach tighten.

"—a triple shot of espresso?"

I took the cup, avoiding her gaze like a damn coward. "Rough morning."

"You? Coach Broody? No."

Her teasing should have made me smile, but it had the opposite effect. It gutted me thinking about the fact that at one point not too long ago, she'd teased me while tangled in my sheets, naked, her lips brushing my jaw as she'd whispered something smart-mouthed into my ear.

"Dani, your herbal tea is on the bar."

That stopped me cold. "Herbal tea?"

She had been a dirty chai latte drinker for as long as I'd known her—they were as much a part of her as her tattoos.

"Mm-hmm," she said, avoiding my gaze. "I'm fighting a bit of a stomach bug."

She turned toward the milk and sugar and began doctoring her tea.

I should have walked away right then. Should have taken my cup of espresso sludge and left her in peace the way she'd asked me to.

Because she had asked.

"Please, don't make this harder than it has to be."

Her words echoed through my brain.

It didn't matter what I wanted. Not when she'd already drawn a line. I wasn't the kind of asshole who crossed lines with women. I'd been raised better than that—by a mother who'd taught me how to listen and a daughter who reminded me every day why it mattered.

But goddamn, it was getting harder every time I looked at her.

Harder to pretend like I didn't still feel her under my skin. Harder to remind myself that though we were both adults, we also had different priorities. I had no business falling for someone who made sarcastic comments about my protein powder and had glitter on her cheek half the time.

And yet, here I was.

Rooted in place like a fucking idiot, spending six bucks on a coffee I wasn't even going to drink, all for a chance to see her.

"By the way, we finally picked a name."

Her brow furrowed. "For what?"

"The sourdough starter."

Her expression shifted instantly, and damn if that didn't make me feel like I'd just hit a walk-off.

"Did you really?" she asked, the faintest trace of a smile tugging at her mouth.

I sighed. "Doughy McIntyre."

That earned me a blink, then a slow grin. "You did *not*."

"Carolina insisted, though I'm pretty sure somebody else gave her the idea."

She tucked a strand of hair behind one ear. "You're welcome."

"New Kids on the Block has become her new background music while baking, and needless to say, her mother is thrilled."

Dani laughed—soft at first, then full-on, the kind that made the rest of the coffee shop employees glance over. She covered her mouth, still giggling. "That's honestly incredible."

I smirked into my cup. "I'm honestly surprised you know who that is."

"Excuse you," she said, feigning outrage. "Just because you remember when MTV actually played music videos doesn't mean I don't have good taste in '80s boy bands."

"Good taste is debatable," I grumbled. "But you make a compelling case."

She rolled her eyes but didn't fight me.

For a second, it felt almost normal between us again, like the weirdness of the last few months had been scrubbed clean by a punny bread name and boy band reference. Like maybe we could go back to the easy banter and stolen glances that had made this whole thing so impossible to walk away from in the first place.

But the second passed, and reality came back just as fast.

Dani glanced at her phone, then gave a little sigh. "I should get back. We still have a lot to finish up before game time."

I nodded.

"Besides, you've got a game to win."

"Damn straight."

She smiled again, smaller this time. Softer. "Give 'em hell, coach," she said around a wink. And fuck, that was all it took to have my cock hardening in my warm-ups.

"Always," I rasped, voice rough.

Her breath hitched just slightly, but I didn't miss it. The way her lips parted, the way her eyes darted briefly down before she caught herself. A flush bloomed high on her cheeks, and she turned so fast it was like she was afraid of what might happen if she stayed a second longer.

Apparently, I wasn't the only one affected by our conversation.

I waited until she disappeared around the corner before heading back toward the field, trashing my untouched cup of coffee along the way.

One thing was for sure—it was the best six bucks I'd spent all week.

Dani

Roasters 10–7

I was more baked than a potato—and not in the fun, legal in twenty-four states kind of way.

It was one of those criminally hot afternoons that only came around every so often in Oregon, even in the springtime. To think, just two days ago, I had been wrapped in a fleece blanket, huddling next to my space heater like a Victorian orphan. Yet here I was, clad only in sunglasses and my favorite black-and-white bikini like Wednesday Addams, sipping something vaguely citrusy and nonalcoholic.

Only in Oregon could you go from seasonal depression to sunscreen in under forty-eight hours.

"This is the life." Nessa beamed from the neighboring chair.

"You're telling me."

"I wonder what it would take to convince Pink to put in a pool at his place."

My lips curved up in a small grin. "Oh, probably just whatever it is you do that makes him groan your name like he's praying to a goddess every other night."

Clarke nearly spit out her drink. All Nessa could do was laugh.

"Do you really want to know—"

"No!" Clarke and I shouted at the same time.

Pink was the closest thing to a sibling I had ever known, and sure, I was thrilled that he and Nessa had found each other, but that didn't mean I wanted to hear about all the nasty things they did to each other.

The three of us had curled up on the daybeds beneath the covered pergola while the guys got in the pool, alternating between conversation and whatever books we were reading on our Kindles. Nessa had talked Clarke and me into joining the monthly book club she hosted at her store, but between my surging hormones and the fact that the main character was a tattooed, single father, I had had to set the book aside.

I could only take so much torture.

A few of the guys were engaged in some sort of hyper-competitive water volleyball match. The rest were scattered amongst the luxurious outdoor kitchen, taking turns manning the grill and margarita station like dads at a neighborhood block party.

And then there was Matty, our esteemed host.

The entire team had thought he was nuts when he'd first purchased the 1920s farmhouse just outside of town, and rightfully so. The place had looked like something out of a true crime documentary—peeling wallpaper around every corner, creaky floors that screamed "unresolved murder," and more than a few questionable stains. Even the Zillow listing had come with a disclaimer that said, *"For legal reasons, we advise against this."*

Six months and a hundred grand later, and the place was nice enough to make any HGTV show host cry. Warm wood accents, black window trim, and rustic-modern everything. If the baseball thing didn't work out, Matty could probably make a pretty penny flipping houses for Pacific Northwest hipsters—he had done most of the renovations himself.

"Yo, Matty," Bennett called out from the patio. "Your dog ran off with my wiener."

"Mo," Matty drawled from the pool. "Don't you dare."

The dog froze in a stance I could only describe as cartoon villainish, long ears dragging on the tile, tail straight out like a periscope. Sure enough, her tiny teeth were wrapped around a hot dog, bun and all.

And then, she lunged.

Half the team erupted into shouts and laughter as Mo barreled across the lawn, launching herself—and Bennett's hot dog—into the pool.

Matty groaned. "That dog is gonna be the death of me."

"Only because you spoil her rotten," I shouted across the lawn.

"She's not rotten," Matty said, dead serious, scooping Mo up into his arms like she was a precious jewel. "She's just a Daddy's girl."

I shook my head, smiling as the guys launched into a debate about whether or not hot dogs should be counted as a type of sandwich. *Sigh.* We had been down this road before. Several times, in fact—the last of which had turned semi-violent when half the team had staged a gas station sandwich fight.

That had been a fun one to explain to Brooks.

Because Clarke and I traveled with the team, we were used to their amusing antics—the half-serious debates, the constant chirping, the weird inside jokes that came from spending half of the year crammed together in hotel rooms and buses.

But today felt different. It felt like family.

The messy, too-loud kind who argued over stupid shit at Thanksgiving and then passed you a slice of pecan pie like nothing had happened. Or so I had been told by friends and Hallmark movies.

Family traditions were as foreign to me as the idea of living on the moon. Even before my mom had passed away, we had never had that kind of closeness that most daughters craved from their mothers. Mostly because she had always been more taken with the *idea* of parenthood rather than the messy, exhausting reality of actually being a parent.

Thankfully, she had missed the peak of family vlogging by about two decades, because there wasn't a doubt in my mind that she would have been a "mommy vlogger," one of the filtered, performative ones who doled out parenting advice between brand deals.

She had wanted a curated version of parenthood, and sadly, I had never fit the aesthetic.

To be fair, I would have made terrible content.

I was too stubborn, too independent, too resistant to be the kind of daughter she'd wanted to shape. I listened to podcasts and watched obscure documentaries. I didn't dress for style or trends, but rather for armor. Black was safer than pink; combat boots were better than ballet flats.

She had never understood my bisexuality either. She didn't even try to. She wasn't cruel about it, but she had looked at me differently after I'd come out. Like I was something off script, a detour she hadn't planned for.

Deep down, I thought she always hoped I'd grow out of it—whatever "it" was in her mind. That maybe one day I would wake up and want the kind of life she had always wanted for herself: a comfortable home, a husband, and a couple of kids who thought just like their mother.

But I was doing okay. Better than okay most days, even if I still carried that invisible ache of having never been quite enough for the one person who was supposed to love me unconditionally.

And now, with a baby of my own on the way, that ache twisted into something sharper.

I didn't just want to be different from my mother—I *had* to be.

I wanted my kid to know, without question, that they were loved exactly as they were, not in spite of it.

A harsh breath whooshed out of me. *Damn.* Who would have guessed that a friendly argument about hot dogs would lead to such heavy thoughts and repressed memories? Now, I was anxious *and* hungry.

"I'm going to grab a snack," I blurted, peeling myself off the lounger and grabbing my oversized tote. "Anybody need anything?

Clarke and Nessa waved me off, and I made my way toward the food table, on the hunt for something salty that wouldn't immediately send my stomach into a tailspin.

That was when Pink spotted me.

"There are pickles in the fridge and ice cream in the freezer," he said, popping a dip-drenched carrot into his mouth. "You know, if that's what you're still craving these days."

I smiled. "Pickles are so first trimester. I'm onto avocados now."

"That seems . . . relatively normal."

"With barbecue chips and chili oil."

He smirked. "Still, anything is better than that pickle-Cheetos-ice cream slop."

"Says the man wearing a flamingo shirt."

He held out his arms and spun slowly, showing off every inch of his white, flamingo-covered shirt, unbuttoned enough to expose his abs and chest hair. The man had zero shame.

"You feeling okay?" he asked, lowering his voice.

"You know, growing a person. Trying to keep down my lunch. Living the dream." I nodded toward the margarita in his hand. "I'd be lying if I said I wasn't dying for a sip of that margarita."

His brow furrowed just slightly, the way it always did when he was clocking something deeper beneath the surface. People could think what they wanted about Jared Pink, but the man had a lot more going for him than boyish good looks and fuck boy charm.

"Have you told him—"

"No."

"But you're going to—"

"Leave it be, Sir Pink-a-lot."

Thankfully, he didn't push. He knew me better than that.

Instead, he just nodded and leaned casually against the table, letting the silence stretch comfortably between us.

Deciding I should throw him a bone, I fished around in my bag and pulled out the grainy black-and-white photo the ultrasound tech had sent home with me after yesterday's visit.

"Here." I held it out to him discreetly, like we were doing some kind of shady drug deal.

"Is this—"

"Your future niece or nephew." I nodded. "But don't go waving it around."

He studied the photo with a kind of reverence, holding it delicately between his fingers like it might crumble if he breathed too hard.

"Well, damn," he whispered, blinking down at it. "Look at that little bean. You think it's too early to say they've got my jawline?"

I couldn't help the laugh that escaped me. "You wish."

"Uncle Pink," he murmured. "I like the sound of that."

Somewhere behind us, Mo let out a low, mournful howl—probably because someone had finally blocked her from nabbing another hot dog.

"That dog is a menace."

Pink grinned. "We should get one."

"Abso-fucking-lutely not." I twisted my lips in thought. "Although, you might be able to talk Nessa into it if you get her a pool."

His eyes lit up. He looked at the photo for another second, then handed it back to me. Or at least, he tried to.

Just as the sonogram slipped between our fingers, a flash of brown and black fur bolted between us.

Fucking Mo.

With ninja-like speed, the floppy-eared chaos demon snatched the photo clean out of Pink's hand and took off at a dead sprint.

"No!" I shrieked.

"Fucking hell, she stole your baby."

We both took off after her—me clutching the front of my bikini top to avoid a nip slip and Pink sprinting at full speed, his half-finished margarita sloshing over the edge of his cup.

Mo bolted across the lawn like a four-legged bandit with a new chew toy, dodging discarded pool noodles, furniture, and anybody in her path.

"Don't chase her," Matty shouted. From the corner of my eye, I saw him pull himself up and over the pool's edge. "She thinks you're playing."

Mo juked left, nearly colliding with Nessa, then doubled back, clearly thinking this was the greatest game ever invented. The sonogram flapped in her mouth like a victory flag.

There was no way I was going to let her win this one.

"Come back, you little gremlin," I yelled, gaining on her. Even in a bikini, I could run circles around these guys. And their dogs, apparently.

Somewhere behind us, Clarke was doubled over, laughing. Matty hollered after Mo, offering to trade her for another hot dog. *Not spoiled, my ass.*

"I swear"—I panted, sprinting across the grass—"if she eats it, I'm never talking to Matty again."

Pink huffed. "And give up access to his pool? Yeah, right."

The race continued. Somewhere behind me, I heard the sliding glass door open, and a few new voices filtered out across the yard, but I couldn't be bothered to investigate. Not while this furry little fucker still had my baby's first photo between her teeth.

The two of us barreled across the grass like a couple of mall cops chasing our perp. And just when I finally had her in my sight, my foot snagged on the edge of a deflated pool floatie.

One second, I was going down, and the next, a pair of strong hands were hauling me back against a well-toned chest.

My breath caught in my throat before I even looked up. I knew that grip, that warm and woodsy smell.

Brooks.

Oh, fuck.

He caught me with one strong arm, the other landing instinctively on my hip as he eased me back onto my feet. His hands were rough and warm, and despite the late afternoon heat radiating off the concrete, his touch sent a full-body shiver straight through me.

I barely had time to recover before I registered just how close we were—or how fucking hot he looked. It wasn't often that I saw him out of athletic wear, but Brooks Bailey-Ward in a pair of jeans was almost too much to handle. The way they clung to his thighs, cupped his crotch. I felt my face get hot, and I knew my blush would give me away any second.

And then there was the backwards hat. *My kryptonite.* The man was a walking, talking orgasm.

When his attention raked over my body, I was suddenly very aware of just how naked I was. And just like that, the heat on my skin had nothing to do with the sun.

"What are you doing here?" I managed, voice low and shaky.

"Heller invited me for a beer," he said, nodding toward the long-haired man standing by the pool.

Brock Heller was a sports journalist turned podcaster turned novelist who had recently stepped back from his journalistic career to focus on writing his next queer romance novel. He was also dating the Roasters' second baseman, Johnathan Tucker.

Brooks looked around the yard, confused. "I didn't realize the whole team would be here."

I stepped back, trying to reclaim my heartbeat. "Yeah, it's an unofficial movie night slash housewarming party."

He blinked, still a little out of sorts, and that was when the yelling started again.

"What the hell?"

Matty's voice rang out from the middle of the lawn. All eyes turned toward him just as he held something up above his head, waving it through the air.

Double fuck.

Mo was now sprawled beside him on the grass, tongue lolling, completely unrepentant.

Matty squinted at the image. "Alrighty, which one of you is knocked up?"

Silence fell over the yard like someone had hit the mute button. Heads spun. Drinks paused mid-sip. Even the music from the outdoor speakers seemed to fade.

And then, slowly, every pair of eyes turned toward me.

Clarke murmured something that sounded like, "Well, crap on a cracker."

Nessa covered her eyes.

And Brooks . . . his eyes ping-ponged back and forth between me and the photo Matty was waving. His hands had dropped from my waist, but I could still feel the heat of them like they'd been branded there.

"Dani?" he asked quietly.

I swallowed, heart hammering.

"Um, surprise," I said, just above a whisper.

Fuck, fuck, fuckity fuck, fuck.

Brooks

"Um, surprise."

I didn't say anything. *Couldn't.* Not when it felt like I had been sucker punched straight in the dick.

It had been years since something—or somebody—had knocked me on my ass. Not since a 98-mph fastball to the collarbone back in Double-A had left me seeing stars and spitting teeth. And then there was the time Carolina had sliced her hand open on a sliver of broken glass. I'd nearly passed out trying to wipe up the blood before the paramedics had gotten there.

But this?

This hit different. And it hit hard, without mercy.

The second Matty had held up that sonogram photo and asked who it belonged to, I'd felt the ground shift under my feet. Every pair of eyes had turned to Dani. And not because of how incredible she looked in her bikini—I had nearly swallowed my tongue when I'd first spotted her running across the yard in the scrap of black-and-white fabric, my favorite bits bouncing and jiggling with every step—but rather because of the guilt coloring her cheeks.

Because she was pregnant.

My kitten was pregnant.

My hands were shaking, my heart was pounding, and I had the sudden urge to vomit all over my shortstop's well-trimmed grass. *Breathe, asshole.* I knew I should have said something. I must have looked like a bumbling idiot, and in front of my team no less, but still, I struggled to find the words.

And all the while, I never took my eyes off Dani.

Her face flushed, her mouth parted like she was about to deny it—or maybe defend herself—but she didn't say a word. She took off, snatching the photo out of Matty's hand and bolting for the house.

I stood frozen for a second too long, my brain still trying to play catch-up with what the hell had just happened. And then, I was moving, too.

I barely registered Pink's wide-eyed expression or Clarke calling out after Dani. I was already cutting through the stunned silence and heading for the sliding glass door.

She was fast, but I was faster. I found her halfway down the hallway inside the farmhouse, pushing open a door like she didn't care where it led, just so long as she could disappear.

Not on my watch, kitten.

I reached it just as she did, slamming it closed behind the two of us. It was a guest room, dressed in recycled wood and at least fifty shades of cream, a stark contrast to the tan, tattooed beauty standing across from me, avoiding my gaze.

"Something you want to tell me, kitten?" My voice came out harsher than I'd meant it to, cracking around the edges.

I stalked toward her when she didn't respond. I needed her to look at me, but her eyes were stubbornly fixed on her feet.

Fuck that.

I stopped when we were toe to toe, tipping her chin back until our eyes finally met. Moisture gathered in hers, but she blinked back her tears. I was mad—fucking pissed, actually—but I knew what that look on her face meant.

Shame. Guilt.

It wasn't something I was used to seeing on her, and I didn't like it one bit. I swallowed past the knot in my throat and forced myself to soften my tone.

"Dani."

She didn't say anything right away, but I could feel the tension radiating off her. Her breath hitched against my chest, shallow and uneven. She blinked up at me, lashes fluttering like she wanted to look away but couldn't—not with my hand still under her chin, tilting her face toward mine.

"I wasn't hiding it," she said finally, her voice hoarse. "I promise."

My thumb brushed her jaw, and I felt it clench beneath my fingers. "Hiding what exactly?"

"You know what."

"I need to hear it." My voice came out low, almost guttural. I was trying to stay calm, but with every second that passed, I felt closer to unraveling. "Because right now, I feel like I'm losing my goddamn mind."

One of her hands fisted gently in the fabric of my shirt, like she needed something to hold onto. Her eyes searched mine, and she gave the smallest shake of her head. Whether it was in denial or fear or panic, I couldn't tell.

"Dani." My pulse thundered in my ears. "Are you having my baby?"

Her lips parted, and for a second, I wasn't sure the words would come out.

"Yes," she whispered. "It's yours."

There it was: the truth laid bare between us.

Dani's having my baby.

I let out a slow breath, trying to keep the floor steady beneath my feet. She was still right there in front of me, still holding onto my shirt like she needed me, even though we both knew that wasn't the case. But her eyes told me that she was already starting to retreat. I saw it in the way her shoulders tensed, the way her lips trembled.

"Fuck, Dani," I said quietly. The breath I let out was shaky. I scrubbed a hand over my mouth, unsure what to do with any of this. The weight of it. "Why the hell didn't you tell me?"

Her breath hitched—just barely, but it was enough.

I knew I'd fucked up the second the words left my mouth. They were too sharp, too raw, too much like an accusation when what I should've offered her was comfort.

Her expression crumpled. "I was going to," she said quickly. "I've been trying to figure out how to tell you for weeks—"

"You've known for weeks?" I asked through gritted teeth. This just got worse and worse.

She winced. "Okay, that sounds bad, but I swear, I was going to tell you. And it was not supposed to be like this. But now that you do know, I just want to make it clear that you don't owe me anything. I'm not expecting you to drop anything for me. Or us, I guess."

Excuse me.

"Seriously, you don't need to be involved at all if you don't want to be."

She said it like she was doing me a favor, like letting me off the hook was some kind of gift. Now, I was pissed for a completely different reason.

"You don't get to say that," I snapped, stepping away from her. "You don't get to decide what kind of father I want to be."

She opened her mouth, probably to argue, but I wasn't finished. "I already have a kid. I already know what this whole thing looks like, how much it means. I'm not some one-night stand you forgot to text the next day. You *know* me. You should know I don't walk away from shit like this."

I gestured between us.

"Did you really think I wouldn't want this?" I asked. "That I wouldn't want you?"

Her mouth dropped open at my directness. I couldn't blame her—it was probably the most words I had ever strung together at once. Definitely not my smoothest move either, but there was nothing smooth about this situation.

This was a fucking mess. And I was in deep.

Her arms wrapped around the slight swell of her belly. *Our baby*. Fucking Christ, she was growing our child. Which reminded me—

"Can I see?"

She flinched when I reached for her hand. More specifically, for the now crumpled photo clutched between her fingers.

All the fire and panic inside me cooled into something heavier. Something sadder. Dani wasn't trying to punish me; she was trying to protect herself—from hope, from heartbreak. From me.

And that was the deepest cut of all.

She followed my gaze, and a flicker of understanding passed across her face.

She uncurled her fingers and placed the sonogram in my hand. It was creased from being held so tightly and a bit torn thanks to Matty's dog, but I could still make it out—the little bean-shaped silhouette in the center no bigger than a strawberry.

Jesus Christ.

I stared at it, mesmerized by this little being I already loved so damn much. The onslaught of emotions rushed over me—awe, terror, gratitude. It was overwhelming, in the best way possible.

And then the dam burst.

"When's your due date?"

"October eighth."

The questions spilled out of me. "And are you taking your vitamins? How's your blood pressure? Have you decided on your birth plan yet? Are you going to stop traveling with the team? That might be too much for your body."

Her mouth dropped open, eyes wide with disbelief.

"Okay, stop," she said, holding up her hands. "Back it up, coach. This is turning into an interrogation."

I scrubbed a hand down my beard, dragging in a breath like it might calm the heat under my skin. It didn't.

"I'm sorry, but this is a big deal. We have a lot to figure out, and I should've been there for you since day one, but I didn't—"

"You didn't know," she cut in sharply. "I got that, Brooks. You've made it very clear that I should have told you sooner, and you know what? You're right. And I apologize for that, but now that you do know, you're acting like I've been completely reckless and incompetent."

"That's not what I meant."

She took a step back. "Are you sure?"

I reached for her again, but she dodged my touch.

"Dani—"

"You don't get to show up and start barking orders like I'm one of your players, Brooks," she said, voice trembling. "I'm glad you want to be involved, but that doesn't mean you get to control me."

"I'm not trying to," I said defensively, but even as the words left my mouth, I wasn't sure if they were true.

Because maybe, just maybe, some part of me *was* trying to control it—her, this, all of it. Not because I didn't trust her, but because the second I saw that sonogram photo, the earth shifted beneath me. The trajectory of my life changed. And I didn't know how to exist in this new version of reality, where the woman I wanted was pregnant and I hadn't been there for any of it.

Again.

I had seen this film play out before and sequels fucking sucked.

I was used to calling the shots, used to having a game plan. But there was no playbook for this. And watching Dani inch closer to the door, desperate for an escape, was starting to feel a hell of a lot like losing.

And I hated losing.

"I need a minute," she muttered, snatching the photo from me and turning on her heel.

I watched her go, my hand still half-lifted in the air. But I didn't chase her this time. I couldn't, not yet at least.

The slam of the door echoed in my chest like a warning shot. My instincts were screaming at me to fix this, to follow her, to force a conversation until everything made sense again. But I knew better. If I pushed now, she would only run farther, faster—and maybe not come back.

If I wanted any chance in hell of being in this kid's life—*and hers*—I needed to figure out how to show up without bulldozing everything in my path.

I wasn't just some guy trying to make things right anymore. I was going to be a father again, and this time, I wasn't going to fuck it up.

Dani

Roasters 16–10

According to the pregnancy app on my phone, my baby was officially the size of a Pop-Tart.

Which felt vaguely . . . threatening.

Maybe it was the sharp corners. Or the frosting that never quite reached the edges. Or the fact that until the last few days, I hadn't been able to look at my second favorite pantry pastry—because nothing beat Entenmann's iced honey buns—without feeling like I needed to hurl since finding out I was pregnant. Thankfully, the constant bouts of nausea had finally started to subside.

Now, I was just hungry, horny, or some combination of the two at all times.

Biology was wild.

Even more wild was trying to pretend like I still had complete control of my hormones while mic'd up at a baseball stadium full of thousands of rabid fans. Fortunately, distraction came in the form of controlled chaos, which was basically my professional love language.

"Your turn, Wes," I called out, motioning our centerfielder over to the sidelines as the rest of the team wrapped up warm-ups. "Your question is, would you rather fight a hundred goose-sized horses or one horse-sized goose?"

He blinked. "*Acho, puñeta*! What kind of psycho came up with that one?"

I nailed him with a look. "Who do you think?"

His eyes roved the field. It only took him a second to spot Pink not-so-subtly waving to him from the bullpen. Wes flipped him off.

"Put me down for the horses," he said, dead serious. "You ever seen a goose up close? Like a *chupacabra* with feathers."

From behind the camera, Clarke snorted. "Does that mean you don't want to volunteer for the Swing for the Fences event at the petting zoo?"

Swing for the Fences, the team's nonprofit organization, aimed to provide opportunities and resources for youth baseball and softball teams in the Pacific Northwest. That included monthly outings with the kids where our players traded batting gloves for picnic baskets, a fishing trip to Tillamook where the kids out-fished the pros, and the infamous sleepover at the stadium that we were all still going to therapy for. Nonetheless, these little snapshots of joy stuck around longer than any final score.

And the guys *loved* the kids. Truly, it was a wonder that none of them had any of their own yet.

Wes shook his head. "Not if geese are involved."

I bit back a smile. "Fair enough. Who do you want us to talk to next, and what do you want us to ask?"

"Diaz. Ask him to pick his favorite Chris Evans movie."

Clarke gasped at the same time I groaned. It was no secret that Diaz worshipped at the altar of Chris Evans. Literally—the guy had a prayer candle with his favorite cable-knit sweater wearing icon and everything. Asking him to choose his favorite Chris Evans flick was like asking a parent to pick their favorite child. Except in this case, the "children" were *Captain America: The First Avenger*, *Knives Out*, and a surprisingly passionate defense of *Not Another Teen Movie*.

"Bold choice," I said, shooting Clarke a look that promised chaos. "You're really trying to cook something up before the first pitch."

Wes grinned, unapologetic. "That's me. Chef Nuñez."

Chef was putting it lightly, more like a *god*.

Wes's authentic Puerto Rican cooking was a staple at most team functions, so it went without saying that I envied the woman who would nab a permanent seat at his table.

I blew a few hot puffs of air into my palms when he jogged off.

Chicago in April was a cruel joke. Wind like razor blades, clouds thicker than last night's cream of cauliflower soup. And I was doing my best impression of a fleece-wrapped marshmallow, layered in thermals, a hoodie, *and* my well-worn pleather bomber jacket.

It was nothing compared to my partner in crime, though. In fact, the only visible part of her was her face, pinkened from the cold. Her ankle-length team parka had been thoughtfully adorned with two glittery pins—one shaped like lipstick and another that read "Bless your heart."

"You look like a Jawa," I teased, tugging on the strings of her fur-lined hood.

"A what?"

"You know, one of those guys from *Star Wars*." Curse me and my random knowledge of nerdy fandoms. "The little dudes with the dark cloaks and glowing eyes."

She rolled her eyes.

"I hate that this weather exists," she grumbled.

I chuckled under my breath. She even sounded like a Jawa. "You say that at every away game that dips below fifty degrees."

"And you better believe I'm gonna keep on saying it." She lowered her voice before adding, "I could dial a rotary phone with my nipples."

Hm, that's a new one.

Movement at the edge of the visiting dugout caught my eye. Diaz jogged over, his jacket half unzipped and his face already bright with curiosity. Much like his celebrity crush, Diaz had the build of a superhero and the disposition of an actual puppy.

Soren came running up behind him, his cheeks flushed from warm-ups, batting gloves tucked into his back pocket.

"Just a few more," I told her. "I promise, your nipples will be fine."

"What's wrong with your nipples, blondie?" Soren greeted, sliding in beside Clarke like he'd been summoned by the sheer force of her grumpiness. Without missing a beat, he unzipped the top of her parka and wrapped his arms around her middle, pulling her against his chest. "Do you need me to take a look at them?"

Clarke made a noise that was half-protest, half-purr. "You're warm."

"Perks of hitting grounders for twenty minutes straight," he said, rubbing his hands over her sides in a way that definitely wasn't workplace appropriate. "Now, back to your nipples—"

"That's enough of that," I interrupted. "Save the nipple talk for somewhere, literally *anywhere*, that's not in front of forty-thousand fans."

I wedged myself between Clarke and the camera set-up. I was desperately in need of a snack, but first, we needed to finish filming our pregame segment for the team's social channels. Today's was a fun trend that had been circulating around the MLB circuit—just a quickfire Q&A with the guys as they jogged off the field during batting practice. The twist was that each player decided on the question for me to ask the *next* player. Some were softballs, and some were chaos. Some were about creepy, hypothetical farm animals.

Diaz was already grinning like he knew what was coming. "All right, Diaz. Wes wants to know your favorite Chris Evans movie."

His eyes widened in mock betrayal. "You really want to get into this?"

I rolled my shoulders, twisted my neck, and pressed record. If we were going to open Pandora's box, we might as well smash the whole bitch to smithereens.

"Let's have it."

Diaz threw up his hands. "You asked for this. First things first, we need to outline the six different eras of Evans. Starting with—"

I tried to stay focused. I really did. Truly, there was almost nothing more entertaining than a verbal dissertation about A-list celebrities.

But my gaze kept pulling toward the dugout like a magnet I didn't remember pocketing.

I didn't see him at first.

Usually, Brooks was one of the easiest guys to spot—tall enough to tower over most guys, black frames catching the light, tattoos snaking down both arms. Plenty of the team had the ink, and a few even had the height, but none of them carried the same quiet, coiled energy he did.

An aura you could feel even when he wasn't looking at you.

And right now, he was looking at a group of kids like they were his own.

He was crouched low, pen in hand, signing a baseball for a boy in an oversized jersey that nearly swallowed him whole. Another two kids were waiting beside him, all wide-eyed and jittery, clutching caps and jerseys.

And Brooks . . . was smiling.

Fucking smiling.

Not the polite, tight-lipped press smile he broke out for photo ops or the half-smirk he used when he thought one of his players was being an idiot. No, this was a real, full-on smile. The kind that crinkled the corners of his eyes and made him look like someone I barely recognized.

I could count on one hand the number of times I had seen that in real life and still have fingers left over.

He looked younger, more at ease—a stark contrast from the man who just last weekend had looked like he might rip out his salt-and-pepper hair when he'd found out he was going to be a daddy again.

Not that I could blame him. That wasn't exactly the pregnancy reveal I had envisioned, and it certainly wasn't the one either of us deserved. I was still trying to figure out how to make it up to him.

"—and then there's the 'lovable fuckboi' era. Starting with *Scott Pilgrim vs. the World*—

We hadn't spoken since Matty's party.

Partly because our schedules had been a mess, and partly because . . . we were both scared of what came next.

I should have known that he would want to be involved. That was just who Brooks was—steady, dependable, the guy who was always there to lend a listening ear to any of his players and who remembered the name of every employee in the clubhouse, even the ones he had only met once. He was a good man, and an even better father.

But knowing that and *trusting* it were two different things.

I had spent the past two decades taking care of myself, counting on nobody but me, and that kind of wiring didn't just switch off. Letting someone in—letting them carry even part of the weight—felt like stepping off a ledge without checking if there was ground underneath.

And I had never been a fan of heights.

I glanced toward the dugout again and froze. This time, Brooks was looking straight at me. No smirk, no frown. Just a steady, unreadable gaze that sent something low and sharp through my chest . . . and made me want to rip my thermal underwear off.

Thankfully, Diaz's voice cut back through the fog.

"—and that's why if I *have* to pick, it's got to be *Knives Out*."

"The sweater is iconic," I said, nodding. "Who do you have a question for?"

He nodded toward Soren, who was too busy focusing on the woman in his arms rather than his teammate's answer. "Ask Sinclair what his favorite yoga position is."

Soren was an avid yogi—that was common knowledge. But Diaz's grin told me there might be more to his question. He jogged off toward the dugout to heckle Wes about his question, and I redirected my attention toward the couple canoodling three feet away.

"Clarke, stop sucking face with your boyfriend and make him tell us what his favorite yoga position is." I held the mini microphone out to him. "And don't you dare say downward dog."

Soren tore his gaze from Clarke long enough to glance at me, then back at her, one corner of his mouth curling like he'd just been handed the setup for his favorite joke. Clarke's eyes narrowed in warning, the faintest flush creeping above the edge of her parka.

"Happy baby," he said finally, voice low and smug.

Fuck, of course it is.

Clarke groaned, burying her face in his chest while I tried—and failed—not to laugh into the mic.

"What does that look like?"

He winked. "Look it up."

Later that night, hours after Chicago had cleaned our clocks and the team bus had hauled us back to the hotel, I had just finished demolishing my room-service grilled cheese when there was a knock at the door.

Fuck.

Clarke was spending the night with Soren, nursing his physical and emotional wounds—and then some. The rest of the team had reserved a boat for a late-night cruise on Lake Michigan.

Personally, I had opted for bed rotting.

The heater rattled in the corner of the room, pumping out air just warm enough to thaw the chill that had burrowed into my bones. I was warm, full, and perfectly horizontal. The absolute last thing I wanted was to swing my legs out from under the covers.

But I did it anyway, slipping into my pajama bottoms on the way to the door. I should have known who would be waiting on the other side.

"Hey," he said quietly.

"Hey, yourself."

Brooks stood in the hallway wearing sweats, a black quarter-zip, and that sheepish, slightly disheveled look he got when he wasn't sure if I was going to slam the door in his face or not.

I knew better than that, though. This conversation had been a long time coming. I swung the door wide and gestured him inside. His lips twitched like he wanted to smile but didn't quite let himself. He simply walked past me, carrying the scent of soap and cold night air with him.

"Sorry about the game today," I said, closing the door behind us.

He shrugged. "We played like crap."

Finally, something we could both agree on. To say the guys hadn't played their best would be an understatement. I was pretty sure we had set a season record for the most pop flies to the infield.

I crossed my arms, partly because it was comfortable, partly because it felt safer to keep some space between us. "So, what's on your mind?"

"I wanted to see how you were. And if we could talk." His gaze flicked back to mine. "And apologize."

"I think we both know I'm the one who owes you an apology."

The words scraped on the way out because letting go of my pride had never been my strong suit. Stubbornness had been my shield for as long as I could remember—it kept me upright when things got hard, kept people from getting too close. *Kept me safe.* And yes, it wasn't always pretty, but it was familiar.

I swallowed past it, forcing myself to keep going.

"I should have told you sooner, regardless of how I thought you might respond. And finding out like that, in front of everybody, was fucked up, so I'm sorry."

"I get it," he said gently. There was no accusation in his voice, just that calm, even tone he used when he was trying to talk someone down from a ledge. "I get why you didn't tell me right away. And I'm not here to make you feel worse about it."

My chest loosened just a fraction.

"But I still want to be a part of it."

I grinned. "Well, you are part of it. You know, *biologically.*"

"That's not what I mean, and you know it." He unraveled my tangled arms and took my hands in his. "I want to be involved in all of it. I'm talking doctor appointments, preparing the nursery, the weird ass stuff no one talks about." His mouth twitched. "Like whatever the fuck happens with your ankles in the eighth month."

Hold up.

"Wait, what's going to happen to my ankles? I haven't made it to that part of my book."

He huffed out a laugh. "Let's save that for another day, yeah?"

I nodded. That was all I could manage when my brain had completely short-circuited from the way his thumbs were dragging lazy circles over my skin. His hands were warm, calloused in the places that came from years of gripping a bat, and the steady pressure against my pulse felt almost hypnotic.

Our tattoos met in the space between our knuckles. His bold black lines and shaded script tangled with the softer, fine lines inked along my fingers. In the low hotel light, they looked like they belonged to the same story. One design bled into the next until I couldn't tell where his ended and mine began.

"Now it's my turn to apologize."

"What? You don't have—"

"I do. I'm sorry for bombarding you with a million questions. I was . . . trying to wrap my head around everything and forgot you were probably doing the same. I didn't mean to make you feel like you were doing it wrong."

"I appreciate that."

He looked away before adding, "I have been through this before, so I do know *some* things, but there's also a lot I missed the first time around. Things I didn't get to be there for with Carolina, and I don't want to miss them this time. Not if you'll let me be part of it."

Something low in my chest tightened, not in a bad way, but in that way that made it hard to find the right words. For so long, I had filed Brooks under unshakable—gruff, stoic, built out of steel and discipline. But right now, with his hands still warm around mine and his voice low and steady, I could see past all that armor.

And underneath it all, Brooks was a gentle giant.

"Okay," I said, my voice quieter than I meant it to be. "We do this together. Just try to give me some grace while I figure out how to do this with someone else in the equation."

His shoulders eased, and the smallest smile ghosted over his mouth. "Deal."

I wasn't sure if I felt lighter because of his answer or heavier because of what it meant, but for the first time in weeks, I didn't feel like I was carrying it all alone. And as reluctant as I was to admit it, that felt pretty good.

"I promise not to take over your life," he added. "But if you need anything—antacids, a midnight snack, one of those massive pregnancy pillows that looks like a pool noodle—just call me, please."

I shook my head. "You don't need to do that."

"But I want to. And I would really appreciate it if you'd let me know when your next appointment is." He smirked. "I think

I owe you another sonogram photo, one without drool and toothmarks."

There it was. Earnest, not pushy, and infuriatingly hard to resist.

"I'll text you the date."

He let out a slow breath, like he'd been holding it since I'd opened the door.

"Thank you," he said, and then, just before he turned to go, he leaned in—hesitating, checking my expression—and pressed a soft, chaste kiss to my forehead. "I don't know if I said it before, but I'm really excited about this. I, uh, would be lying if I said I hadn't thought about you having my baby once or twice."

That stunned me into stillness.

He didn't linger. Didn't ask for more. Just gave me one last look—one full of longing and gratitude—and walked back toward the elevator. I must've stood there for a full minute, forehead tingling, heart confused, stomach doing Olympic-level flips.

He slowed a step, glancing over his shoulder. "Oh, and kitten?"

"Hm?" I choked out.

"I love the pajamas."

His eyes flicked to the cartoon cats in witch hats covering my pants. *Kittens.* The corner of his mouth curved up before he turned away again, leaving me with an open mouth, racing pulse, and the unsettling feeling that maybe—just maybe—trusting him wouldn't be as impossible as I had thought.

Brooks

Nongame days were supposed to be quiet, dull, reserved for reviewing scouting reports, analyzing game footage, and catching up on my endless stream of emails. And yet here I was, on my hands and knees, crawling around my office, desperately searching for Mr. Chomp, my daughter's favorite toy.

When we'd stepped off the plane from Chicago two nights ago, the first thing waiting for me hadn't been a good night's sleep, but rather a voicemail from my ex-wife.

Carolina's stuffed dinosaur was missing.

I had barely made it to the team bus before being informed—in long, grueling detail—that bedtime had been a disaster. I was on strict directives to *"locate the blue, one-eyed menace before Friday."*

Because for a six-year-old, losing a stuffed dinosaur wasn't just an inconvenience. It was an existential crisis. Mr. Chomp had been with our family since Allie's baby shower. He had survived juice spills, airplane turbulence, and one unfortunate run through the dryer that had left him looking like he had been to war and seen some shit.

Which meant if I didn't find him, I wasn't just letting my kid down. I was breaking an unspoken father-daughter pact.

"I gotta give it to you, man. This pregnancy stuff isn't for the faint of heart."

I looked up from beneath my desk, narrowly avoiding knocking my head against the heavy wood. Brock Heller was parked in a chair across from me, legs crossed as he flipped through one of the pregnancy books I had picked up this week like it was the *Guinness Book of World Records*.

"Did you know some pregnant people can develop a weird craving to chew ice, clay, or even laundry starch?" he read, eyebrows climbing. "It's called pica."

"Sounds like a choking hazard," I muttered, running a hand along the back edge of the credenza. "In the event that Dani starts eating laundry starch, I'll be sure to let you know."

After a trip to the emergency room.

Brock smirked, flipping to another page. "Oh, here's another one. How many weeks is she?"

I did some quick mental math. "About nineteen."

"Your baby has fingerprints by the end of the first trimester."

"Huh," I said, crouching to check under a filing cabinet. "A tiny, wrinkly criminal."

"Dude, don't mock the fetus."

I grunted in acknowledgment, reaching behind the cabinet, springing up with excitement when my fingers brushed something lumpy and suspiciously fuzzy. One victorious tug later and I emerged holding the battered, one-eyed dinosaur like it was a trophy.

"Mr. Chomp, reporting for duty," I cheered.

Brock arched a brow at the frayed blue fabric. "That thing looks like it's been through a woodchipper."

"Yeah," I said, dusting him off and setting him on my desk. "And somehow, he's still the most important member of my household."

"Does that mean we can go to lunch now?"

I nodded.

To some people, the two of us might have made an unlikely pair. It wasn't every day that a head coach bonded with a sports reporter, especially not one like Brock Heller, who chose his words without mercy. But after a few conversations, we'd realized that we had a lot more in common than our shared love of the game.

We also both ate vegan.

The man could recite pitching stats from memory and debate oat-milk brands in the same breath. The only difference was that Brock wasn't a purist. The guy had a weakness for cheese that would make a dairy farmer proud.

I shut my laptop and reached for my jacket. "Mediterranean?"

"Works for me."

"I just need to stop off at the weight room first," I told him. "Make sure the guys are staying on top of their shit."

He smiled. "Sounds good."

Yeah, I bet it does.

Something told me that his eagerness had less to do with my favorite falafel truck and everything to do with his boyfriend. He and my second baseman had gotten together last summer, and they were still going strong nearly a year later.

We took the stairs down to the weight room. The clanking of plates and low hum of friendly trash talk filled the air even before we rounded the final corner.

"That doesn't count," one of them complained. "His chest didn't touch the floor."

"Oh, quit your bellyaching, fucker."

That was Matty. There was no mistaking his drawl.

By the time we stepped through the doorway, the picture came into focus. In the middle of the rubber-matted floor, Bennett, Matty, and Pink were locked in what looked like a push-up death match—palms planted, backs ramrod straight, faces set with that grim, competitive determination usually reserved for the bottom of the ninth.

They had arranged themselves in a loose circle, heads pointing toward the center like some sort of weird athletic sundial, each one trying to outlast the others.

Bennett's jaw was clenched, sweat dripping down his temples, past his cochlear implants. Pink, predictably, was running his mouth between reps, tossing out insults like beaded necklaces at Mardi Gras. Matty looked like he was out to prove a point, eyes narrowed, counting under his breath as if sheer willpower could keep his arms from giving out.

Off to the side, Soren leaned against a weight rack, arms crossed, smirking like he was watching a nature documentary. Tucker was next to him, one hand on the barbell resting across his shoulders, clearly invested in the outcome but too smart to join in.

Brock and I paused just inside the doorway, the air thick with the smell of chalk, sweat, and the fragile male ego.

"Let me guess," Brock murmured. "Loser has to wash the other guys' jockstraps?"

"Something like that," I said, though with this group, it could just as easily end with someone having to wear a ridiculous T-shirt for a week.

Case in point, last week's squat contest had ended with Bennett having to rock a leopard print thong under his shorts during batting practice—we were all still trying to scrub that mental image from our brains. And then there was the time that Roman had had to change his walk-up song to Taylor Swift's "Look What You Made Me Do," though, in my opinion, he had enjoyed that one a little too much.

Matty took the cake, though. He had lost the homerun contest during spring training and as such, had to host what the guys now referred to as *The Most Extra Dinner in Baseball History*. That meant renting out a private dining room at some five-star steakhouse, showing up in a tux, and presenting everyone with personalized menus. He had even gone the extra mile and hired a Michelin-starred baker to craft bread loaves in the shape of miniature baseball bats.

Tucker peeled himself away from the weight rack and strolled over, a towel draped around his neck. He leaned in toward Brock like he was about to share state secrets.

"This time," he said, voice low and conspiratorial, "the loser has to get a spray tan. I'm talking *Jersey Shore* level orange."

Brock's brows shot up. "That's just cruel."

I glanced over at the push-up circle, where Pink was already starting to wobble but still trash-talking like he was in the lead. "Who are you rooting for?"

Tucker rested his hand on Brock's shoulder and grinned. "Orange is the new pink."

Brock snorted.

"Alright, break it up," I called, stepping farther into the room.

Bennett's head snapped up mid-rep, sweat dripping onto the mat. "Coach, we were just—"

"Save it," I said. "I don't remember this being a part of any-body's strength training program."

Pink gave one last grunt, knocked out two shaky push-ups, and collapsed onto his stomach like he'd been shot. Matty lasted three more—purely for the show—before rolling onto his back with a grin.

"Looks like you're heading to the tanning booth, Pinky boy," Soren called, smirking.

"Fuck off," Pink shot back, rolling to his feet and grabbing his water bottle.

While the others continued razzing him about whether he should go with a subtle pumpkin spice latte shade or full-on Oompa-Loompa, I leaned over to Brock. "Give me a few min-utes?"

"Sure," he said easily, slipping an arm around Tucker's waist without missing a beat. Tucker didn't even look away from the scene in front of us, just reached up and twirled a finger through Brock's hair like it was second nature. "I'm in no rush."

I crossed the room, catching Pink next to the squat racks. "Walk with me."

He gave me a quick, curious glance but followed as I steered us toward a quieter corner at the opposite end of the room. "Is this about the spray tan? Because I'm already planning to wear long sleeves for the next month."

I waited until we were out of earshot of the others before laying my cards on the table. "It's about Dani."

"In all seriousness, coach, it's probably best I stay out of whatever's going on between the two of you." He quickly added, "Just so long as you understand that I'm not going anywhere. Dani is practically family, so that little bun in her oven might as well be my niece or nephew. Treat them right and we're cool."

His tone was easy enough, but there was a thread of warning underneath. This wasn't the first time he'd given me "the talk" about treating his friend right.

When Pink had first found out about us last year, he had spelled out in no uncertain terms what would happen if I hurt her. No raised voices, no dramatics, just a calm, pointed reminder that Dani deserved nothing less than the world. Not the best delivery, but it had made me look at him with newfound respect. Dani was lucky to have someone like Pink in her corner.

"I have no intention of fucking things up with her again." He nodded. "But you live with her—you have the best read on how she's really doing."

He tilted his head, studying me like he was taking my measure. "You want intel."

"I want to know if there's anything she needs." And even though I knew I would probably regret it later, I somehow found myself adding, "I have a feeling that she's more likely to share that with you than me."

"That'll come at a price."

I folded my arms. "What do you want?"

Pink's grin tilted.

"Wall sits."

I blinked. "Excuse me?"

"Wall sits," Pink repeated, like it was the most natural sentence in the world. "It's like you always say, coach. You gotta make them earn it."

That was how I ended up with my back flat against the cement wall, knees bent at ninety degrees. Pink dropped down beside me with a little too much confidence for someone who'd just lost a push-up contest.

"Alright, coach. What do you want to know?"

"Cravings," I said without missing a beat.

"It used to be hot Cheetos and ice cream, but she's recently moved onto avocados and peanut butter. Oh, and she pretends she's over pickles, but I caught her drinking straight out of the jar the other night."

Well, anything was better than laundry starch.

"How about sleep?"

"She's getting it . . . mostly. But she's waking up more at night. And when she's up, she's raiding the kitchen like a raccoon."

"Noted," I said, keeping my breathing even.

He blew out a breath. "Her back's been bothering her. She won't admit it, but she's been stretching more, walking a little slower. Take it from me, though—don't make a big deal out of it or she'll bite your head off."

Another thirty seconds and his legs started to shake.

Mine didn't. *Sucker.*

"You're annoyingly good at this," he muttered.

"Comes with the job," I said, settling in. "Anything else I should know?"

Pink's jaw flexed.

"Is she still jogging?"

"Five miles, nearly every day," he answered between broken breaths. "I don't know how she does it."

We hit the two-minute mark, and Pink's hands went to his thighs like that would stop the burn.

"Fuck, are you even trying? My quads are on fire."

"Trying," I said, "would imply there's effort involved."

"Show-off," he muttered, finally springing up and shaking out his legs. "Fine, you win. But you better use that info wisely."

I pushed off the wall, barely winded. "Appreciate the tips, Pink. Or should I say, *Orange*?"

He fixed me with a pointed glare. "I knew I should've kept my mouth shut."

"That would be a first."

Pink stalked off toward the showers, muttering under his breath, and I stood there for a second, running over everything he'd just told me. I had gone into the conversation looking for crumbs, but he'd handed me a full scouting report—cravings, sleep, exercise, the back pain she wouldn't admit to. It was all useful information, the kind of details I could act on.

Starting now.

When I stepped back into the hall, Brock was exactly where I'd left him, still tucked under Tucker's arm and looking entirely unbothered by the wait. "You two done having your little quad contest?" he asked.

"Yeah," I said, falling into step beside him. "We need to make a stop on the way back from lunch."

"For what?"

I let a small smile slip. "I've got some shopping to do."

Dani

Roasters 22–14

"I'm just saying, if the kiss cam lands on us, we should totally make out," June announced as we wove our way down the stadium steps.

Kaylani arched a brow, one hand clutching her protruding belly. "Need I remind you that I'm a soon-to-be married woman and this kid is due any day now?"

"Ryan will understand." She tilted her beer toward us. "What about the rest of you?"

Nessa shrugged. "I have a boyfriend."

"I have a husband," Jo added.

"I am heterosexual," Bella said, though she didn't sound convinced.

June arched a brow. "Was that a question?"

Bella blinked at June's expression. "Well, I've only ever kissed two men, so I'm not really sure if I'm attracted to women or not."

I bit back a smile. Pink's younger sister had moved to Rose City last fall after taking a leave of absence from college, and she had won us all over almost instantly. Even though she was a decade younger than I was, she had maturity and self-awareness that I admired.

I pitied the idiots who thought autism was anything less than a superpower. Bella's directness was something to be envied. She processed everything in straightforward terms—no dancing around it, no dressing it up to make other people more comfortable. Just pure honesty, like she was reading from her own internal rulebook.

June's lips twitched like she wasn't sure whether to laugh or press for more details. "All the more reason for us to make out in front of thousands of strangers, don't you think?"

Bella gave a little nod, clearly filing away June's reasoning like it was useful data. "Excellent point."

Nessa rolled her eyes. "Oh my god. If I promise to kiss you on camera, will you leave the poor girl alone?"

June smirked into her drink. "No promises."

I snorted. "Lord, you guys are going to get banned before the first pitch."

It was one of those picture-perfect game days at the Roasters' stadium. Bright blue sky, sunlight glinting off the upper deck, just enough wind to whip your hair into your beer and send stray napkins skittering across the concourse. On the field, players jogged the warning track, worked through stretches along the foul lines, and snapped warm-up throws across the infield. A couple of outfielders were tracking lazy pop flies under the sun, while the bullpen guys leaned against the railing, talking and spitting sunflower seeds like they had all the time in the world.

Today marked our second annual "Rose City Proud" day at the ballpark. The event honored local businesses, including Nessa's bookstore, Jo's bakery, Would Smell as Sweet, and June's vintage trailer resort, Bed of Roses, all of which would be featured on the jumbotron between innings. The three of them had been invited down to the field pregame for photos, and they were still riding the buzz of having their logos splashed across a stadium full of fans.

Kaylani was just along for the ride . . . and ballpark snacks. Because where else could you enjoy a slice of deep-fried marionberry pie while watching men in too-tight pants play with balls?

By the time we reached our seats behind the dugout, the place was already humming. Bella settled into hers crisscross applesauce style and pulled out her Loop earplugs, not that they were any match for the stadium noise. Nessa, June, and Jo filed in beside her, their arms loaded with enough concessions that it made me wonder if they had all skipped breakfast *and* lunch. The smell of melted cheese and fryer oil immediately drifted down the row, making my stomach growl despite the bag of boring ass trail mix in my fanny pack.

That left Kaylani on the aisle, who lowered herself into her seat with the air of a queen claiming her throne. Talk about a walking, talking example of pregnancy propaganda. She looked ten times better than I felt.

I had yet to experience that "pregnancy glow" I had heard so much about, but Kaylani was practically the poster girl for it. Her warm golden-brown skin caught the afternoon light like she'd been airbrushed, and not a single strand of her glossy black hair dared to be out of place. She looked like she'd stepped straight out of a maternity photoshoot in one of those chic, neutral-toned wrap dresses rather than someone waddling into a ballpark for deep-fried pie.

May we all be so lucky.

"Wow, we're practically on the field," Jo squealed. While Bella and Nessa had ties to the team through Pink, Jo was by far the biggest baseball fan of our friend group. "Thanks, Dani."

June zeroed in on our backup catcher not ten yards away. "Incredible views."

I had pulled some strings with the ticket office to make sure they had prime behind-the-dugout seats, even blocking off an extra one for Clarke and me to tag-team between innings. It wasn't exactly a hardship—especially when the view came with a side of eye candy in uniform.

And black-rimmed glasses.

"So," Nessa said, twisting in her seat to look at me. "What was in your latest Triple D package?"

My brows scrunched together. "My what?"

"Triple D. Your daily Daddy delivery."

I buried my face in my hands.

Kaylani leaned back, resting her hands on her belly. "Ooo, do tell."

"There's nothing to tell."

"She's gotten, like, six care packages this week," Bella said flatly, not even looking up from her phone. "Sometimes two in a day."

I turned toward her slowly. "Traitor."

Bella shrugged. "It's not a secret. They're usually sitting on the porch when I get home."

June sighed wistfully. "God, he's like the UPS guy, but hotter."

That earned a round of knowing smirks from the group.

Bella wasn't exaggerating. Brooks's surprise packages—most of which he had delivered himself, usually in the dead of night—had started last week, after the team had gotten back from our series in Chicago.

It had been little things at first—a jar of overpriced pickles that was big enough to feed a defensive line, a bottle of bougie (and vegan) prenatal vitamins, a pair of ridiculously soft socks that I had taken to wearing to bed almost every night. Because apparently, I was the one pregnant person who ran cold—more like freezing—instead of hot, shivering under layers while everyone else complained about hot flashes.

Then, the boxes had started getting bigger—a weighted blanket that I may or may not have napped under for two days straight, a heating pad shaped like a cat that had come in clutch after a particularly grueling bus ride. And then there was the night my phone buzzed with a text from him.

Brooks

Need me to grab you more avocadoes?

Me

> I'm pregnant, Brooks. Not bedridden.

Brooks

> **Is that a no?**

I'd been curled up on the couch, dressed in my rattiest pair of period-stained sweatpants, and watching reruns of *Dateline*. Without thinking, I shot him another message.

Me

> You know what I really want? A slice of Jo's maple pecan bread.

It had been an impossible ask. I'd known that. Would Smell as Sweet had already closed for the night; there wasn't another bakery for forty miles. And yet, three hours later, there'd been a knock at my door—and a still-warm loaf waiting on the porch, wrapped in a tea towel.

It had gotten to the point where I couldn't go outside without half expecting to find him there, arms loaded up with salty snacks and nipple balm like some kind of pregnancy-themed Santa Claus.

Mm, another bearded Daddy...

Damn, these hormones were getting out of hand. Two rounds with my go-to vibrator this morning weren't cutting it.

"Don't keep us hanging," Nessa said around bites of popcorn. "Not to go full Brad Pitt, but 'what's in the box?'"

I chewed on my lower lip. "Oh, nothing too exciting. Just a seventy-two pack of cereal boxes."

June blinked rapidly. "Seventy-two?"

"I kind of have a thing for Frosted Flakes right now," I said, nodding.

Nessa smiled. "The man knows your love language."

I rolled my eyes, but there was no hiding my smile. "My love language is 'not having to cook dinner if I can help it.'"

Kaylani shifted in her seat, one hand flying to her belly. "Oh, there it is again."

"Is he kicking?"

"More like tap dancing." Her grin was soft and a little dazed as she looked at me. "Want to feel?"

I hesitated for half a second, unsure if I was intruding on something intimate, but curiosity won out. Leaning over, I placed my palm against the smooth curve of her stomach, the fabric of her wrap dress warm from the sun.

"Right there," she whispered, guiding my hand a little lower.

A second later, a firm, fluttery thump pressed back into my palm, quick and certain, like a tiny knock from the inside. I glanced at her, eyes wide, but she was still watching me with that knowing, serene smile only pregnant people who were further along seemed to have.

It felt impossibly small and huge all at once, the kind of moment that didn't just happen in passing. The kind you remembered.

I hadn't felt that yet—not from the inside, anyway—but I had started noticing the subtler shifts.

During the first trimester, my body had felt mostly the same, aside from the constant nausea and tits so sore I'd wanted to file a formal complaint. But the second trimester had flipped some invisible switch.

My skin was more sensitive, my boobs had pulled a full-on Grinch and "grown three sizes," and my hips felt . . . different. Looser somehow, like my body was already making room for the inevitable. Worst of all, my jeans didn't button anymore.

It wasn't bad, exactly—aside from the jeans. Just new. And new had always made me a little uneasy.

"Wow," I murmured, pulling my hand back. "That's wild."

Kaylani beamed. "You'll get there soon enough. Also, feel free to hit me up with any random pregnancy questions you might have. I know I'm still learning as I go, but I've got a few months on you."

I did have questions. *Lots* of them.

Like, was it normal for my feet to feel weirdly sore first thing in the morning? Was there an actual medical reason why lemonade tasted like it had been blessed by the gods? And how the hell was I supposed to give up sleeping on my stomach?

But there was one burning question that had been sitting in the back of my mind all week, tapping insistently until I couldn't ignore it. The kind that made my cheeks warm just thinking about saying it out loud, especially in the middle of a crowded ballpark.

Kaylani's gaze sharpened, like she could hear my brain working. Nessa caught the expression too, her brows lifting in intrigue. "Oh boy," she said, leaning in. "You're thinking about something. Spill it."

"Yeah," June added, grinning. "That's an *I'm about to ride something and it's not a Peloton* kind of face. Out with it."

"Peer pressure," Nessa coughed.

Fuck it. There was nothing to be embarrassed about. I might as well get this over with.

"Fine. Lately, I've been feeling extra—"

"Horny?" Kaylani finished for me.

"Yes. That's normal, though, right?"

Her mouth curved. "Oh, completely. Second trimester, your hormones are in overdrive. Seriously, Ryan and I went at it for three months straight like we were teenagers."

June let out a low whistle. "I've never been prouder, Kay."

Jo's brows shot up. "*Ay, mami.* Three months? My back would give out."

Kaylani just laughed. "Not the way we're doing it."

A flicker of something—jealousy, maybe—pinched in my chest. Jars of pickles and fuzzy socks could only get me so far.

I needed to get fucked.

Sure, the care packages were thoughtful, and I wasn't about to knock free snacks, but they didn't keep me warm at night. They didn't bend me over the bed, wrap their hands through my hair, and drill me into the mattress until I screamed. No wonder people usually coupled up before they got pregnant. There were some things you just needed a partner for—sex being right up there at the top of the list.

And right now, my body was practically begging for it.

"You know, I bet a certain someone would be willing to help you out with your . . . situation," June offered, wagging her eyebrows suggestively.

"Uh-huh," Nessa agreed, pointing her hot dog at me for emphasis. "Didn't Brooks say you could tell him if you needed *anything*?"

My face warmed. "I don't appreciate the way that you're waving that wiener at me."

She grinned devilishly before taking a bite that could only be described as downright pornographic.

"Besides, you know that's not what he meant."

"Sweetheart," June said, "that's exactly what he meant."

Jo nodded sagely. "Let the man fulfill his promise. It's a win-win."

Bella glanced up from her phone just long enough to add, "Statistically, sex during pregnancy is safe."

Et tu, Bella?

I covered my face with both hands, laughing despite myself. "You guys are awful."

"Awfully smart," Kaylani said, leaning back with a Cheshire catlike grin.

The idea was more than a little tempting.

Brooks and I had been there before—*many* times—his lips on my skin, his tattooed fingers wrapped around my throat, the weight of his body pressing me into the mattress. And it had been good.

Every. Fucking. Time.

So good, in fact, that it didn't have to mean anything. After all, we had messed around for months without it being anything more. At least, that was the lie I kept trying to sell myself.

Then again, nothing about Brooks was simple, and pretending otherwise was just asking for trouble. Sleeping with him now, in the middle of all . . . this, could turn into a full-blown mess before I even had time to catch my breath. I had more than myself and *my* feelings to think about now.

Mama's little parasite deserved their father. I wasn't going to jeopardize their relationship just because I couldn't control my libido.

No, the safer plan was to keep my distance, to ride out this hormone surge until my body stopped behaving like a sex-starved maniac. That meant no more late-night texts, no more lingering looks across the dugout, and *definitely* no more fantasizing about riding his cock in that ridiculously big leather chair in his office, the one that looked like it belonged to a mob boss instead of a baseball coach.

I shook the thought from my head just in time for June to lean forward, eyes sparkling. "So, Kaylani, how exactly *are* you and Ryan doing it? And please, be as detailed as possible."

Jo clapped his hands. Nessa leaned in, hot dog forgotten. Even Bella tilted her head with mild interest.

Kaylani grinned sheepishly. "Well, there was this one time where I was on my side—"

And just like that, the first fifteen minutes of the game became a crash course in pregnancy sex positions, complete with hand gestures, questionable metaphors, and more than one double entendre that eventually made the family in the row ahead of us turn around.

Brooks

Roasters 28–19

I t was a wonder that there weren't more pregnant body-builders.

Between the gear, the gadgets, and the random "must-haves" that promised to make life easier while simultaneously making your load heavier, it was like training for a fucking strongman competition.

Without the glory of a medal, no less.

Mothers didn't get half the trophies, pay raises, or standing ovations they deserved—hell, they were lucky if anyone even noticed they were carrying the whole damn team on their backs.

The package in my arms was big enough to block half my view of the cobblestone path leading up to Dani's townhouse, but that didn't slow me down. I had scored the holy grail of maternity gear: a U-shaped pillow the size of a small canoe, with enough fluff to swallow her whole. According to the *Baby Bumps and Lumps* subreddit, which, as of late, had become my how-to guide, it was *the* pregnancy pillow of all pregnancy pillows, and I could believe it. I had gone to four different stores to find the damn thing.

Hell, I had nearly bought one for myself. The damn thing had nearly swallowed me whole when I'd tested it out at the store. It was like napping inside a cloud. If the new maternity pajamas I'd nabbed for her felt half as soft, I might need a set of those, too.

Dani had recently mentioned in passing that her skin had been extra sensitive lately, so I'd gone down a three-hour internet rabbit hole until I'd found the kind every mom-to-be blog swore by.

Some might've called it overkill, but I called it giving a damn.

I climbed the front steps to her and Pink's townhouse, careful not to scuff the box against the railing, and reached for the doorbell.

"You just missed her," a soft voice muttered from behind me.

I turned to find a twenty-something woman standing in the narrow strip of grass between the side-by-side townhouses. Her chocolate-brown hair had been pulled into a loose braid over one shoulder that fell nearly to her waist.

"Excuse me?" I asked.

"Dani. She left about twenty minutes ago for her doctor's appointment," she said flatly, gaze already drifting back to the book in her hands.

What the actual fuck?

A sharp pang landed in my chest, unexpected and unwelcome. "She didn't tell me she had one today."

The brunette shrugged. "Sorry."

I just stood there for a second, my brain trying to process the onslaught of emotions—fear, anger, hurt. I thought we were past this. I thought we had finally found our footing. We had texted nearly every day for weeks now, and not just about her cravings or potential baby names—which, surprisingly, we mostly agreed on—but about random, normal couple shit. Like we were a random, normal couple rather than . . . whatever we were.

We had even shared a meal together a few times when our schedules had aligned. Just last night, she had invited me in for dinner when I'd dropped off some of the parenting books I had finished reading. One minute, we'd been swapping books, and the next we'd been eating meatless chili on her couch while watching game highlights.

It wasn't perfect, but it had felt like progress. So, what the hell had changed between then and now? Why was she pushing me away again?

It didn't make sense.

Hell, it didn't even sit right.

I'd bent over backwards this past month, partly because I'd wanted to, but mostly because I couldn't stand the idea of her thinking she had to go through any of this alone. And sure, maybe I overdid it sometimes with the questions or the care packages, but damn it, I thought we were over this stage where she shut me out.

Now, it just felt like I'd been benched without warning.

"Do you know what time her appointment is?" I asked the woman with the book, trying to keep my voice casual.

She nodded. "In ten minutes. Dr. Kong's office."

The knot in my chest pulled tighter. If I left now, there was still a chance I could catch her while she was still sitting in the waiting room, flipping through outdated parenting magazines.

Calls could be dodged. Texts could be ignored. But a face-to-face confrontation in the gynecologist's office? That would be harder to walk away from. If she thought I was just going to shrug this off and let her keep me in the dark, she was wrong.

"Thank you—"

"Bella. Jared's sister."

"Jared Pink?"

Bella rolled her eyes. "The man, the myth, the asshole."

I liked her better than her brother already.

"I appreciate your help."

I shifted the package under one arm and took off for my truck without waiting for her response. One thing was for sure: I was going to make it to that appointment whether she wanted me there or not.

And then, we were going to have a conversation about what she and this baby meant to me—one she couldn't sidestep, one that needed to happen before this turned into a pattern.

The receptionist barely got out a, "Room seven—" before I was halfway down the hall, scanning the frosted-glass placards until I saw her name.

I didn't bother knocking.

The door swung open to reveal Dani on the exam table, swaddled in one of those flimsy paper gowns that did absolutely-ly nothing to hide how vulnerable she looked. Her hair was pulled into two messy knots and her bare legs—minus the pur-ple-and-black striped skeleton socks that *should not* have been a turn-on—dangled off the edge.

Her eyes went wide. "Brooks, what are you doing here?"

"What am *I* doing here?" I shut the door behind me, temper-ing my voice but not my irritation. "How about why didn't *you* tell me about your appointment?"

She swallowed audibly. "I promise, it wasn't like that."

"Then what was it like?"

"I was— I mean—" She glanced toward the counter where a tray of metal instruments had been laid out like torture devices. "This wasn't supposed to happen today."

I took a step closer. "The appointment?"

She nodded, chewing her lip. "The anatomy scan was sched-uled for next week, but last night I noticed some . . . bleeding." Her gaze flicked up to mine, quick and careful. "I called the doctor's office this morning, and they told me to come in. Just to be safe."

A cold weight slid down my spine.

That word—*bleeding*—hit me square in the chest, knocking the wind out of whatever argument I had built during the car ride over. A minute ago, I'd been pissed about being left out. Now my gut was twisting for an entirely different reason, every worst-case scenario I'd ever heard of clawing its way to the front of my brain.

"And you didn't think to tell me?"

Her mouth opened, then closed again. "I didn't want to worry you if it was nothing."

I took a deep, cleansing breath, attempting to channel my inner yogi . . . even though I had only taken a few classes with some of my players. She still didn't get it. She still didn't understand that this wasn't just about the baby for me—it was about *her*, too. That every part of this—every part of *her*—mattered to me more than she seemed to realize.

Enough was enough. It was time I made myself clear.

I lowered myself until we were nearly eye to eye. "Oh, kitten," I said quietly, the word heavier than usual. "You still don't get it, do you?"

Confusion flickered through her emerald eyes, but there was something else there, too—want. She nearly jumped up from the table when my hand skittered across her middle.

"This, *us*, is not nothing. Every second, every heartbeat, every curveball this pregnancy throws at us, I want to know. I need to know. And I'm not letting you go—not now, not ever. This isn't just about the baby, Dani." My voice dropped, rough with conviction. "I'm in this for as long as it takes. And please, believe me when I say that I'm prepared to play the *fucking* long game if I have to."

She blinked rapidly. Before she could respond, the door swung open again and, presumably, Dr. Kong stepped inside. "Oh! You must be Dad."

"Brooks," I said, dwarfing her palm in mine. "Great to meet you."

"Dr. Emilia Kong."

She was a curvy woman, with warm amber-brown skin and sharp, blunt bangs that skimmed her eyebrows in a perfectly straight line. She couldn't have been more than thirty—hell, she looked barely old enough to rent a car—but the crisp precision in her voice and the confident set of her shoulders left no doubt she knew exactly what she was doing. A white coat hung open over a Barbie-pink blouse, the stethoscope around her neck catching the overhead light.

"How are we doing today? I heard you were experiencing some bleeding."

Dani nodded silently. Her fingers twitched against the edge of the paper sheet, shoulders drawn tight like she was holding herself together by sheer force of will. I could see the hesitation, the weight of everything pressing in.

I reached for her hand, lacing my fingers through hers in a quiet promise. "Is that something we should be concerned about, Dr. Kong?"

"Not at all." She flipped open the chart in her hands. "Your blood pressure is solid, your iron levels are well within range, and your blood count looks great. Weight gain is exactly where we want it for this stage—right in the healthy zone." She glanced at Dani with a reassuring smile. "From what I'm seeing here, there's nothing alarming. The spotting could be from something as simple as increased blood flow or activity."

Her hand relaxed in my grip.

"Now, I know we had your anatomy scan on the calendar for next week," Dr. Kong said, rolling her stool toward the machine in the corner, "but since you're already here, would you like to take a look?"

"Please," I answered without hesitation.

At the same time, Dani said, "Yes."

Dr. Kong smiled at our chorus of agreement. "All right then. Let's get you set up." She snapped on a pair of gloves and wheeled the ultrasound cart closer. "Have you decided if you want to know the sex or not?"

I glanced at Dani, unwilling to answer for her. She worried her bottom lip between her teeth, eyes flicking between me and the doctor like she was weighing the pros and cons.

"Your call, kitten," I said softly. "I'm good either way."

She hesitated for another beat, then gave a small shrug. "We're already here, right? Might as well find out."

"Sounds good to me," I said, my pulse kicking up for reasons I couldn't quite explain.

Dr. Kong nodded and gestured for Dani to lie back. "I'm going to lift your gown up just a little bit."

A moment later, the gel hit her skin, and Dani made a small noise of surprise. "Wow, that's surprisingly warm."

Dr. Kong laughed. "Warming gel," she explained. "Best innovation in the past twenty years."

The doctor moved the wand across her stomach with practiced ease, eyes scanning the monitor. The screen filled with shifting gray static until, slowly, the faint contours of a tiny body emerged. Arms, legs, head—imperfect but undeniable. My breath caught in my throat.

"There's your baby," Dr. Kong said warmly. "Heartbeat's strong—152 beats per minute. That's perfect."

I couldn't take my eyes off the screen. For all the conversations, all the plans, all the thinking ahead, nothing had made this feel more real than seeing that tiny body wriggling around in there.

"How cool is that?" Dani asked.

My eyes met hers with wonder. "Amazing."

"Everything looks great," Dr. Kong continued. "Now, let's see if your little one wants to cooperate and give us a peek."

The wand tilted, the image shifted, and I realized I was holding my breath. Dani's fingers tightened around mine.

"Well," Dr. Kong said after a moment, a small smile tugging at her lips. "Your baby is *definitely* not shy. I can say with complete certainty, you're having a girl."

The words hit me like a fastball straight to the heart. My grin was instant, wide enough to make my cheeks ache. "A girl," I repeated, words tinged with awe. "I love girls."

Dani let out a shaky laugh, her eyes glassy as she stared at the screen. "She's so small," she whispered, voice breaking on the last word.

"She's perfect," I corrected softly.

And she was.

I must have pictured a thousand different versions of our baby, but now I could see her—tiny and fierce, just like her mother.

Dr. Kong smiled at the two of us, then glanced at the door. "Congratulations to you both. Want me to make a recording for you?"

"Please," I answered quickly.

Dani sniffled. "Thank you, doctor."

She tapped a few buttons, and the machine began recording a short loop of the sonogram. The little figure on the screen kept moving, heart flickering, limbs shifting like she was trying to find the comfiest side of the uterus.

"I'll step out and give you a moment," Dr. Kong offered before slipping out, the quiet click of the latch leaving us alone in the small, warm room.

For a long beat, neither of us said anything. We just sat there, fingers still threaded together, our gazes fixed on the little girl flipping and kicking on the screen like she had all the time in the world.

For a moment, the only sound in the room was the steady, reassuring thump of our daughter's heartbeat. Then Dani turned to me, eyes still wet, and something in her expression shifted—like whatever walls she'd been holding up had finally crumbled.

Before I could say a word, she launched herself forward and crashed her mouth to mine.

The kiss deepened fast—*too fast*—her fingers tangling in my hair and dragging me even closer. And still, it wasn't enough. She twisted on the table without missing a beat, paper crunching with every move until finally, she could wrap one leg around my waist, locking us together.

We were clumsy and desperate, groaning between kisses, but there was no mistaking the heat sparking under the surface. Her mouth was hungry, demanding, teeth nipping my bottom lip before she soothed the sting with her tongue.

My fingers dug into her hips, sliding under the flimsy paper gown, inching closer to her heat, and then—

The ultrasound cart groaned under the weight of Dani's other foot. She froze, eyes wide and cheeks flushed. "Whoops."

We stared at each other, panting.

"Dani, I—"

"Don't you dare stop," she whispered, her voice shaky. Her hands fisted in my shirt, dragging me closer. "Please, Brooks, I need this. I'm on fire and I have been for weeks. Fucking make me come. *Please.*"

I searched her face, the flush in her cheeks, the intense determination burning in her eyes. She wasn't kidding. This wasn't just want—it was *need*, bone-deep and aching. My breath hitched, and for a heartbeat, I thought about telling her we couldn't do this, at least not here.

But then her fingers curled tighter in the fabric at my chest, her forehead pressing to mine, and I knew I was already lost.

"You need me, kitten?"

"Yes."

I flicked a finger through the tuft of dark curls at the top of her pussy, drawing a line down to her clit.

"You going to let me fuck this pussy with my fingers until you come?"

She groaned. "*God, yes.*"

With her legs still wrapped around my waist, I settled her upper body back until she was laid flat on the exam table. Her gown gaped open at the middle. I pushed the material up to her waist, baring her lower half to me.

"I've missed this gorgeous cunt." I traced a finger along her outer lips, teasing, not quite dipping inside.

"Hurry, please."

She arched her back, trying to push herself into my hand. Normally, I would've made her wait—*beg*—but desperate times called for a desperately fast finger fucking.

And I was all too happy to give it to her.

I pressed two thick fingers inside her, pressing them deep. "Goddamn," I growled. I barely recognized my own voice. "You feel like hot fucking silk."

Her head fell back against the table and a moan broke free.

"You gotta be quiet, kitten." I flicked my thumb over her clit. "At least this first time."

She nodded and reached above her head, bracing her palms against the wall to get the friction she needed.

There was no more talking after that.

The paper on the table crunched with every flick of my fingers. Our muffled moans and broken breaths filled the room. I curled my fingers inside her, stroking that swollen bundle of nerves, watching her eyes roll back and her jaw fall open.

Voices filtered in from the hallway, but I was well past caring.

"You're close," I said. It wasn't a question.

She bit her lip and nodded. "Don't stop."

"Wouldn't dream of it."

I picked up the pace, adding a third finger to her channel and thrusting rhythmically. There was nothing practiced or measured about my technique. No, this was raw, primal.

And somehow, that made it hotter.

I pressed the heel of my palm against her clit and fucked her faster. Her pussy tightened around my fingers, and her entire body shook.

Almost there, kitten.

I watched the flush creep up her neck, her skin gleaming with a sheen of sweat, her lips red and plump.

Goddamn, I wanted to take her mouth. But not now. Not when her thighs were trembling around my waist. Not when she was too busy grinding against my hand, fucking my fingers like she had something to prove.

She was a fucking vision.

I couldn't look away, not from her face or her tits bouncing beneath her paper gown or her hips flexing and moving with every stroke.

She was almost there. And because I was an impatient bastard—that, and I knew that we were working on borrowed time—I dropped my head forward, capturing her nipple through the thin gown.

"Oh, fuck." She moaned. "I'm coming."

"Good girl," I gritted against her tit.

Her body arched off the table, her palms flattening hard against the wall as her orgasm tore through her. I pressed my free hand over her mouth, swallowing the cry that broke from her throat.

When I looked up, her head was thrown back, her whole body shuddering as pleasure crashed over her.

It took several long moments for her to come back down. And when she finally sagged against the table, the tension easing from her body, I pulled my fingers free. She gasped when I sucked them clean, licking them thoroughly the same way I longed to lick her pussy.

That would have to wait for later.

The ultrasound machine was still whirring, and we had maybe another thirty seconds before we risked getting caught. I tucked her gown back into place, trying—and failing—to ignore the way her pussy glistened.

I cupped her face, brushing a lock of hair behind her ear. Her eyes were heavy-lidded, her cheeks flushed, and she had the sated, content expression of a woman well-fucked.

I couldn't help the smug smile that spread across my face.

She laughed softly. "Careful, your ego is showing."

"It's not my fault you're gorgeous when you come."

My thumbs swept over her cheekbones, and I memorized the sight of her like this—messy, glowing, and mine.

"So . . . ," she started, her voice softer now, a hint of pink creeping up her neck. "Where do we go from here?"

A slow, knowing grin tugged at my mouth. I leaned in, letting my lips brush her ear. "We go to my place," I told her. "Because I'm not finished with you yet, kitten—not even close."

Dani

I was never going to look at a doctor's office the same way ever again. I had already been teetering on the edge of lust and logic for weeks now, but seeing Brooks watch our daughter flicker to life on that ultrasound screen had officially broken me.

Fuck logic. And fuck me, too.

We barely said a word on the drive back to his place, both of us strung tight, buzzing with excitement for what was still to come.

And come . . . and come and come.

Brooks's hand didn't leave my thigh the entire ride, thumb drawing loose circles against my leggings that had me shifting in my seat, squirming under the weight of his smirk. By the time he pulled into his driveway, my pulse was a steady roar in my ears.

The front door barely clicked shut behind us before Brooks had pinned me against it, his mouth crashing down onto mine like he'd been holding back for weeks instead of the twenty-minute drive.

More like twelve minutes.

Apparently, I wasn't the only one desperate to get his cock inside me. Then again, only one of us had come—embarrassingly fast, I would add—in my gynecologist's office. And yet, I was still burning up.

Heat.

That was all I could register. Heat from his hands on my hips, from his chest pressed against mine, from the way his tongue plundered my mouth.

My bag slid from my shoulder and hit the hardwood with a dull thud, already forgotten. I barely had time to gasp before his arms hooked under my thighs and he lifted me clean off the floor. I wrapped them around his waist on instinct, the muscles in his back flexing under my palms as he carried me up the stairs.

"Where are we going?" I whispered against the shell of his ear, half-dizzy from want, half from the way he carried me like I was nothing.

"Bed," he growled, voice sure and determined. "I want you laid out for me. I need to see all of you."

The world blurred. Stairs, hallway, the faint scent of his laundry detergent—competent men were my kink—and then, we outside his bedroom.

"You good with this?" he asked, his forehead brushing mine.

My pulse stuttered, heat pooling low in my belly. The fact that he still felt the need to ask while my heat was soaking my panties made me ache. I didn't deserve this man or his reverence.

I dragged my mouth across his jaw, nipping the edge of his beard. "More than okay."

He kicked the door open wide and laid me back on the bed with reverence that contrasted the hungry way his lips trailed down my neck.

The mattress dipped under his weight as he came over me, bracing one forearm beside my head while the other slid up my thigh. His mouth was everywhere—along my jaw, down the curve of my neck, across the swells of my tits—each kiss harder and hungrier than the last.

"Fuck, kitten," he rasped against my skin, the scrape of his beard sending a shiver down my spine. "I want you so bad."

"How do you want me?" I purred.

"Naked," he said between kisses. "Under me." *Kiss.* "Over me." *Kiss.* "Riding my fucking face."

"I pick D, all of the above."

His rumble of laughter felt like an electric bolt straight to the clit. Better than any vibrator I'd ever had.

"Clothes on or off?" he asked, voice low. His thumb traced the waistband of my leggings, patient even as his eyes darkened with need.

"Off," I breathed.

"Everything?" His lips ghosted over mine, brushing the words against my mouth like he was spelling out every fucking letter. "Because once I start, I'm not stopping."

"Good," I whispered back, tugging at the hem of his shirt. "I don't want you to."

His grin turned feral. "Careful, kitten. I'm gonna hold you to that."

A shiver rattled down my spine when his fingers slipped beneath the lace edge of my panties, finding me wet and aching. He groaned with approval and claimed my lips again, swallowing my moan as his fingers started a slow, deliberate rhythm that had me arching off the bed.

It was like his fingers had been made for this, for playing my body like it were a piano made solely for him. They worked over my clit, rubbing circles just hard enough to have my eyes rolling back in my head. I was already close to coming a second time today, and that was the biggest surprise of all.

Well, maybe the second biggest; letting Brooks diddle me in the doctor's office definitely took the cake.

What was it about this man and his magical fucking fingers?

"Off," he ordered, voice like gravel.

His hands were already at my hips, hooking my leggings and panties down my thighs before I could breathe a reply. He kissed a path after them, hot mouth dragging along sensitive skin, leaving me trembling before he even got where I needed him.

By the time he settled between my legs, I was clutching fistfuls of sheets, desperate and shaking. He looked up at me once—just once, pupils blown wide—before lowering his head and sealing his mouth over me.

The first stroke of his tongue tore a cry from my throat. I hummed deep when he licked up the length of my sex. Slow, deliberate, like he was savoring every second, every taste. Then faster, deeper, lips and tongue working me over with precision that made my toes curl.

A moan slipped past my lips, my vision darkening.

"*God,* you're good at that," I cried, seeing stars when he nipped my clit.

He laughed, and the vibrations sent me skyrocketing.

"That's it, kitten," he growled. "Fuck me back. Take what you need."

"*Brooks.*"

Had his mouth always been this dirty? I didn't think so. Then again, it was hard to think about anything other than how his tongue felt when he dragged it through my folds and pressed inside.

And how his fingers felt when they finally joined, curling inside me and hitting the spot that made my eyes cross.

My hips bucked against his face, and he growled like the taste of me was a reward he'd kill for. His grip on my thighs tightened, pinning my legs open wide as he devoured me, no mercy in sight.

"Tell me you missed this, Dani." He kept his pace steady, tongue and fingers moving together, and the heat grew unbearable. "Tell me that you've dreamed about me fucking you. Filling you. Making you mine."

He knew it without me saying a word. I was gasping for air, writhing uncontrollably, soaking his sheets.

"*Please,* Brooks." I gasped, grinding shamelessly against his fingers and tongue. "Please don't stop."

He didn't. Just worked his fingers faster, tongue stroking and tasting. The room was silent save for the filthy, wet sounds of his mouth, the creak of the mattress as my hips moved, and the pained sounds pouring from me.

He sucked on my clit and stars danced behind my eyelids. I was going to come. Again. Harder than before.

And this time, I was not fucking quiet.

My orgasm ripped through me. It was like lightning striking the earth, all heat and fire and the sharp taste of metal. The world shattered.

I wasn't typically a multiple orgasms kind of girl—especially not without the help of a toy or two—but it had been too long since somebody had made me feel this good, and frankly, my dear, I just didn't give a damn.

June and Nessa had been right. There was nothing wrong with giving in and enjoying myself with someone who loved my body, who loved—

Not going there.

I was still trembling when he finally lifted his head, lips slick, beard damp, wearing that smug, satisfied smirk I half-wanted to slap off his face.

"Delicious," he rasped, kissing the inside of my thigh.

"Get naked." I panted. "Now."

His smile was sin personified. "I don't know, kitten. I'm enjoying the view from down here."

Without a word, I sat up and tugged my shirt over my head before unhooking my bra and tossing that aside, too. Brooks's mouth dropped open when he got his first unobstructed glimpse of my tits.

"How's *that* view?"

His eyes darkened. "You better not be asking me to choose between these tits and your juicy pussy."

Little did he know that there was no need—he could have all of me.

He reached for me, but then paused. "Are they sensitive?" he asked, voice rough, gaze still locked on my breasts like he couldn't decide whether to worship or devour. Like I was the most beautiful woman he had ever seen.

"Kind of," I admitted, cheeks heating even as my nipples tightened under his stare. "I used to barely fill an A-cup, and now . . ."

I gestured toward the thick mounds, vaguely self-conscious, though his hungry expression made it clear he didn't see anything to be embarrassed about. I was still getting used to them myself—the way my clothes hung differently off my body, the way they painfully bounced during my morning runs.

Brooks sat back on his heels, dragging a hand through his hair as if steadying himself. "Show me."

I reached for his wrist and guided his palm over one breast, shuddering when the warmth of his hand met sensitive skin.

"Gentle," I whispered, guiding his touch, showing him the pressure that made my back arch instead of flinch. And he obeyed—a novelty for Brooks—brushing his thumb over my nipple in slow circles that sent sparks shooting to my core. His mouth followed, warm and tentative at first, as he waited for my reaction.

"*Yes.*" I gasped, threading my fingers through his hair and holding him closer. "Just like that. Not too hard—"

My words broke into a moan as he sucked lightly, drawing the peak between his lips with careful precision. Brooks lifted his head just long enough to meet my eyes.

"You guide me, kitten. I'll give you exactly what you need."

Sweet Jesus, this man is going to wreck me.

My breath hitched when his mouth closed over my other nipple, tongue circling, sucking with just enough pull to make my toes curl. My back arched off the mattress, pressing me closer to him.

"Brooks . . ." His name came out broken, a plea *and* a curse.

He groaned low in his chest, the vibration sparking through me, then moved back to the other breast, lavishing the same slow attention until I was writhing beneath him. His hand splayed across my belly, thumb brushing along the small curve that cradled our daughter while his mouth dragged me higher and higher.

"Fuck, Dani. You're so perfect like this," he rasped against my skin. "Soft, sweet, swollen with my baby. These tits—"

He nipped my nipple lightly with his teeth and I nearly screamed.

"—are mine now."

Something snapped in him then. The patience, the care, the restraint—it all went up in flames. He pushed up onto his knees and stripped off his T-shirt. I barely had time to take in the hard lines of his torso, the tattoos spanning his arms and neck, and the light dusting of hair that disappeared into his waistband before his mouth was on mine again, his hand cupping the back of my neck.

We both reached for the buckle of his belt, shoving at his jeans and boxer briefs. Finally, he kicked them the rest of the way off and climbed over me, pressing me into the mattress.

But this time, it was my turn.

Maybe it was hormones, maybe it was the weeks of pent-up wanting, but I wasn't about to let him think he had all the control.

"I want to be on top," I demanded, pushing at his shoulders until he sat up. I shoved him back against the pillows, the surprise in his eyes only fanning the fire in my chest. His cock was throbbing, leaking against my thigh, and I wrapped my hand around him with a deliberate squeeze.

"Dani—" he groaned, head lolling back.

"You and that perfect cock of yours broke me, Brooks." I swung a leg over him, straddling his hips. "Nothing else will do—my fingers, my vibrator, my favorite alien tentacle dildo."

"Your what?"

"None of them are good enough. I need your cock."

"Fuck, kitten."

I rocked forward, letting him glide through the slickness between my thighs, teasing the head of his cock over my clit. He
grunted, his hands coming up to palm my bare ass. "You can't
just say stuff like that."

I smiled against his lips and reached back to stroke him again.
He was so thick and long, his length spanning the width of my
palm.

I wanted him inside me.

Now.

With another rock of my hips, he notched himself at my
entrance, and my breath caught. We both watched, transfixed,
as I lowered myself onto him. There was no suppressing my
moan when he slipped inside, one inch at a time.

Slowly, so slowly, I rolled my hips and rose up, feeling every
inch of him drag against my walls. I sank back down, taking him
deeper this time. His hands flew to my hips, fingers biting into
my skin hard enough to bruise.

My next tattoo, maybe?

"Fuck," he hissed, eyes blown wide when my walls clenched
around his length. "What were you just thinking about that
made your pussy squeeze me like that?"

I bit my lip. "My next tattoo."

His brows pinched together.

"Your fingermarks on my thighs."

I didn't think his eyes could get any darker, but they did.
He grabbed a fistful of my hair and brought my mouth to his,
kissing me like a man possessed.

It was hard and fast and filthy, the kind of kiss that stole my
breath and my soul *and* made me forget my own name.

I bit my lip, rolling my hips in a slow, deliberate circle. "You
like that?"

He let out a wrecked laugh. "Too much."

That was all the encouragement I needed. I leaned forward,
palms braced on his pecs, and set the pace, rising and falling,
grinding down until sparks danced across my skin. He tried to

thrust up, to take the rhythm back, but I pressed him flat with a smirk.

"Not this time, coach." I panted, breathless but grinning.

"I'm dying here, kitten." His thumbs slid up to stroke circles across my nipples, and I nearly lost it right there.

"Shut up, you love it."

I did it again. And again, rising and falling on his cock with slow, deliberate movements, relishing the way his jaw went slack and his breath stuttered.

I rode him harder, faster, nails digging into his muscles. The sounds of skin slapping, our ragged breathing, his filthy praise, they all blurred into something primal.

"*Fuck*, Dani," he growled. "You're going to wreck me."

"Good." My voice was sharp, breathless, shaking with need. "I want you wrecked."

His head tipped back against the pillows, veins straining in his neck as he tried and failed to hold back. I leaned forward until my warm breath fanned his neck.

"I want you to remember me every time you breathe."

I bit him.

Like a fucking vampire. And apparently, Brooks had a thing for undead bloodsuckers because that was all it took to send him over the edge.

His hands flew to my hips, dragging me down harder, rougher, while his cock pulsed deep inside me. He cursed loud and raw, hips bucking once, twice before he spilled inside me, hot and endless.

I collapsed onto him, both of us panting, slick with sweat. Wrapping me up in those big, tattooed arms, he held me there like he had no intention of letting me go.

He pressed his lips to my temple, still breathless, still trembling beneath me. "Fuck, kitten," he murmured, voice hoarse. "Round one goes to you."

I laughed weakly against his throat, still trying to catch my breath. "Round one?"

His hand slid down my spine, settling on the curve of my ass, giving it a lazy squeeze. "You didn't think we were done, did you?"

I stayed draped over him, limp and buzzing, listening to the way his heartbeat thundered beneath my ear. His skin was warm and damp, carrying a salty scent mixed with the clean bite of soap and the faint spice of his cologne.

"You smell good."

He chuckled low, his fingers combing lazily through my tangled hair. "You're sex drunk. I smell like sweat and cum."

"Mm, I think Gwenyth Paltrow makes a candle for that," I muttered into his skin, smiling despite myself. "Besides, you should be thanking me for the privilege of licking my pussy."

His laugh rumbled deeper. "Are you putting me in my place, kitten?"

"You know it." I shifted just enough to look up at him, smirking when I caught the wrecked, satisfied look still painted across his face. "Consider it your penance."

"For what?"

"For making me fall asleep at night thinking about you," I said softly, more truth than I'd meant to give away.

Fucking hormones.

His grin softened into something dangerous, something that made my heart squeeze. He kissed me once, slow and deep, before laying us down and tugging the blanket over us both. He was still buried inside of me, and I had no doubt we were making a mess of his bed, but for once, I couldn't be bothered to care.

Instead, I curled against him and relaxed.

Minutes ticked by in a haze of warmth, our breathing evening out, the world shrinking down to just this bed, this moment. His hand drifted lower, resting on the soft swell of my belly. I felt him go still, his thumb brushing back and forth like he was tracing something only he could see.

"We're having a little girl," he whispered, the awe in his voice pulling at something deep inside me.

I closed my eyes, letting the words settle over me like a second blanket. His daughter. *Our* daughter.

"Yeah," I murmured, my throat thick. "We are."

His arm tightened around me, protective and reverent, and I let myself drift off, falling asleep to the steady rhythm of his heartbeat and the promise of something more.

Something that, dare I say, might feel like forever.

Brooks

The first thing I registered when I woke was softness. Smooth, supple skin plastered against mine, a cascade of blue-black hair spilling across the pillow and tickling my chin, the soft curve of her ass nestled against my hips like she'd been made to be there.

She had, even if she didn't know it.

I had lost myself in Dani's softness half a dozen more times last night. First, in the shower, with her moans echoing off the tiles. Then again with her bent over the bathroom vanity, turned toward the mirror so we could both watch her tits bounce with every punishing thrust of my hips. And once more, after our three a.m. snack in the kitchen.

While she ate the last of my vegan mac and cheese—slathered in pickle juice—I ate her pussy, laid bare on my kitchen island.

Every place in this house felt like it had her scent, her sounds, her body stamped into it now. And yet, with the morning light seeping through the blinds and her ass tucked tight against my cock, all I could think about was how ready I was to start all over again.

I pressed forward just enough to hear her sleepy little hum, the kind that went straight to my balls. Her hand slid back blindly, finding my thigh and squeezing.

"Mm, good morning," she murmured, voice rough with sleep.

"Morning." I kissed the back of her neck, grinding into the slick heat of her, and *fuck,* it would have been so easy to slide right back in. "You hungry?"

She laughed low, husky. "Are we talking about food or your dick?"

"Both? Either?"

Her laugh buzzed against my chest, and I buried my face in her hair, breathing her in. She smelled like sleep and sex and the faintest trace of my body wash. *Mine.* Every part of her was mine, and I was hers, even if we hadn't put words to it yet.

She shifted against me, rolling her hips back just enough to tease me with that sweet friction. "You know what I really want?"

"Tell me," I said, my hands gliding over the gentle swell of our baby, tracing the place where our daughter grew, before drifting up to cup her breasts.

She arched into my palm, gasping softly when I rolled her nipple between my fingers. "A nice, big, *juicy* helping of . . ." She paused, lips curling in a wicked grin over her shoulder. "Blueberry pancakes. With extra butter. And bacon. Lots of bacon."

I groaned, half in frustration, half in amusement. "Kitten, you can't talk about bacon when I'm this hard. That's cruel and unusual punishment."

Her laugh was low and husky, vibrating through me. "Priorities, coach."

"Fine," I muttered, grinding into her just enough to make her gasp. "But after pancakes, I'm eating you again."

I smiled against her shoulder, about to prove to her just how serious I was, when—

The front door opened.

Dani stiffened in my arms, twisting to look at me with wide eyes.

"Oh, shit," I muttered, every ounce of blood draining straight from my cock.

The unmistakable pitter-patter of little sneakers hitting hardwood echoed down the hall. "Daddy!" Carolina's bright voice carried through the house, seconds before my bedroom door creaked open.

With barely enough time for me to roll out of bed and slip my discarded jeans up and over my bare ass, I tugged the comforter up and over Dani's shoulders just as my daughter appeared, her backpack still hanging off one shoulder.

"There you are!" She beamed. She stopped dead when she saw Dani in my bed, then looked at me with all the blunt honesty only a kid could pull off. "Miss Dani?"

Dani made a strangled noise and yanked the blanket up to her chin. Her cheeks flushed for reasons Carolina couldn't possibly guess. "Hi, Carolina."

If my daughter thought it was odd that one of her dad's coworkers—the "pretty lady with the good snacks"—was sitting in his bed first thing in the morning, she didn't show it. Instead, she darted across the room like a bullet, dropping her backpack with a thud.

"Daddy, can we make pancakes? The lemon-blueberry ones, like last time?"

Over her head, Dani's eyes found mine.

Blueberry pancakes. Jesus.

I bit back a laugh.

"Sure, cutie," I said, ruffling Carolina's curls. "We can do that."

A polite throat-clearing in the hallway had me freezing in place. *Allie.* My ex-wife leaned against the doorframe, keys dangling from her hand, her gaze flicking from me—shirtless, half-hard under my jeans—to the woman hiding under my comforter.

Her brows arched. She didn't look mad, more amused than anything, actually. Which was somehow worse.

"Well," she said lightly. "This is . . . new."

"Allie—" I started, but Carolina was already bouncing in place, tugging at Dani's hand.

"Dani, you have to help us. Daddy always burns the first batch."

Dani's nervous laugh cracked, and I could see the panic flaring in her eyes. She didn't know whether to stay or run.

I stepped in quickly, squeezing Carolina's shoulder. "Why don't you go pull the stuff out of the pantry? We'll be there in a few minutes."

"Okay!"

Carolina skipped out, humming happily, backpack abandoned. The second she was out of earshot, Allie's arms crossed over her front.

I exhaled, raking a hand through my hair. "Can we, um, step outside for a sec?"

"Uh-huh."

Allie didn't move right away. Her gaze flicked from me back to Dani, whose knuckles were white against the comforter bunched at her collarbone. Then, to my absolute horror, Allie smiled. Not the sweet, beaming smile I remembered from the early days of our marriage, but something sly and knowing.

"I guess I should at least say hello before I get dragged into whatever this is." She stepped closer, extending her hand toward the bed. "I'm Allie. Carolina's mom. And you are . . . ?"

Dani's eyes widened like she wanted the mattress to swallow her whole. Nonetheless, she lifted a hand free of the blanket and shook Allie's, her cheeks redder than the Roasters' jerseys. "Dani Bernal, social media manager for the Roasters."

Allie shot me a look. "And you said you would never date a coworker," she teased.

Blood roared in my ears. "Allie—"

She lifted her caramel-colored hand, cutting me off with that same amused calm. "Relax, B. I'm not here to give you grief. Just . . . surprised." Her mouth twitched, fighting back a smile as she flicked her gaze between us again. "Walk me to my car."

Dani made another small, strangled sound, and I shot her an apologetic smile. Then, with one last suspiciously friendly glance in Dani's direction, Allie turned on her heel and headed for the stairs. I followed her out, pulling the door gently closed behind me, heart still hammering.

Allie's boots clicked softly on the stairs as we made our way down, her silence somehow heavier than words. I trailed just behind her, my pulse still thundering. Carolina's chatter carried faintly from the kitchen—drawers opening and shutting, the thud of a chair dragging across the tile.

Allie pushed open the front door, stepping onto the porch like she needed fresh air just to process. Her car sat at the edge of the driveway, still idling. She leaned against the porch railing, arms crossed, watching me with that same bemused, sharp-eyed look she'd had upstairs.

"You know," she said finally, "when I suggested you get back out there, I didn't expect—" She gestured vaguely toward the upstairs window. "That."

I blew out a slow breath, bracing one hand on the porch post. "I know. And trust me, *that* isn't what you think it is."

"Really?" Her eyebrow lifted, tone somewhere between skeptical and curious. "That wasn't your daughter walking in on you and a woman, naked in your bed?"

"No, it was," I admitted, meeting her gaze head-on. "But it's more than that, Allie. Dani isn't just a random fling."

Her lips parted, just slightly. "Okay."

My throat tightened, but I forced the words out, low and certain. "She's pregnant. With my kid."

For a beat, all I heard was the wind shifting through the trees and Carolina's off-key humming inside my kitchen. Allie blinked once, then twice, like she needed to make sure she'd heard me right.

"Well," she said finally, her voice dry but not sharp. "That's . . . a hell of a curveball, Brooks."

"I know," I admitted. My pulse was pounding so hard I could hear it in my ears. "I didn't exactly plan for it either. But I'm all in. I want this baby with Dani. But you need to know that nothing is going to change with Carolina and me. She's still my priority, my whole damn world. That's never up for debate." I paused, jaw clenched. "This doesn't take away from that. It adds to it."

For a minute, she just looked at me, like she was weighing every word. Then her shoulders softened, her lips tugging into something that wasn't quite a smile but wasn't disapproval either. "You couldn't just hook up with some rando from a dating app like the rest of us, could you?"

I huffed out a laugh that came out half-relief, half-nerves. Allie was one to talk. She and her live-in boyfriend, Mitchell, had met on a dating app marketed toward artists, and they were still together, two years later.

"You know I don't do casual well."

"I do." She gave me a long look, then added, "You look different, B. Lighter, happier."

The weight in my chest loosened a notch. "I am. I didn't plan for any of this, but Dani— She matters to me."

Allie nodded, her braids sliding over her shoulder as she tilted her head. "You're sure about this? About her?"

"Dead sure," I said without hesitation. "This isn't just about the baby. I want her in my life."

Her lips parted like she wanted to argue, then pressed into a thin line. I could see the wariness there, but also the trust. Because if there was one thing we had always managed, even when everything else between us had fallen apart, it was showing up for Carolina as a team. There was no reason for this to be any different.

She exhaled, shoulders dipping. "Alright," she said finally, a huff more than a word. "We'll figure this out. Just, please don't leave me blindsided when it comes to telling Carolina, okay?"

"Never," I promised. "I want her to hear it from both of us."

"I agree," Allie said. "But not today. We'll come up with a plan when Mitchell and I get back from Palm Springs. I want her to understand that whatever changes are coming, she's still our priority. That can't change."

"I'm not going anywhere," I said firmly.

"I know." Allie's gaze softened again, and for the first time since she'd walked in, there was no judgment in it, just under-standing. "Congratulations on the baby, by the way."

"Thanks." My mouth tipped into a goofy, lopsided grin. "It's another girl."

Her brows shot up, surprise giving way to warmth. "That's wonderful. Carolina's going to be over the moon."

The image of my daughter's face when she finally found out made me smile. Carolina had been begging for a sister since she'd been old enough to talk.

"Yeah," I said quietly. "She's gonna be a great big sister."

Allie's smile lingered as she slipped her sunglasses back on, keys jangling in her hand.

We said our goodbyes, and I stepped back as she slid into her car, giving her a small wave as she pulled out of the driveway. For a long moment, I stood there on the porch, watching until her taillights disappeared through the thick cover of trees.

Then I exhaled, shoulders easing.

Time to face the real circus.

I shut the door quietly behind me and started toward the stairs, intent on checking on Dani and hopefully reassuring her that the sky hadn't fallen just because my daughter and ex-wife had caught her in my bed. The last thing I wanted was to give her any reason to run again.

I was halfway up the steps when the sound of clanking pans and laughter drifted from the kitchen.

Dani.

Carolina, too. Their voices melded together better than lemon and blueberry. Which, speaking of . . .

I froze in the doorway of the kitchen. Dani was perched on one of the barstools, hair a little mussed, cheeks still flushed, wearing yesterday's leggings and one of my old T-shirts that swallowed her frame. Across from her, Carolina sat with a juice box, blinking up at her like she was a real-life Disney princess.

A mixing bowl sat between them, half full of beige batter. Carolina's spring-like curls bounced as she stirred with serious concentration, her little arm working the whisk like she was powering the whole operation. Dani leaned over, steadying the bowl with one hand, laughing when a fleck of batter dotted her wrist.

"Did you know," Carolina said, eyes narrowing in deep thought, "that if you don't sift the flour, your pancakes could turn out lumpy?"

Dani's lips parted on a surprised smile. "Really?"

"Daddy never sifts, but I do. Also, room temperature eggs are the secret to fluffy batter. That's what Mary Berry says."

"Hm," Dani mused. She leaned in, *really* listening, her chin propped on her hand like my kid was a world-class chef instead of a six-year-old with a Spice Girls shirt. "This Mary Berry sounds like she really knows her stuff."

"Yup." Carolina gave a decisive nod. "Now we need to let the batter rest for at least ten minutes."

"Ten minutes?!" Dani repeated, feigning outrage. "I don't know if I can wait that long."

"That's what cartoons are for," Carolina said wisely, licking a smear of batter off her knuckle before Dani handed her a towel. "Do you like cartoons, Dani?"

"I do. Especially *Scooby-Doo*."

I leaned against the doorframe, unseen for now, drinking it all in—the domesticity of it, the sound of their voices mingling like talking about their favorite cartoons was an everyday occurrence. Dani looked completely at home perched there in my kitchen, wearing my shirt, indulging my daughter's pancake TED Talk like it was gospel.

And fuck if that didn't do something to me.

It shouldn't have been erotic—my daughter stirring pancake batter, Dani laughing, soft and easy—but I couldn't shake the memory of her spread out on that same counter last night, gasping my name while I feasted on her pussy. The contrast made my blood run hot.

But beneath the hunger was something else, something steadier. Watching them together, I couldn't help but look forward, not just back. The vision was clear as day. The four of us—Carolina, me, Dani, and the little girl we were bringing into the world. Pancakes, cartoons, messy batter on small fingers, and a life where my kitchen always sounded like this.

Warm and bright and full of love.

I swallowed hard, shifting my weight before they could catch me staring like a lovesick fool.

Carolina tilted her head suddenly. "Do you know how to make a birthday cake, Dani?"

Dani froze. Her fingers tightened around the bowl, a quick flash of panic flickering in her eyes. "I've baked a few before."

"But like, a *real* one?" Carolina pressed. "With the layers and sprinkles? Daddy said that he would help me this year, but he burns pancakes, so . . ." Her little nose wrinkled.

Dani opened her mouth, then closed it again, fumbling for an answer that might satisfy my daughter. Her eyes darted quickly, like she wasn't sure if she was supposed to answer that.

"Oh, you have to come to my party, too!"

That was my cue.

"Hey," I said, pushing off the doorframe and crossing the room. Both of their heads swiveled toward me. Carolina grinned. Dani shot me a look over Carolina's head, something between *help me* and *don't you dare laugh*. "What's this I hear about birthday cakes? I thought we were making pancakes."

I just smirked, sliding a hand over the back of Dani's chair as I leaned down to kiss the top of my daughter's head.

Carolina's little mouth tugged into a tiny pout. "We can do both."

"Pancakes first," I told her. "Go wash the berries, please."

The moment Carolina dashed off toward the sink, Dani straightened, smoothing her hair like she'd just realized where she was. Her eyes flicked toward the hall, the front door, anywhere but me.

Shit.

I caught the shift in her posture, the panic blooming in her eyes like she was about to bolt. Sure enough, the second Carolina was distracted, Dani slid off the stool and padded toward the other room, barefoot and quiet.

I moved faster.

"Kitten." My hand pressed flat to the wall above her shoulder, caging her in against the pantry. She froze, wide eyes flashing up at me. "Where are you going?"

"I shouldn't be here." Her voice cracked, the words brittle. "Not like this, with her—"

"Don't do that. Don't run." I leaned in, keeping my voice low. "Not after last night."

Her throat bobbed. "Brooks—"

"Dani, you have to stay for pancakes," Carolina's voice rang out from the kitchen. "Daddy, make her stay. *Pleeeassee.*"

Apparently, the universe was in on the joke, too.

Dani pressed her lips into a thin line, torn between fight and fold. I watched the emotions flicker across her face, one after another like flipping pages—panic, guilt, longing. The urge to bolt was there in the tight set of her shoulders, but so was the softness I had felt last night, the tenderness when she'd whispered my name like it meant something more.

She wanted to run, but she didn't want to leave.

Not really.

Her gaze darted toward the kitchen, where Carolina's singsong voice carried on about berries and cartoons. When she looked back at me, her eyes were glassy, full of everything she couldn't put into words.

"It's just breakfast," I said, softer now, close enough that my breath skimmed her temple. "Carolina already adores you, and I know that you want her to have this—to know her sister when she gets here."

Her breath hitched. For a heartbeat, I thought she'd shove past me, vanish out the front door, and slam it shut behind her. Instead, her shoulders dropped, the tension in her frame breaking like a dam. She sagged back against the wall, lips parting in defeat.

"Besides, you said you were hungry."

She blew out a shaky laugh that sounded nothing like amusement. "Unbelievable. You're guilt-tripping me with your daughter and her pancakes."

I shamelessly grinned.

Dani glared, but the color in her cheeks betrayed her. "Fine, but we're *talking* about this later," she hissed, rolling her eyes heavenward. "I guess I'm staying for pancakes."

I brushed my thumb across her jaw, leaning in just enough to let her know I wasn't letting go. "Damn right you are."

Dani

By the time afternoon sunlight slanted across the living room, I was almost convinced I had stumbled into an alternate universe. One where I wasn't just the weird, goth girlie sneaking out of a hookup's house at dawn or hiding from awkward run-ins with ex-wives, but rather, someone who might actually be exactly where she was supposed to be. That was the only explanation for the scene playing out in front of me.

Coach Brooks Bailey-Ward—the man, the myth, and the baseball legend—was sitting cross-legged on the carpet with his massive hands splayed obediently across a towel while his six-year-old daughter painted his nails.

Hot pink with glitter.

"Hold still, Daddy," Carolina ordered with the seriousness of a brain surgeon. "You're smudging."

"Not smudging," he grumbled, though the twitch in his jaw gave him away. "My hand is falling asleep."

"You've only been sitting there for five minutes," I teased, dipping a brush into the sky-blue polish I'd claimed for his other hand. "Be glad she didn't want to do your makeup."

His gaze slid toward me, heavy-lidded and sharp, but there was no real bite in it. Just warmth, and maybe something else? The kind of look that made my stomach somersault even as my brush trembled over his thumbnail.

Carolina, blissfully unaware, hummed to herself while she finished his pinkie. "You look beautiful," she declared with a satisfied nod.

Brooks raised a brow at me. "Beautiful, huh?"

"Oh, definitely," I said, keeping my tone solemn. "The glitter really brings out your eyes."

He groaned under his breath but didn't pull away. Instead, he let Carolina grab his hand and blow dramatically on the wet polish. Watching the two of them together, so unguarded, so easy—it did something to me I couldn't quite name.

For the first time all day, the thought of running didn't even cross my mind. And the three of us—four, if you counted our baby girl—had had quite a day.

After Brooks had cornered me by the pantry and used his BDE, aka "big dad energy," to convince me to stay, I had nearly bolted again when I'd realized the state of my clothes.

My leggings and panties were absolutely wrecked after yesterday's . . . activities. But that didn't faze Brooks. If anything, it inspired him. I was still trying to recover from my mortification when Brooks had wordlessly traded a pair of his sweatpants, the drawstring cinched tight at the waist, for my soiled clothing, which he had immediately tossed into the washing machine with the rest of his laundry. Now, I would *never* be able to shake his delicious scent from my body.

The lemon-blueberry pancakes had been next level. After the first batch, that was, which Brooks had accidentally burned, just like Carolina had predicted. Afterward, the three of us had piled on his oversized couch, sticky plates balanced on knees, cartoons humming in the background while Carolina filled me in on how to feed her sourdough starter, and I schooled her on why Velma was objectively the best member of the Mystery Inc. team.

From there, it was onto *The Great British Baking Show*, where I learned quickly that Carolina was as ruthless a judge as Paul Hollywood. Only, she gave out hugs rather than handshakes.

Just like me. We were both huggers.

Through it all, Brooks had just laughed, his arm stretched along the back of the couch, his hand toying with the edge of my shirt—well, his shirt—in a way that felt both casual and deeply intentional. Like he wanted me to know that he was close, but not as close as either of us wanted.

It was the best kind of torture.

And now, with the sun sinking lower and the day winding down, Carolina had decided she was finally old enough to give her dad a manicure.

I was the tiniest bit jealous.

I couldn't remember the last time someone else had painted my nails. Even back in high school, it had never been like this. I would have given anything for my mom to sit with me like Brooks was with Carolina. To let me curl up against her shoulder and feel her arms tight around me while we picked out colors and pretended like everything was okay.

That ache in my chest—the one that never really went away when I thought about what I hadn't had growing up—softened when I let my hand drift down to the curve of my belly. My daughter wasn't going to feel that emptiness. Not ever.

She was going to know what it felt like to have arms around her, steady and safe. To be chosen, every single day. To laugh in the kitchen while pancakes burned and cuddle on the couch beneath blankets and sticky plates.

She was going to have what I never had, because I was going to give it to her.

I was going to be different. For her.

Carolina clapped and sat back to admire her handiwork. "Perfect."

Brooks showed off his pink-and-blue glittered fingers. It was hard to believe that those were the same massive fingers that had been inside of me yesterday. And this morning.

"What do you think, kitten?"

I bit back a laugh. "Pink and blue are definitely your colors."

Carolina crawled across the towel, fishing in her little bag of polish. "Time to do your toes."

Panic flitted across his face.

"Pass me a green, Carolina," I said sweetly, leaning back against the couch. He shook his head but sat back, resigned. *Smart man.*

For a minute, it was all laughter and glitter and the faint squeak of polish brushes against Brooks's toenails. But while I watched him play along, grumbling and rolling his eyes, yet never once pulling away, I couldn't help but feel something stir low in my belly.

This wasn't just a man humoring his daughter. This was the man—the *only* man—who had shown up for me again and again, even when I hadn't asked him to. Even when I had tried to push him away. Both times. And now, here he was, letting his daughter paint him like a canvas without a single complaint.

Maybe it was time *I* showed up for *him*.

I cleared my throat lightly. "Hey, Carolina?"

"Mm-hmm?" she answered, tongue poking out as she carefully applied a coat of purple glitter to Brooks's big toe.

"For your birthday party," I began, watching Brooks's head lift slightly at my words. "I was thinking, what do you think about letting each of your friends have their own mini cake to decorate? That way everyone gets to make something special that they can take home, and you can still have your big cake to eat, too?"

Her eyes lit up like the Eiffel Tower. "Mini cakes? Like on *The Great British Baking Show*?"

"Exactly like that," I said, smiling.

She squealed, flinging her arms around me in a sticky hug that smelled like acetone and maple syrup. "That's the best idea ever! Thank you, Dani."

When I looked up, Brooks's gaze was already on me, soft and unreadable but full of something that made my pulse stumble.

Carolina bounced on her knees, polish brush still in hand. "Does this mean you're going to come to my party?"

Her earnest little face nearly undid me.

I blinked, stalling because I hadn't thought that far ahead. "Um, when is it?"

"The last Saturday of the month," Brooks answered quickly, his voice low but steady, eyes never leaving mine. It wasn't just a date on the calendar—it was an open door. An invitation. A sign he wanted me there, too.

Carolina wiggled closer, grabbing my hand with glitter-stained fingers. "Please, say yes."

That lump rose in my throat again, equal parts nerves and warmth. There it was, laid out as simply as blueberry pancakes—a chance to be part of something bigger than just stolen kisses and a surprise pregnancy.

"Yes," I said softly, giving her hand a squeeze. "I'll be there."

Carolina squealed, launching herself into my lap, and Brooks's chuckle rumbled low across the space between us. His eyes met mine over her coiled curls, and the weight of his smile nearly knocked the air out of me.

Because we both knew this wasn't just a birthday party I was saying yes to.

I was already curled up against his headboard, pillow hugged to my stomach, by the time Brooks came back from tucking Carolina in. He shut the door with a quiet click, tossed his sweatshirt on the catchall chair in the corner, and crossed to the bed.

"She's out," he murmured, a soft smile tugging at his lips. "Didn't even make it past the first page of *Goodnight Moon*."

I smiled faintly. "She had a big day."

"We all did."

He sat beside me, close enough that the mattress dipped but not so close that he crowded me. I could feel the weight of his gaze on me, but I kept my eyes trained on the pillow in my lap. There was already a seventy-percent chance—okay, ninety-five—that I might burst into tears at any second. At least this way, I wouldn't have to watch him, watch me cry.

"Can I be honest with you for a minute?"

"Kitten," he said softly, "you can be honest with me for as long as you need."

The words clogged in my throat, but I forced them out. "I'm scared. About what happens when the baby comes, about us. I've fought too hard to build a life, a career, an identity—and I'm not willing to give all that up when I become a mom."

I couldn't bring myself to look at him just yet. My cheeks burned with embarrassment, but I didn't back down. It was all the truth, after all.

"I think— I *know* that there's something here between us, but I don't want to disappoint you. I'm not cut out to be a stay-at-home mom who only hangs out with the other baseball WAGs, so I need you to know that if that's what you're looking for, I might not be your girl."

I finally worked up the nerve to raise my head, only to find him studying me like I was a puzzle he was determined to solve. His lips pressed together in a thin line as he seemed to work through his response.

"I don't want you to give that up," he started, leaning forward and bracing his forearms on his thighs. "Not for me or anyone."

My heart squeezed, sharp and aching. The ache intensified when he reached forward, laying a palm flat on my stomach.

"The woman I fell for was already whole *before* this baby. I wanted you long before I knew you were pregnant, Dani."

I chewed on my lower lip. "But what if she's the only reason you're saying any of this?"

He reached for my hand and laced our fingers together. His thumb brushed over my knuckles, slow and deliberate, but then, he went quiet. Long enough that the back of my neck prickled.

"What?" I asked softly, trying to read his face. His jaw was tight, his mouth pressed flat like he was holding something back.

I couldn't believe it. For the first time since we'd met, Brooks Bailey-Ward was nervous. And that made me feel even more uneasy.

"Just tell me, please. I can take it."

His grip on my hand tightened, enough to ground me. He shook his head, finally letting out a breath. "Blue donuts."

I blinked. Of all the things. Was he speaking in code?

"Huh?"

He leaned back against the headboard beside me, his mouth twitching into the faintest grin. "The first day you came into the training facility. It was a Tuesday, and you were sitting cross-legged on the bleachers, waiting for me to finish grilling my pitching staff. And all I could see were your bright blue socks with little donuts all over them."

I let out a startled laugh. "You remember my socks?"

"Kitten, I couldn't stop looking at your damn socks. I thought, who is this woman sitting here with hair black as midnight and socks that look like a Saturday morning cartoon?" His grin widened, softening his whole face. "You made me curious before you ever opened your mouth."

My lips parted, but I had no idea what to say. That seemed to be happening more and more lately. Only around Brooks, though.

He squeezed my hand again. "So don't tell me this is only about the baby. She might be a part of it, but those ridiculous blue donuts? They had me long before you ever let me inside you. You're the one I want, Dani."

The lump in my throat nearly broke me. "I think you mean Sandy."

His brows furrowed. "Sandy who?"

"You know, the song from *Grease*?" I sang a few bars for him—badly, I might add.

"I've never seen it."

"You've never seen *Grease*?" I asked with disbelief. "Well, that decides it. Now, we definitely can't be together."

A slow smile spread across his face, and he reached out to run a fingertip along my jaw. I turned my head, kissing the pad of his finger, and he sucked in a breath.

God, I was a tease. I couldn't help myself, though. Everything about this felt so good, so right.

"We can take it slow," he said. "You keep being you, and I'll keep proving I'm not going anywhere."

"You make it sound so simple."

"It is." His hand squeezed mine, firm and grounding. "Trust me."

I stared at our joined hands, his big palm engulfing mine, the glitter polish from earlier still faintly shimmering under the lamplight. The tension racking my body loosened just a fraction, enough to let hope in.

"I don't want to turn into my mom, Brooks." The words tore out of me before I could second-guess them. "What if one day, our daughter looks at me and feels the same emptiness I did?"

Brooks was quiet for a moment. His throat bobbed. His tongue darted out to wet his lips, and when he spoke, his voice was raw.

"I think about my dad every damn day," he said. "He played ball his whole life, and he was good—great, even. But he was never home. The game came first, always. And you know what? I swore to myself when I went pro that if I ever had a family, I wouldn't do that to them."

I blinked at him, stunned by the vulnerability in his voice. "So, we're both . . . scared of being our parents."

"Yeah," he admitted, his mouth curving with something that wasn't quite a smile. "But that doesn't mean we will be. You and me, kitten, we get to decide what kind of parents we want to be, what kind of people. Together."

The word *together* sank into me like sunlight, chasing away shadows I hadn't realized were still clinging. I swallowed hard, my throat thick, but nodded. "You really believe we can break the cycle?"

He didn't even hesitate. "We already are."

Something heavy unknotted inside me, loosening a little more with every word. His thumb brushed over my knuckles, slow and steady, before he shifted closer and rested our linked palms over the gentle swell of my stomach. Not grabbing, not claiming—just holding, anchoring both of us to the promise we'd made.

For a long moment, neither of us moved. It wasn't heavy, though—it was grounding. His hand on my belly, mine laced through his, both of us breathing in sync like we'd stumbled onto something bigger than ourselves.

Then, Brooks's mouth tilted into a crooked grin, mischief sparking in his eyes. "So, I know I said we should take things slow, but . . . does that mean you can't spend the night again?"

I huffed out a laugh, shaking my head. "I can stay."

The relief that spread across his face made my heart stutter. He leaned closer, lips brushing my ear as his voice dropped low, hungry. "I like it when you call me coach."

A shiver danced down my spine. I smirked, tilting my head just enough to catch his gaze. "Good, because I was thinking that maybe tomorrow, you might let me . . . play with your balls."

His laugh vibrated against my skin, but when he lifted his head, his eyes were molten, locked on mine like I'd just handed him the win of his life.

"But tonight," I said softly, steadying myself against the weight of his gaze, "I just want to cuddle."

His brows lifted, surprise flickering in his eyes, but he didn't let go of me. "Just cuddling?"

I nodded, feeling my throat tighten. We had gone about this thing ass backwards—sometimes literally—from the very beginning. Every time we'd collided, it had been fire first, our bodies running miles ahead of the rest of us. Sex had been our language, our escape, the one way we knew how to reach each other when everything else felt too overwhelming to name.

But sitting here with him, my pulse thrumming in every place his hand touched me, I realized that if we wanted this to last—if we wanted a shot at forever—we couldn't just keep burning. We needed something steadier, softer. The kind of foundation that came from choosing each other . . . even when our clothes stayed on.

He didn't argue, didn't push, just shifted closer until his shoulder pressed against mine. "If cuddling is what you want," he said quietly, "then cuddling's what you'll get."

Finally, I could breathe again.

"And you should know that I'm one hell of a cuddler, kitten."

I let out a shaky laugh. "Is that right?"

His arm slid around my shoulders, tugging me against him until I was curled in his warmth. "Mm-hmm," he murmured into my hair. "I've got all the stamina in the world where you're concerned, even when it comes to cuddling."

I hummed against his skin. "Stamina, huh? Bold claim from someone born before CD-ROMs."

"Okay, now you're going to get it."

His chuckle rumbled against me as he pressed a slow kiss to my temple, then another to my lips, gentle and unhurried. I melted into him, breathing in the steady rhythm of his heartbeat, our laughter fading into quiet. Wrapped up in his warmth, I let my eyes drift shut, content to fall asleep with his arms around me.

And for once, I was happy to eat my words. Brooks was indeed a world-class cuddler.

Brooks

Roasters 33–23

"I fear I might be having pornographic thoughts about my breakfast."

Brock's fork clattered against his plate. "Tuck, baby," he said softly, resting his hand on his boyfriend's shoulder. Intricate metal rings adorned every finger, catching the light. "You can't just say that kind of stuff in New Hampshire."

"They don't have sexual thoughts about French toast in New Hampshire?" Tucker asked, genuinely curious. Syrup glistened at the corner of his mouth like evidence.

"I don't think they have sexual thoughts of *any* kind in New Hampshire," Soren muttered around his coffee, which he held like it had personally wronged him.

Pink snorted, nearly choking on his omelet.

I cut into my pile of vegan breakfast hash, enjoying the easy banter that ping-ponged around the table like it was a free comedy show. Not that I would ever be caught dead at a comedy show—impromptu crowd work was my biggest nightmare.

A pregame breakfast with my team, on the other hand, that I could manage any day of the week. Matty had picked the place this time, so I knew it meant he was looking for cozy conversation rather than something showy and extravagant.

There was nothing extravagant about Flapjack Fantasy. The barn-to-brunch spot smelled like maple syrup and woodsmoke. Sunlight filtered through tall, stained-glass windows, spilling across mismatched tables that looked like they'd been salvaged from every antique store in the Granite State.

It was a tradition during away series—dining together before our final game on the road. Between tonight's game and the red-eye flight back to Portland, we had a long day ahead of us—all the more reason to load up on coffee and carbs.

Brock swiped his fork through Tucker's blueberry French toast and lifted it to his mouth. He chewed thoughtfully before announcing, loud enough for the entire table to hear, "Damn, that *is* fucking good."

It was open season after that. Chairs scraped across the floor as half of the team flocked around Tucker like rabid vultures, itching for a chance to snatch a bite of his meal.

"Back off, assholes." Tucker leaned over his plate, trying to block their synchronized attack. He waved his fork like a dagger, ready to stab the next teammate who tried to steal a bite. "It's not my fault you didn't read the Yelp reviews before ordering."

"Yelp reviews," Pink said with a snort, plucking a stray blueberry from Tucker's plate anyway. "Listen to this guy. He'd be lost without the internet holding his hand."

"I don't need the internet for that," Tucker shot back. "Not when I have a hot partner with a huge, pierced—"

Brock stuffed a forkful of his breakfast poutine into Tucker's mouth. Unruly laughter broke out amongst our side of the table. I should've known better than to take the seat at the head next to Brock. His boyfriend clung to him like a fucking barnacle. Where Brock went, Tucker followed, and where Tucker went, his roommate, Roman, usually wasn't too far behind. And so on and so on, until I was seated at a table with the entire Roasters starting roster.

Roman smiled into his coffee. "Now, this is my kind of breakfast talk."

Matty leaned back, draping an arm around the back of the chair beside him like he owned the place. "Speaking of girlfriends," he drawled. "Mine's pissed I didn't bring her out here this weekend. She's obsessed with barn weddings, so this place would've been like her Super Bowl."

Pink groaned, and Soren smacked him across the stomach hard enough to knock the wind—and his mouthful of bacon—out of him.

"How are things going with . . . Lila?" Soren asked.

Between the twitch of his jaw and the way he said her name, I had a funny feeling that Soren wasn't a fan of Matty's girlfriend.

"Honestly, not great," Matty answered solemnly. "I think it's time to end it."

A round of half-hearted nods circled the table. No one looked particularly surprised—or upset.

"About damn time," Pink muttered, stabbing at his omelet.

Wes arched a brow. "We were wondering how long it was going to take you to figure that out."

"This has been a long time coming, dude," Tucker said. "The real question is how are you going to break the news to your devil dog?"

That drew a round of laughter, though it was the kind that came with a few side-eyes. Nobody said it out loud, but the truth hung in the air—there wasn't a man at this table mourning Lila's exit.

Matty leaned forward, resting his forearms on the table. No elbows, though—he was a Southern gentleman, through and through. "So, what you're saying is that none of you liked her?"

"Nope," Pink said, popping the "p."

Soren coughed into his napkin. "She was . . . fine."

"Fine like gas station sushi," Roman offered, earning a snort from the rest of the table. "No offense, man."

"We just know you deserve better," Diaz said flatly.

He lifted his coffee cup to his mouth, but not before I caught a flicker of relief in his eyes. *Interesting.* The kid had been Matty's shadow since day one, the first to volunteer for fielding drills with him. Hell, the two of them had shared a hotel room for half of last season.

And judging by the ghost of a smile tugging at his lips from the opposite end of the table, I couldn't help but wonder if there might be something more to their dynamic beyond friendship, at least from Diaz's perspective.

I made a mental note to keep an eye on that.

Pink leaned back in his chair, stretching his long legs under the table. "True love is out there, boys. Nessa's flying out next month for our Michigan series, and then we're going to drive to the Upper Peninsula and go blueberry-picking. That's true love."

"Clarke's the same way," Soren said wistfully. "Last week, she dragged me to this pop-up fashion show. I thought I would be miserable, but it turns out, I kind of liked it."

Pink smirked. "You liked it because she sucked your dick on the limo ride home."

"How the fuck did you—"

"Women talk, bro."

Soren didn't even bother denying it, just sipped his coffee with that satisfied look of a man who knew he was whipped and didn't care.

I couldn't blame him.

The table rippled with a chorus of laughs and mock kissing noises, but none of them meant it. Beneath the jokes was something quieter, more grounded. A couple of my guys had found partners who steadied them, who gave them something more than the game. And as much as I tried not to think about it, I couldn't help but picture Dani filling that same spot in my life.

We had been "taking it slow" for a couple of weeks now, spending the bulk of our time getting to know each other—beyond our bodies—while also figuring out our parenting style. She had spent most game-free evenings at my place, making dinner with me, sneaking vegan recipes into the rotation like she was testing out how many things she could do to tofu. In turn,

I had spent hours massaging her swollen feet while watching whatever musical she decided I "needed" to see, starting with *Grease* and *Grease* 2—she was still giving me shit for saying I preferred the latter.

She had also found a mini-me in Carolina, who had taken to her like a duck to water. The two of them had bonded quickly over cartoons, 90s boy bands, and a sworn alliance against any vegetable that wasn't drowned in ketchup.

But it wasn't just their shared taste in shitty music and condiments that made me smile. More than once, I had walked in on Dani with her laptop open, quietly watching YouTube tutorials about caring for Black hair—how to detangle, how to protect curls overnight, how to braid without breakage. She never announced it, never made a show of it, but I still noticed.

And as the father of a biracial daughter, I couldn't put into words what that meant. It wasn't just about hair. It was about Dani seeing my girl fully, honoring every part of her identity. That extra step, the intention behind it, was proof enough that Dani wasn't just sliding into my life. She was choosing to love all of it.

It was in those quieter moments, though, when it was just the two of us that we traded pieces of our pasts. She'd told me about her strained relationship with her mom and the loneliness of raising herself even before she'd passed away. I'd talked about the regrets I had when it came to my first few years of parenthood, and how I was determined to do better this time around, with her *and* our baby girl.

We had covered a lot of ground in two weeks. Every tattoo, every scar—physical *and* emotional—now had a story. Slow wasn't easy, but it was rewarding. It was teaching me what it meant to show up in ways that had nothing to do with sex or grand gestures. And the more we leaned into that, the more I wanted to find ways to keep proving—to her, to myself—that I was in this for the long haul.

Which was how I ended up sitting at a breakfast table in rural New Hampshire, surrounded by half my damn infield, about to do the unthinkable—ask them for relationship advice.

"Coach." Soren's voice cut through my thoughts, sharp as always. He gave me a look like he'd been reading my mind for the last ten minutes. "You're doing that thing again."

"What thing?" I grunted.

"Oh, you know, that thing where you pretend to listen but you're actually . . . brooding." He gestured with his fork. "It's giving Mr. Darcy."

Tucker nodded. "Colin Firth or Matthew Macfadyen?"

"Macfadyen," the entire table echoed without hesitation.

Was that a compliment? *Damn, I really need to watch something beyond the Bravo network.*

Pink leaned forward, elbows braced on the table. His eyebrows wiggled, and he looked downright giddy. "Oh, shit. Is this about Dani?"

I dragged a hand over my face. Lord help me, I was really doing this. "Fine," I said, glaring at all three of them in turn. "Yes, it's about Dani. And yes, I could use some advice."

Eight heads swiveled toward me in unison. Tucker even set down his fork, leaving room for Brock to snag the last bite of his French toast.

Soren chuckled low, clearly enjoying the show. "Well, damn. I didn't have that on this season's bingo card."

Normally, I'd have shut down their teasing.

I wasn't in the business of letting my guys poke into my personal life, but the thing was, I was stuck. Dani was special, and if I wanted to keep her, if I wanted to prove to her that I wasn't going anywhere, I needed some tips. And as much as I hated to admit it, the three knuckleheads closest to me—Soren, Pink, and Tucker—were the only men in my clubhouse who knew what being in a real relationship looked like.

"Cut the shit," I muttered, though I didn't push them away. "Things are good—better than good—but I need to show her I'm in this for the long haul and I don't know where to start."

"But you're having a baby together," Tucker said, as if it were new information.

"I'm well aware." I spoke through gritted teeth.

They waited, forks poised, expressions expectant. *What do I have to lose?*

"I've told her shit I've never told anyone else, not even my ex-wife," I started, keeping an even tone. "I've bought out half the baby stores in Portland because apparently, babies need a fuck ton of stuff. She gets along with my daughter like they've known each other forever. We cook together, we do bedtime together, and we even made it through putting a changing table together without wanting to kill each other."

"Sounds like you're already halfway down the aisle," Tucker said, resting his hand over Brock's.

"Yeah," Pink added. "Building furniture together is definitely a cornerstone of every healthy relationship."

Soren smirked, eyes gleaming. "I have a question."

"Shoot."

"When was the last time you took her out on a date?"

I swallowed hard. "What?"

"*A date,*" Soren repeated slowly, like he was explaining algebra to a toddler. "You know, dinner, a movie, mini golf. Literally anything that doesn't involve your couch, your kid, or PBS Kids playing in the background."

My stomach dropped.

Fuck. Me.

All this time, all these months, and I had never asked Dani out on one fucking date. What the fuck was wrong with me? Had it really been that long since I wooed a woman? Answer, yes.

Come to think of it, I hadn't been on a date in years, not since well before Carolina had been born. By the time I met Allie, we were already a decade deep into our careers, both of us too busy to waste time on candlelit dinners or late-night walks. We dated off and on for a few years, circling each other whenever my schedule allowed, until it finally got to the point where we had to choose—commit or breakup. We got married the following year, more out of practicality than whirlwind romance.

Carolina came a year after that. Diapers, bottle schedules, doctor visits—our lives had filled up with all the new demands of keeping a tiny human alive. Nights out had turned into nights in, and "date night" had meant splitting takeout while the baby monitor crackled between us on the couch. Eventually, even that had stopped. We hadn't carved out time for each other anymore. We'd been comanaging a household, partners in logistics instead of romance.

Maybe that had been the start of the end. We hadn't dated each other, not really; we'd just gotten by.

And now here I was, years later, realizing far too late that I'd walked into the same trap again. This time, though, I had someone I desperately didn't want to lose. Dani wasn't just the mother of my future kid. She was someone I wanted to *choose* over and over, the way I hadn't done with my ex. She deserved the chase, the effort, the full weight of my attention.

"Shit," I muttered, raking a hand through my hair.

Soren smirked, clearly delighted. "Welcome to the twenty-first century, coach. We date now."

Pink leaned forward, eyes lit with mischief. "You know what she would love? A trip to the farmer's market. Women eat that stuff up. Fresh flowers, homemade candles, some guy playing sad acoustic covers—it's a date factory."

Brock jabbed his fork in my direction. "Or a bookstore. You could pick out books for each other to read."

"I don't know," Soren said. "She's really into the whole true crime podcast thing. Maybe there's something there?"

"What do you want him to do? Murder somebody and then let her solve the case?" Pink taunted.

"It's not your worst idea, Stinky Pinky."

"Jesus Christ," I muttered, but I couldn't help the way my lips twitched.

Their voices blurred together as they continued volleying suggestions across the table, half-teasing, half-serious, but underneath it all was the truth I couldn't ignore.

There were only so many times I could tell Dani that I wanted to be with her; I needed to *show* her. Not with another baby blanket or another night cuddling on my couch, but with something that made her feel chosen.

Because Dani deserved that—to be chosen out loud, publicly—and I was going to make sure she knew I already had.

Dani

I couldn't remember the last time I'd been this nervous about a date. Which was ridiculous, considering the man in question had already seen me naked—*many* times. And yet somehow, this felt different. More important. Like everything we had been dancing around for months was finally coming into focus.

"Stop chewing on your lip. You're going to ruin your lipstick." Nessa flicked my chin lightly, a makeup brush clamped between her teeth as she dug through the mess on my bathroom counter.

I groaned, tipping my head back against the doorframe. "I can't believe I let you talk me into this."

Her eyes met mine in the mirror, sharp and smug all at once. "Because I'm the only one around here who knows how to do a proper cat eye, and because you'd show up in sweatpants if I didn't intervene."

"I can't help it if ninety percent of my clothes don't fit right now."

Sweatpants had become my second skin during the past month. More specifically, Brooks's sweatpants. The same pair I had borrowed—well, *stolen* because I had no intention of giving them back—the first night I'd stayed over at his place.

And thank fuck for them because somewhere between weeks twenty-one and twenty-two, my belly had popped. That meant no more hiding beneath oversized sweaters, no more fastening my jeans with a paper clip, and no more pretending like the only reason I had put on ten pounds was because of my daily bowl of ice cream.

I was pregnant—visibly, undeniably pregnant. Every time I caught my reflection in the bathroom mirror or one of the windows at the Roasters' facilities, I did a double take. Sometimes it scared me, the way my body was changing faster than I could keep up. Other times, I rested my hands against the swell, waiting, hoping to feel my little girl kick—according to the books, it would be any day now.

When nearly everything made me sweat, itch, or break out these days, Brooks's sweats gave me comfort. Even after two washes, they still smelled faintly like his detergent. Sliding into them at night made me feel like he was wrapping me up, holding me close, even when he wasn't there.

And maybe that was why I was so nervous.

Because for all the comfort I had found in his clothes, in his house, in the way he made me feel safe, tonight was special. Tonight was about stepping out with him in public, just the two of us, a declaration without saying a single word.

Brooks was taking me out. On a real date.

Cue inner teenage girl squeal.

And of course, he had done it the most Brooks way imaginable: blunt, decisive, and with zero room for argument.

It had started with a text exchange two days ago:

Brooks

> Do you have plans Friday night after the game?

Me

> Other than a pint of ice cream and the new ID docuseries about those kids who murdered their parents, not really.

He had followed that one up with the detective emoji. I didn't know what had been more surprising—the fact that Brooks wanted to take me on a date or the fact that he used emojis.

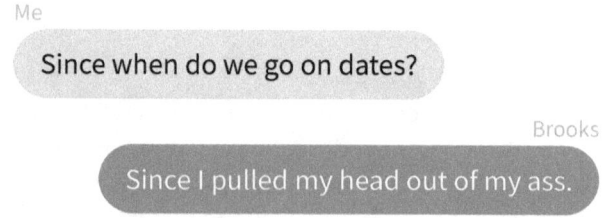

I'd stared at the screen for a solid five minutes, trying to figure out if he was joking. But then another text had come through:

Brooks

> Wear something warm and comfort-able. I'll take care of the rest.

It hadn't been flowery or over the top—it was just him—and yet, that had been all it'd taken to light me up. And it had had nothing to do with the pregnancy hormones.

"This is cute," Nessa said, holding up a green-and-pink floral-print maternity dress I had found on sale last weekend. It was a tad *SpongeBob SquarePants* with a pinch of *The Brady Bunch*, and something about it had called out to me. "Not too fancy, not too casual."

Nessa had been rooting through my closet like a woman on a mission for nearly an hour.

"He said to dress warm."

"Fucking Oregon," Nessa grumbled. Having been born and raised in Rose City, she knew the Pacific Northwest weather better than the rest of us. "Show me the rest of your new maternity wear haul."

I pulled a dozen or so hangers off the rack. "Don't laugh, I went full suburban mom chic."

Nessa's eyes lit up as I held up a pair of dark-wash maternity jeans with the stretchy belly panel. "Oh, those are hot. Look at you, already leaning into mom jeans. But like, slutty mom jeans."

I snorted. "I'm pretty sure that's not what the marketing department had in mind."

She plucked a clingy knit top from the pile, holding it up against me with a thoughtful hum. I tried not to squirm under her appraising stare, but my cheeks still warmed.

"I'm pretty sure Brooks won't care," she said, wagging her brows.

That's what I'm afraid of.

It was getting harder and harder to take things slowly with him. Every time his hands slid over my stomach—casual, reverent, like he couldn't help himself—I felt more wanted, not less. Like the extra softness, the new fullness, the growing curves only made me more magnetic to him. *Irresistible.* And when I caught the hunger in his eyes when I changed into pajamas, it was enough to undo any insecurity I had been clinging to.

She tossed a chunky sweater onto my bed. "Girl, it doesn't matter. You could show up in a potato sack and that man would still look at you like you hung the moon."

My cheeks warmed. "You really think so?"

"Take it from me," Nessa said, her voice softening before she leveled me with a look. "When a man like that sets his mind on treating you like a queen, don't fight it."

I scoffed lightly, more out of habit than conviction. "I don't need a man to validate me."

"Exactly," she shot back without missing a beat, jabbing the sweater at me like a weapon. "You don't. You're still the same badass bitch who takes no shit and runs circles around half the people I know. You can be strong and independent *and* let someone spoil you at the same time. One doesn't cancel out the others."

Her words landed sharp but steady, and I felt something in me loosen—the part of me that had always been afraid of losing myself if I leaned too hard on someone else.

I stared at the collage of colors draped across my bed. They were all too safe, sweet, something you might wear to brunch with your parents. *We can do better than that.* Tonight, I wanted to own every curve, every softened edge of me. I wanted to make Brooks sweat, to remind him who he had been chasing all these months.

And I knew exactly what outfit would do it.

I slipped past Nessa, digging deep through the hangers until my fingers found the fabric I had shoved out of sight weeks ago. When I pulled it free, the hanger clinking softly against the rod, Nessa let out a low whistle.

"Well, shit," she said, eyes going wide, a grin curling slow and dangerous across her face. "Now we're talking."

I laughed nervously, pressing the fabric against me in the mirror. "You don't think it's too much?"

She scoffed. "Dani, that dress is too *everything*, and I mean that in the best way possible."

"Too everything," I echoed, smiling wide. "Just the way I like it."

I smoothed the material against my skin, imagining Brooks's reaction when he saw me in it. Tonight, he was going to get a lot more than his kitten. He was going to get the whole damn lioness.

A knock rattled my front door, sharp and certain, and for a heartbeat I just stood there, palms clammy against the smooth pleather of my jacket, trying to remember how to breathe.

When I finally opened the door, Brooks was standing there in dark jeans and a steel colored button-down that did sinful things to his shoulders, his hair still damp from a shower. But the way his gaze swept over me—slow, deliberate, hungry—left no doubt as to who had been knocked off his axis.

His mouth opened, then closed again. He blinked hard, like maybe I'd gut-punched him.

Just the reaction I'd been going for.

"Holy shit." The words left him roughly, reverently. "Kitten."

Heat climbed up my throat, but I lifted my chin anyway. "Do you like it?"

"*Like* it?" He dragged a hand down his face, shaking his head like he couldn't believe I had had the nerve to ask him something so offensive. "You're killing me. That dress—" His voice cracked low, like gravel sliding across stone. "It should come with a warning label."

I glanced down at myself. The electric blue, ribbed body con dress had just enough stretch to hug every curve, from the slope of my tits down to where my belly rounded out. The hem hit mid-thigh, giving way to my tattooed legs, sparkly black socks, and platform sneakers.

Not exactly my warmest outfit, but what was a little frostbite in the name of foreplay?

When I looked back up at him, I couldn't help but smirk—he was still staring. And because I was feeling extra bold, I summoned my inner lioness, went up on my toes, and pressed my lips softly to his.

"You'll survive," I breathed.

His laugh was half-groan, half-growl. "Not sure I will."

He reached for my hand, thumb brushing over my knuckles as he tugged me close. "And for the record, that blue—" His gaze flicked up to the streaks in my hair, then back down the line of my body. "You're beautiful."

Something fluttered low in my chest. Not nerves this time. *Power.*

I could feel the weight of his gaze, hot and heavy, lingering on the swing of my hips as we walked back toward his SUV. By the time he reached around to open the passenger door, my cheeks were already flushed.

"Such a gentleman," I teased, slipping past him. But the heat radiating off his body as he steadied me by the waist made my breath catch.

Once inside, I barely had time to buckle my seatbelt before he was sliding in next to me, settling his broad, warm hand on my bare thigh like it belonged there.

The engine rumbled to life, headlights cutting across the street, but my brain barely registered the direction he was driving. All I could think about was the weight of his palm against my skin, the absentminded stroke of his thumb, the way every shift of the car made his grip tighten just enough to make me shiver.

The silence stretched as we drove, the low hum of the engine and the quiet rasp of his thumb against my skin filling the air. My nerves should've been buzzing, but instead I felt . . . steady. Grounded. And maybe just a little too distracted by the heat of his hand to keep pretending I wasn't curious.

"Are you gonna tell me where we're going?" I finally asked, glancing sideways at him.

His mouth curved, the corner of his lips tipping into that smug, little half-grin that had undone me more times than I could count. "No."

I narrowed my eyes. "No?"

"Patience, kitten." His gaze flicked from the road back to me, heavy with amusement. "You'll find out soon enough."

Easy for him to say when his hand was sliding up just high enough on my thigh to scramble all rational thought. By the time we turned down a side street on the edge of Rose City, my pulse was practically vibrating in my ears.

When he finally pulled to a stop, I blinked out the window, my brows knitting together. He must've taken a wrong turn because the scene ahead was nothing short of a horror movie—a sagging Victorian with peeling paint and cracked windows, its porch leaning under the weight of time.

Or maybe the weight of evil.

Where the fuck were we?

"Umm," I said slowly. "Are you planning to murder me?"

Brooks laughed, the sound rumbling deep in his chest. I wasn't sure whether I wanted to smack or straddle him. Maybe both.

Before I could ask if this was some kind of weird prank, a figure emerged from the shadows. An older woman in a floor-length calico skirt, a white blouse buttoned to her chin, and a bonnet that looked like it had time-traveled straight off the Oregon Trail.

I startled, gripping the door handle. "Oh, fuck. It's a ghost. Brooks, it's a *fucking* ghost."

He smiled, clearly delighted by my confusion. "No, it's Janice."

"Janice?" I repeated, staring as she waved primly at us, the hem of her skirt brushing the weeds. "Janice who?"

"Janice is the president of the Rose City Historical Society. Probably knows more about this city than anyone alive." His eyes glittered with mischief as he reached for my hand. "I hired her to give us a private ghost tour."

I blinked at him, then back at Janice, who, for all intents and purposes, looked ready to churn butter any second now.

"We're doing a ghost tour?" I asked, my voice pitched somewhere between disbelief and awe.

Brooks only lifted one shoulder in a shrug, like this was the most obvious thing in the world.

"You love all that true-crime, murder-doc shit. I figured this was right up your alley."

This man. My man.

My heart did a stupid little flip, the kind that left my chest feeling too tight and too warm at the same time. Most guys might've gone for dinner or a movie or—*gulp*—bowling, but not Brooks. No, he had gone straight for haunted history because he knew me. And for all the jokes about how terrifying the house looked, for all the creep factor of Janice standing there like she'd just come off a wagon train, I couldn't stop the smile tugging at my lips.

"You ready to bust some ghosts?" he asked.

I nodded, squeezing his hand back. "Are you? I know you're not into spooky shit."

"I'm into you," he said, very matter-of-fact. "So, I think I'll be okay."

Fuck. It should've been illegal to be this turned on while staring down a bonneted woman.

"Don't worry," I whispered, leaning across the console. "I'll protect you."

His grin cracked wide, boyish and cocky all at once. "I'm counting on it."

Ninety minutes later, we stumbled out of the creaking house, both of us laughing so hard, my stomach ached. Between the ghost stories and "cold spots" and Janice's commitment to staying in character, it had all been so absurd, and at the same time, oddly perfect.

"Okay," I wheezed, clutching his arm for balance. "You cannot tell me that door slamming shut by itself wasn't creepy as hell."

Brooks shook his head, trying—and failing—to look unbothered. "Just a draft, kitten. Old houses creak. That's all it was."

"Uh-huh," I teased, narrowing my eyes. "Then why were you the one clutching my jacket like your life depended on it?"

"I was making sure *you* didn't run screaming out the door." His grin tugged wider, smug and playful. "You're welcome."

I rolled my eyes, but the warmth in my chest betrayed me. We were ridiculous, teasing each other like teenagers after prom, but I couldn't remember the last time I'd felt so light. His laugh lingered, low and rough, like it was meant for me alone. And that made my chest squeeze more than any ghost story or creaking floorboard ever could.

Janice gave us a knowing smile as she packed up her lantern and historical pamphlets, muttering something about young love and "spirits approving."

"I have to give it you," I said, my hand sliding easily into his, our fingers lacing like we'd been doing it for years. "Best first date ever."

Brooks's grin softened, losing some of its cocky edges, and for a moment we just stood there under the creaking oak, his thumb sweeping lazy circles over my knuckles. The night air felt charged, like the city itself was holding its breath.

Then it happened.

A tiny flutter low in my belly, like butterfly wings brushing from the inside out. I gasped and froze, my free hand flying instinctively to my stomach.

His eyes snapped to mine. "What's wrong? Are you okay?"

"I think she just—" I swallowed the lump in my throat. "Oh my god, Brooks."

I grabbed his hand and pressed it flat against me, holding it there, waiting, holding my breath, until finally—

Another flutter, stronger this time.

Our baby girl.

Brooks went utterly still. His eyes widened, then shimmered with something so raw it knocked the breath out of me. "Holy shit," he whispered reverently. "I felt her, Dani."

Tears stung at the corners of my eyes, hot and uninvited. I laughed through them anyway, the sound shaky and full. "Guess she likes spooky ghost shit, too."

Brooks bent down, pressing his forehead to mine, his palm still anchored over the life growing inside me.

"Best first date ever," he murmured back.

Brooks

I had been dreading this day for weeks—more than any high-pressure, bases-loaded situation or postgame interview after a shutout. Six-year-olds had that kind of insurmountable power.

Allie sat cross-legged on the couch, her dark curls pulled back into a sleek puff, the kind of no-nonsense style that meant she'd been chasing deadlines all morning. She looked calm—calmer than I was, at least—like she had already rehearsed every possible outcome. Which, knowing her, she probably had.

Carolina was in her room, humming loudly enough to carry down the hall, probably elbow-deep in a bucket of markers and pipe cleaners. She had no idea her world was about to tilt on its axis.

"You ready?" Allie asked, raising one perfectly skeptical brow.

"Define ready," I muttered.

Her smile was small, almost gentle. "She's going to be fine, B. You know how much she's always wanted a little sister, *and* she already adores Dani. She still hasn't shut up about that apron Dani got her."

My lips turned up. Dani and I had taken a cooking class with Nessa and Pink last week, a double date that had had disaster written all over it, given how many sharp knives and open flames had been involved. Somehow, we'd made it through the evening with everyone's limbs intact—a personal victory, in my opinion—and a small souvenir for Carolina: a gingham apron that reminded me of something out of *The Wizard of Oz*. Carolina had been practically glued to the apron ever since, parading around the kitchen like a tiny sous-chef, bossing us around with the authority of Gordon Ramsay.

"She lectured me about gluten-free flour substitutes on the way to school last week," I marveled while pacing the rug. "Are we sure she's our kid?"

Allie held her hands up in front of her. "Don't look at me. You're the vegan."

The sudden thud of little feet padding down the stairs had me adjusting my hat, low enough so the brim bumped my glasses. Carolina's soft hum turned into an off-key Disney ballad and my throat closed up.

Showtime.

"Here we go," Allie murmured, like we were about to pull off a heist instead of talk to our six-year-old about her future sibling. "Caro, can you come here for a minute?"

The humming stopped. A few seconds later, Carolina padded in, curls slightly frizzy from whatever craft project she'd been buried in. She climbed onto the couch between us, suspicious as a cat.

"Am I in trouble?"

"No, cutie," I said quickly. "Not even a little."

She studied us with curiosity, then plopped back dramatically against the cushions, clearly bracing for whatever bombshell we were about to drop.

I took a breath and squatted in front of the couch. My knees cracked in protest, a sharp reminder that I'd spent two decades crouched behind the plate, calling pitches and eating foul tips for breakfast. Some habits—and the aches that came with them—never went away.

Allie gave me a sharp nod, one that said *you've got this.*

"You know how you've always wanted a little sister?"

"Uh-huh." Her eyes widened instantly. "Wait, are you getting me one for my birthday? Like, for real?"

"That's what we wanted to tell you," Allie said gently. "Daddy and Dani are having a baby. You're going to be a big sister."

Carolina gasped so hard I thought she might pass out. Then she flung herself upright, knees digging into the couch cushions. "Oh my gosh, oh my gosh!" She turned to me, eyes round as saucers. "Do I get to name her?"

I laughed, relief loosening the knot in my chest. "You can definitely give us ideas."

My heart lurched when her excitement faltered suddenly, her little mouth twisting into a frown.

I knew this was going too well.

"Wait a second," she said. "If you and Dani are having a baby, does that mean that you and Mommy aren't my mom and dad anymore?"

Allie pressed her fingers to her lips, trying to hold back a laugh. I scooped up Carolina and sat back down on the couch with her in my lap.

"Cutie, we will *always* be your mommy and daddy. That's never going to change. You're just going to have a little sister who looks up to you, too."

"It just means even more people to love you," Allie added, smoothing a hand down her curls. "You're not losing anything, honey. You're gaining."

We all are.

Carolina considered our words, gnawing her lip the same way her daddy did—my team knew that look well. It was the universal signal that I was grinding through a decision, weighing the odds pitch by pitch.

Eventually, she puffed out her chest and said, "Okay, but only if I get to teach her how to bake. *And* she has to share my markers. *And* she can't touch Mr. Chomp."

If that's all it takes, I'll buy a dozen Mr. Chomps.

"Deal," I said, kissing the top of her head, sending her into another fit of giggles.

I'd braced for confusion, tears, attitude, but no, my kid squealed—actually fucking squealed—bouncing so hard the cushions groaned beneath her. Her arms shot around my neck, squeezing so tight my eyes burned. "I can't believe it. This is the best birthday present ever."

Allie leaned back against the couch, soft smile, eyes glistening with unshed, happy tears. When Carolina finally hopped down and darted off to her room—no doubt to start sketching out some elaborate plans for "big sister training"—Allie turned to me.

"I told you," she said gently. "You were worried for nothing."

I dragged a hand over my face, exhaling hard. "I guess so."

Her gaze softened even more, landing on me with a kind of fondness I hadn't seen in years. "I'm really happy for you, B."

I blinked, caught off guard. "You are?"

"Of course." She shifted closer, her voice low and steady. "You deserve this, to have someone who makes you feel whole. Just because things didn't work out between us, doesn't mean that you don't deserve to be happy. You know that, right?"

I did. I'd known it for a long time, but hearing her say it like that settled something deep inside me. I hadn't realized how much I wanted Allie's blessing—or maybe just her acknowledgment—to believe I could really move forward.

For so long, I had carried the weight of failing her, of failing us, like it was proof I wasn't built for forever. But this—her encouragement and affirmation that I still deserved something good—it chipped away at the guilt I'd stacked up like bricks, weighing me down.

"Yeah," I said quietly. "I know."

Allie squeezed my hand, the kind of touch that came from years of knowing someone better than they knew themselves. "I know you. Stop waiting for the other shoe to drop. You've got a daughter who's over the moon, another on the way, and a woman who clearly cares for you. Life's too short, so you might as well lean into the good stuff."

Thirty minutes later, I was still sitting on the couch. Allie had already taken off, Carolina was busy packing her game-day bag with toys and coloring pages, and I was staring at my phone, thumbs hovering over Dani's name.

We had a home game tonight, so I could've very easily waited to tell her in person. But the weight in my chest was too full, too urgent, and I needed her to know right now. Needed her to be the first one I told—like it wouldn't be real until I shared it with her.

Finally, I typed it out.

> Me
>
> **Just told Carolina.**

Her reply came almost instantly, three little dots blinking before her words appeared:

> Dani
>
> **And . . . was she excited? Did she cry? Have we ruined her life?**

> Me
>
> **Yes. No. Definitely not.**

> Dani
>
> **Haha, so it went well, then?**

> Me
>
> **You could say that. She's already coming up with baby names and rules about art supplies and toys.**

She shot back an incoherent mix of emojis, ranging from a castle to an avocado to a water droplet, which I assumed meant something about crying.

Me

> I'll tell you more after the game.

I hesitated before adding:

Me

> Thanks for making me feel whole.

I hovered over send for half a beat, then hit the button before I could chicken out.

Dani

> You make it easy. Kick some ass tonight, coach! I'll be the one carrying your baby. xx

I exhaled, sinking back into the couch cushions.
And I'll be the one falling in love.

We pulled off a clean win—5-2 against the Revs—and the buzz of the stadium still crackled in my veins as we funneled down the tunnel toward the locker room. Victory always carried a charge, but tonight it felt lighter, easier, like the whole place was grinning with us.

That, and I was still riding the high from my pregame conversation with Dani, one that had ended with a sloppy kiss behind the stadium's coffee roastery.

"Can we talk about that double play?" Roman shouted, voice echoing off the concrete walls. He thumped his chest like he'd just saved the world instead of turned two. "Play of the night, right there. You're welcome."

Groans and laughter ricocheted around him.

"Please," Bennett shot back, slinging an arm around Roman's meaty shoulders. "If you hadn't bobbled the damn throw in the first place, we wouldn't have needed a miracle double play."

"That was strategy," Roman said, all mock offense. "Gotta keep the fans on their toes."

"Strategy my ass," Soren barked. "You tripped over your own fucking shoelaces."

"I'm just saying," Roman pressed, grinning ear to ear. "Y'all owe me for locking down the tying run."

A chorus of overlapping protests rang out, but one by one, their grins gave them away.

"Fine," Pink said eventually, even more dramatic than usual. "You get MVP."

Roman puffed up instantly, ready to soak in the glory. That was until Pink clapped him on the back hard enough to make him stumble.

"And since you're MVP, that means the first round is on you tonight."

The whole tunnel exploded in laughter.

Roman's jaw dropped. "No, that's not—"

"MVP! MVP!" the rest of them chanted, drowning out Roman's protests. He flipped them off, but they all knew it was good fun, nothing more. He was laughing just as much as the rest of them, doomed to his fate as designated wallet for the night.

I hung back a step, taking it in—the sweat, the smiles, the way a win stitched my guys tighter together. My chest swelled with that familiar pride. Nights like this were a reminder why the grind was worth it.

The noise carried us around the corner—straight into an ambush. A gold, sparkly ambush.

Dani and Clarke were waiting, blocking the path to the locker room with matching grins that spelled trouble. Clarke had her phone directed toward the guys, and Dani—*my* Dani—held up a shiny sheet of gold stars that sparkled under the fluorescents.

"Step right up, gentlemen," Dani cried out in a fake gameshow host-like voice. She spread her arms wide. "Come collect your stars and compliments."

"What's this?" Bennett asked, trotting over to her.

"Positive reinforcement," Clarke said matter-of-factly. "New content for socials."

"And because I said so," Dani added, her smile wide and merciless as she smoothed a star onto Bennett's cap. "For stealing second like your life depended on it."

The guys erupted with laughter. Bennett blushed red to the roots, muttering a thank you as if she had just knighted him.

The rest of the guys hustled in her direction, all of them smiling from ear to ear. One by one, Dani slapped stars onto their jerseys, helmets, and even a forearm or two, matching each one with some off-the-cuff praise about their gameplay. It was ridiculous and silly and exactly the kind of thing that loosened the last bit of tension out of the room.

I hung back, leaning against the wall and watching her work. It didn't matter that half the team smelled like dirt and sweat. She hugged them all, chirped out praise that had them puffing their chests, teased just enough to keep it playful, and every one of those idiots left grinning like they'd just won the lottery. I never thought I would see the day—grown men, professional athletes who could crush a baseball into orbit, *preening* under some gold stars from Office Depot.

Dani had that effect, though—light and effortless and good—and damn, if I didn't love watching her do her job, even if it meant waiting until the very end to get my turn.

Just so long as she left a little sunshine for me.

Every time she reached up on her toes to stick a star on someone's cap or laughed at some half-baked grumbling, I felt the tight pull of pride in my chest. She belonged here, with this team. She was just as much a Roaster as the rest of them.

The tunnel emptied out quickly. Dani and Clarke worked their way through the line of sweat-soaked men, and one after the other, the guys ducked into the locker room, ribbing each other about which of them had earned the best star. *Fucking children.* They could literally turn anything into a competition.

I waited until the last pair of cleats scuffed past us before stepping forward.

"What about me?" I asked, lifting my chin.

Her brows shot up, blue streaks catching in the overhead light as she blinked at me. "What?"

"Where's my star?"

She laughed, startled, like she wasn't sure if I was joking. It was a fair assessment—normally, I avoided all things social media like the plague. I *never* volunteered for goofy content, *never* played along with whatever trend the league was chasing that week, but something about tonight, about seeing her so damn alive and effortless in her element, made me want in.

Her voice softened. "You . . . want one?"

I stepped closer, close enough to smell the faint trace of her new favorite lotion—the one I had given her in one of my many care packages—under the tang of rosin and pine tar lingering in the air.

"I think I earned it."

Her eyes searched mine and a smile broke out across her face. Slowly and much more deliberately than the rest, she peeled another gold star from the sheet and pressed it to my chest, just above the team logo.

"There," she said quietly. "For not losing your mind in the ninth when the bases were loaded."

My hand covered hers before she could pull away. Her cheeks flushed, and for a second, the whole tunnel felt too small, too charged. I angled my head, lowering my voice just enough that Clarke, still fiddling with her phone, wouldn't catch it.

"Am I your star, kitten?"

"Of course," she murmured, voice light enough to sound like she was joking. "Brightest one on the team, no contest."

I smirked, ready to take the compliment and run with it, but then she leaned in, her breath brushing the shell of my ear.

"And don't tell anyone," she whispered, the sweetness in her tone curling into heat. "But nobody wears those baseball pants better than you."

My pulse spiked. I had the sudden urge to back her up against the wall and kiss the ever-loving shit out of her until neither of us could breathe. Then Clarke cleared her throat pointedly.

"I hate to interrupt, but we've got to upload this before the algorithm forgets we exist."

Dani snorted, pulling her hand back, but not before I caught the quick flicker of promise in her gaze. The kind that said we would finish this business at a later date.

I let her walk ahead, watching the swing of her hair, the star sheet still clutched in her hand. She thought she'd gotten the last word, but no—tonight, in every way that mattered, I'd already won.

I was her star.

Dani

Roasters 41–25

I was in hell. Barbie pink, sickly sweet, candy-coated hell.

Half a dozen first graders hyped up on sugar tore through Brooks's backyard like monsters, each one smeared with more frosting than they had managed to keep on their cakes.

The party had started out well enough. The tent we had rented, a gleaming white beast with bunting strung along the edges, looked like a *Bake Off* fever dream come to life. Three folding tables had been lined with mixing bowls, piping bags, and sprinkles of every shape, size, and color. And at the center of it all was a slightly saggy banner—thanks to Pink's questionable knot-tying skills—that read "Carolina's Star Baker Birthday."

Everything had gone according to plan. That was until the great frosting apocalypse had broken out. One second, we'd been decorating cupcakes, and the next, a buttercream war had broken out near the drink station.

After that, it had been every star baker for themselves.

Piping bags had turned into projectile weapons, sprinkles had been scattered across the grass in pastel swirls, and from my vantage point, there were at least two kiddos belly-sliding across the lawn to dodge buttercream bombs, leaving neon-green smears in their wake.

Talk about a showstopper.

And it wasn't just the kids; the Roasters had gotten in on the action, too.

Matty had a streak of neon-blue icing across his cheek like war paint, courtesy of a sneak attack from some kid from Carolina's gymnastics class. Bennett was crouched over a table, painstakingly rolling out fondant flowers with a six-year-old like it was the most serious thing he'd ever done. Tucker was doing his best to "referee" the war, booming out rules that nobody listened to. And Soren, of all people, was seated in a folding chair the size of a booster seat, solemnly judging a plate of cookies presented by three kids who had declared themselves a baking team.

Nessa had taken up perch in one the lawn chairs off to the side, sipping a vodka soda like she was above the chaos, only to shriek when Pink nailed her in the shoulder with a dollop of neon-blue buttercream. Her revenge was swift and merciless, a piping bag blast that left his beard stained like he'd lost a fight with a Smurf.

"Chaos," Clarke muttered from beside me, filming the whole circus for posterity. "Pure chaos."

"You can say that again."

"And to think, you've got another one of those monsters cooking up in your coochie."

Maybe I should have been mortified. Brooks and I had worked so hard on this party, down to the matching aprons and tablecloths. Instead, my cheeks ached from smiling. That was the moment it hit me, somewhere between the shrieking and the frosting-splattered chairs. This wasn't chaos at all; it was family. Messy, loud, ridiculous family, the kind that found its rhythm somewhere in the sugar rush and laughter.

And they were all mine.

Yours, too, baby girl.

I rubbed my hand over my belly, calming the flutters coming from inside.

Every kick reminded me I wasn't alone—that I would never be alone ever again—and that she was here, with me, steady and sure in a way that anchored me when the world spun too fast.

No matter how loud it got outside, she gave me quiet on the inside, a reminder to breathe.

She must get that from her daddy. And speaking of daddies . . .

My gaze found Brooks on the opposite side of the tent.

And he wasn't wielding frosting like a weapon. No, he was surrounded by a gaggle of kids—Carolina and two others hanging off his shoulders like he was a human jungle gym. His laugh carried over the chaos, deep and warm, the kind of sound that vibrated low in my chest.

My thighs pressed together almost on instinct.

Fuck, I wanted him. Bad.

And I wasn't talking about some cute make-out session behind the coffee roastery or a goodnight kiss after one of our dates. No, I wanted to drag him inside, drop to my knees, and lick every ounce of royal icing off his royal cock.

Then again, that might permanently scar a few of the kids, and that was not a conversation I wanted to have with any of their parents. Alas, the royal cock sucking would have to wait.

We hadn't had sex in weeks—not since my stupid suggestion to slow things down, which I had regretted every day since—but we had slept together. Nearly every night the Roasters were in town, and even a few away series, too. What a waste of a hotel room. To think, we could have been smashing all of those headboards—

Don't go there.

This was Carolina's day. The last thing I needed was to spontaneously combust from horniness in the middle of a first-grade birthday party.

It was getting obscene, the way I couldn't stop thinking about him, staring at him. Brooks had always been handsome—annoyingly so, in fact—but there was something about him here, surrounded by frosting-streaked kids, that just undid me.

The way he crouched down until his eyes were level with theirs, patient and kind. The way he didn't flinch when Carolina smeared a cupcake across her hand before giving him her version of the Paul Hollywood handshake. The way his laugh rumbled, warm and genuine, like this—chaos, sugar, and squealing children—was exactly where he belonged.

It was porn.

Absolute, filthy dad porn, if such a category existed.

"You're staring again," Clarke singsonged.

"I am not," I said, way too fast.

"You so are," Pink chimed in from behind us before guzzling an entire water bottle. There was still a faint trace of blue on his cheeks. "You've got the look."

"What look?"

He smirked. "The 'I want him to rail me with his *Bake Off* tent pole' look."

My mouth dropped open. "I do not—"

"Oh, honey," Clarke cut in, nudging my side. "You absolutely do."

I tried to tear my gaze away. I really did. But then Brooks threw his head back and laughed, and one of Carolina's friends tugged on his sleeve to whisper something in his ear, and he listened—really listened—with that big, beautiful, ridiculous heart of his. And I was gone.

Melted buttercream on the pavement.

"Case closed," Pink mumbled.

I swallowed hard, cheeks blazing, and that was when Brooks glanced over. Our eyes met across the lawn—his crinkling at the edges, like he already knew I was watching. He always knew.

Something reckless slipped loose in me. Before I could stop myself, I dipped my finger through the frosting topping my lemon cupcake, shot him the tiniest, most dangerous smirk, and licked.

His whole body stilled, just for a second. Then, one brow arched, slow and deliberate, promise written clear across his face.

Rut-roh.

I ducked my head, pretending to ignore my racing pulse. My friends' laughter buzzed in my ears, but the heat crawling up my neck had nothing to do with embarrassment.

I needed air. Or maybe a cold shower. Or both.

"Bathroom break," I muttered, waving vaguely toward the house before anyone could comment. Clarke shot me a knowing smirk but mercifully let me go.

I slipped out from under the tent, weaving past the frosting-slick battlefield until the squeals and shrieks dimmed behind me. Out on the fringe of the yard, with only the faint smell of sugar clinging to the summer air, I finally exhaled. My hand drifted to my belly again, and I let my baby's kicks anchor me, reminding me to breathe.

"You look like you're about three seconds away from making a getaway."

I gasped, turning toward the voice.

Allie stood a few feet away, perched casually against the pergola, sipping from a can of sparkling water. To say that Brooks's ex-wife was an intimidating creature would be an understatement—the woman was flawless.

Early-forties, maybe, with skin the color of rich espresso and cheekbones sharp enough to slice through concrete. Her hair had been swept into a sleek braid that not even buttercream chaos could touch, and she wore a sundress that managed to look both effortless and editorial. Damn. Leave it to me to discover that Brooks and I had the same taste in women.

"Busted," I admitted with a nervous laugh. "If I start scaling the fence, promise you'll distract the kids?"

She smiled, and for the first time since we'd met, I realized how much softer she seemed outside of the co-parenting logistics and birthday chaos. "Trust me, I've been there," she said, her voice genuine. "Carolina's having the time of her life, and that's what matters."

"She's amazing, you know. You've clearly done something right."

Allie tilted her head, eyes tinged with humor. "Thanks. Though, if you'd seen her at four, taking me down in a gingerbread house contest, you might call it something else."

I laughed, tension melting further. "Intimidation tactics? Pretty sure she inherited that from you."

She smirked. "You'd be surprised how much she gets from her dad."

My stomach flipped, but not in the way I'd feared. It wasn't jealousy in her tone, just truth. Ancient history. I had been bracing for something prickly or awkward, especially after our first encounter in Brooks's bedroom, but this seemed almost . . . normal. Comfortable, even.

"Don't worry, you're holding it together pretty well."

"Pretty well?" I raised a brow, gesturing toward the questionable stains smeared across my so-called slutty mom jeans.

Allie chuckled. "Trust me, I've seen worse."

She glanced toward the tent where Carolina was taking cover behind Brooks as he fended off another sprinkles ambush. "You know who to come to when you have questions." She looked back at me, adding, "About anything."

My eyes widened. "I appreciate that. I kind of hoped that by the time I became a mom, there might be a handbook for the whole thing."

"I get it," she said, nodding. "And for the record, there's no handbook for Brooks either. Just a lot of patience, pasta, and reminding him that sometimes he doesn't have to be perfect."

I huffed out a laugh, caught off guard by how much I needed to hear that. "Good to know."

She lifted her can in a mock toast. "Speaking of men who don't deserve us, I'm getting married again."

It took me a second to process. "Wow, really? Congratulations."

Her grin widened. "Thank you. And before you ask, yes, Carolina already knows. Mitchell actually asked her before he asked me. Got down on one knee and everything."

My hand flew to my chest. "Stop it, that's ridiculously cute. My hormones can't handle it."

"She said yes before I did," Allie relayed with a shake of her head, but her smile was fond, her gaze tender as it flicked back toward her daughter shrieking under the tent.

And just like that, the air between us shifted—lighter, easier. No sharp edges, no competition. Just two women, bound by the same little girl, standing shoulder to shoulder on the edges of delicious chaos.

Later that night, the house finally stilled. Gone were the shrieking children and frosting bombs and rainbow-sprinkled madness. All that remained was the faint hum of the ceiling fan and the steady sound of Brooks brushing his teeth in the en suite bathroom.

I'd showered, scrubbed off what felt like two pounds of sticky residue, and pulled on one of his shirts. And like the rest of the clothes I had stolen from him, it swallowed me whole, the hem brushing my thighs, the sleeves hanging past my elbows. Who needed a shopping spree when you had access to your own personal Brooks Brothers?

Minus the brother. Brooks had two stepsisters.

When he finally crawled into bed beside me, I expected him to immediately pull me into his arms. Instead, he grabbed my ankle and tugged until both my feet were in his lap.

"Woah," I said when he dragged me halfway across the bed. "What are you doing?"

"Taking care of you." My eyes rolled back into my head when he started kneading slow circles into my arch, his thumbs strong and sure. "You were on your feet all day."

I melted back against the pillows with a groan I wasn't proud of. "Holy shit."

He smirked, eyes glinting as he worked over another knot. "I'm serious, kitten. You're doing too much."

I let my eyes fall shut, caught between bliss and exhaustion. "Your ex is getting married again," I murmured, changing the subject. He could scold me all he wanted tomorrow, but tonight, I was gonna soak up his hands on my body.

"I know." His voice was quiet, steady.

"Do you ever think about getting married again?"

The words slipped out before I could stop them, like my mouth had gone rogue while my brain was still catching up. Where the hell had that come from? We'd never discussed marriage before. Hell, we'd never even defined whatever our relationship was.

Dating, sure. Sleeping together, technically, but only in the most literal sense of the word. But marriage? Love? Those conversations lived in a box labeled too soon, shoved somewhere behind the part of my brain currently consumed with hormones and cupcake wars.

And yet here I was, throwing it out there like it was no big deal. Like my heart wasn't thudding in my chest, waiting for him to flinch.

His thumbs stilled, just for a beat, before he said, "To you? Sure."

My eyes flew open. "How do you say something like that so casually?"

He leaned over, brushing his lips against my temple, his voice rough. "Kitten, you should know by now that there's nothing casual about my feelings for you."

Heat shot straight through me, pooling low in my belly. My thighs pressed together under the hem of his shirt, which suddenly felt dangerously short.

Brooks noticed.

His hands slid up from my feet to my calves, slow and teasing, his gaze fixed on mine. "You're thinking about it now, aren't you?"

I swallowed hard. "About what?"

"That shirt. Coming off. My fingers touching you, fucking you. How long it's been since I had you under me." His voice dropped, gravel and sin. "Too damn long."

My pulse spiked, traitorous and eager. "You're awfully confident for a man who just spent the day losing a cupcake war."

His grin turned wolfish as his hands pushed higher, skimming bare skin. "Sweetheart, I always win where it counts."

My breath hitched, every nerve lighting up. Take me now. I wanted to drag him down over me, fist his shirt in my hands, and erase the weeks we'd spent holding back like fucking idiots thanks to me and my stupid mouth. I was already arching into him, needy and reckless.

"Brooks . . . ," I pleaded.

His mouth brushed mine, featherlight, enough to spark but not satisfy. The heat coiled low in my belly, fierce and demanding.

I wasn't above begging. Not when his hands were sliding higher, his voice turned to smoke and gravel in the dark, and every inch of me ached for him to finally, finally stop holding back.

The thing was, I wasn't a woman who begged. Not for favors, not for attention, not for anyone. I'd learned long ago what it cost to need someone more than they needed me. Begging was a weakness. Surrender.

But with Brooks?

It was trust. It was laying myself bare and saying take me apart and put me back together. I would let him do both, so long as I got to do the same, too. Turnabout was fair play.

But before I had a chance to literally get down on my knees and beg him the way we both wanted, he pulled back.

I blinked, stunned, chasing his mouth without meaning to.

"Please don't look at me like that." His thumb traced the line of my jaw, tender in a way that gutted me. "You've been on your feet all day, and I'm not about to push you when you're this tired."

"But I want—"

"Oh, I know what you want," he murmured, pressing a kiss to my forehead that was somehow both infuriating and unbearably sweet. "And believe me, I want it too. But when I finally get inside you again, kitten, I'm not stopping."

His certainty and restraint were somehow even sexier than if he'd just rolled me under him and given us the ride we were both craving. My chest ached with equal parts adoration and sexual frustration.

Mostly sexual frustration.

Brooks smirked at the look on my face, thumb still stroking along my jaw. "Don't forget, I was in the trenches today, too. Cupcake wars, six-year-olds hopped up on sugar? I'm not twenty-two anymore. That shit nearly killed me."

A laugh burst out of me, sharp and helpless, even as heat still pulsed low in my belly. "What happened to all that stamina I've been hearing about?"

"I left it under the tent, buried under six feet of fondant," he said, grin flashing.

"You're impossible."

"And you love it," he murmured into my hair, smug and tender all at once.

Unfortunately for me, he was right.

Brooks

Roasters 42–27

I had just finished wrapping up a meeting with the front office when my phone buzzed. Dani's name lit up the screen, and I grinned like a damn fool.

It still caught me off guard sometimes—how far we'd come in the past few months. There'd been a time when it had just been me, hammering her inbox with texts like a teenager with his first crush, and now we talked every day. And that didn't begin to cover all the hours we spent in my house, in my bed.

It felt easy in a way that nothing else ever had. Progress, sure, but the kind that made my chest ache with how much I wanted to keep it.

I answered with a smile already in place. That was, until I heard her voice.

"We don't have a crib, Brooks."

No hello. No breath. Just a rush of panic straight into my ear.

"Dani—"

"Or a baby registry. Everyone keeps asking me about my registry, and I haven't even decided what website to use. Or what to put on it. There are like five thousand kinds of bottles, Brooks. Five. Thousand. What if the baby hates every single one? What if she doesn't even latch onto my nipples?"

I froze halfway to the door, suddenly thankful that I hadn't taken the call on speaker. I didn't need any of the guys to hear about her nipples.

"And what if she *does* latch but I don't make enough milk? What if I forget to pack a diaper bag? Not that we even have a diaper bag. Also, have you seen how expensive diapers are? *Fuck,* I'm going to be the worst mother in the world and she's not even here yet—"

"Kitten," I cut in, sharper than I meant to because my heart had already started sprinting. "Are you hurt?"

"What? No. But I—"

"Are you bleeding, in pain? Is the baby okay?"

"No, she's fine. I'm fine," she snapped, but her voice cracked, thick with tears. "I just . . . I don't know what I'm doing, Brooks. I was just getting used to being pregnant, and now there's only a few months to go and—"

Relief slammed into me hard enough that I had to grip the doorframe. She was okay. The baby was okay. But still, her voice had that edge, raw and frantic, like she was circling the drain.

"Stay put," I said, already moving. "I'm on my way."

"Brooks, you don't have to—"

"Too late," I muttered, shoving through the door and jogging to my truck. "You called me, kitten. That means you're stuck with me."

I had a whole staff of coaches who could handle practice for the rest of the day without me breathing down their necks. Hell, they would probably prefer it that way. This time tomorrow, I'd be on a plane to Miami for a nine-day road series, but right now, there was nowhere else I needed to be.

More than that, Dani had called *me.*

Not Pink or Clarke or one of her Dungeons & Dragons friends, but me. I wanted to be the one Dani called when the walls closed in, the steady hand she reached for when she felt like she was falling. If she trusted me with that, then we could figure out the rest.

"Stay the phone on with me, kitten."

For the next twenty minutes, I listened to fifteen more variations of the same spiral, everything from how she was supposed to know which stroller was safest, to whether the crib sheets needed to be organic cotton, to the horror of her friends planning some cringeworthy baby shower theme. Because these were the things that kept my blue-haired, goth girl up at night—some bullshit games where people guessed her belly measurements or licked melted candy bars out of diapers.

None of them were life and death scenarios, but that didn't mean that to her, it didn't feel like the sky was falling.

Don't worry, kitten, I'll hold it up for you.

About halfway through my drive, she ran out of stuff about bottles and breast pumps and jumped straight into the big-picture shit. How we were going to split time between her place and mine, how the baby would know which house was hers, whether she'd grow up confused or resenting us.

I didn't tell her the part sitting heavy on my chest: that what I *really* wanted was for there not to be two houses at all. But that was a conversation for another day. Right now, she just needed me to be steady.

By the time I bound up her steps, I thought I'd heard it all. As it turned out, I didn't even get the chance to knock.

The front door yanked open and there she was. Barefoot, red-eyed, shoulders sagging like the weight of the world was on her.

"I killed Doughy McIntyre," she choked out.

I blinked. "Who?"

"The sourdough starter, Doughy McIntyre." Her bottom lip wobbled, another tear sliding down her cheek. "Carolina trusted me to keep it alive while she was at camp, but I left it in my car, forgot all about it, and now it's dead. How can I be expected to take care of a baby when I can't even remember to take care of a doughy blob?"

My hand dragged over my face, and when I looked back at her, she was sniffling so hard I couldn't even laugh.

"Kitten," I said, stepping inside and cupping her damp face with both hands. "You're crying over bread."

"*Starter*," she corrected miserably, shoulders shaking. "It's not just bread, Brooks. It's like a pet—a *yeast* pet—and I killed it."

This time, there was no way to stop the crack of laughter that shook my chest. She tried to swat me, but I was faster, dragging her to my chest and circling my arms around her waist. She collapsed there, sobbing and hiccupping, her fists knotting in my shirt.

"You scared the hell out of me," I muttered against her hair, holding her tight. "Yeast pets I can handle, but I thought—" I broke off, pressing a kiss to the crown of her head. "Never mind what I thought. You're fine. The baby's fine. We can figure out the rest."

She let out a strangled laugh that was half-sob, half-relief. "Sorry."

"It's okay," I admitted, rubbing slow circles over her back. "Now, sit down before you cry yourself into dehydration. You tell me everything that went wrong today, and we'll fix them."

"But the starter—"

"Fuck the starter. I'll buy her another one. I'll buy her whole a fucking bakery."

That got a small laugh out of her, and I felt her start to unclench against me, the tension bleeding out of her shoulders.

"Come on," I said softly, steering her inside and nudging the door shut behind us. I guided her to the couch and crouched in front of her, taking her hands in mine.

"I know what'll make you feel better."

Her watery eyes met mine, wide and searching. "Crying some more?"

I huffed a laugh and shook my head. "Let's make a list."

"A list?"

"You love lists," I reminded her, squeezing her hands. "Let's make a list of everything we still need to do. Anything we need to buy, build, or whatever—we'll write them down and knock them out, one by one."

Her throat worked as she swallowed, staring at me like I'd just offered her oxygen. "But there's still so much—"

"We've got three-and-a-half months, kitten." I leaned in, brushing a kiss to her temple. "Plenty of time. In fact, we can tackle a couple today. You know, baby steps."

Her laugh came out watery, but real. "When did you get so corny?"

"Anything to make you laugh, kitten." I reached for the notepad and pen sitting on the coffee table and pressed them into her hands. "Let's start with a crib."

She sniffled, looking down at the blank page. For a moment, she just stared. Then, she wrote in shaky but determined letters.

"Perfect," I said, nodding like we were planning a championship lineup. "What's next?"

Her gaze flicked to me, softer now, steadier. "Registry."

"I'll ask Allie if she has any recommendations." I grinned. "Don't you feel better already? And tomorrow, during my flight, I'll research how to resurrect our yeast pet."

"And what if it's a lost cause?"

I shrugged. "Rest in yeast, Doughy McIntyre."

That earned me a laugh so sudden, she covered her face with the notepad, shoulders shaking. The sound loosened something in my chest. "There she is," I murmured, tugging the pad down so I could see her smile. "We're gonna figure this out. All of it. Together."

She muttered something under her breath.

"What was that?" I asked.

"Nothing."

Her eyes darted around the room, catching on the plant in the corner that had overgrown its pot. I closed the distance between us, tipping her chin up with a finger. "Kitten."

She groaned like a teenager caught sneaking out. "Fine, I can't . . . shave my legs anymore, okay? I can't even *see* my legs anymore."

The flare in her eyes warned me that there would be hell to pay if I even cracked a smile. "That's it?"

"That's it?! Brooks, I've officially hit rock bottom. I can't even handle the basics. I'm hairy, hormonal, and homicidal."

I bit back a grin, but what struck me harder than the dramatics was the look in her eyes—wide, wild, like she was teetering on the edge of another spiral. Maybe what she needed wasn't a pen-and-paper solution. Maybe she just needed to get out of her head for a while, to breathe, laugh, remember there was more to her than panic and planning. A distraction, not a strategy.

"C'mon," I said, settling back on my heels. "Let's get out of here."

Her head snapped up. "What? Brooks, I look like a raccoon that lost a fight with a mascara wand."

"You look perfect," I replied, already hauling her up from the couch. "And trust me, where we're going, nobody gives a damn about your mascara or your legs."

Suspicion narrowed her eyes. "Where are we going?"

I only grinned, grabbing her sandals and tossing them at her feet. "Field trip, kitten. You'll see."

The bell over the door dinged as I pushed it open, holding it wide for Dani. Her eyes bounced around the nondescript room with peach and yellow accents, looking at it like it was another dimension, rather than the local cat rescue.

"Wha— You brought me to a cat shelter?"

"I brought you to *the* cat shelter," I said around a nod.

Pawsitive Vibes also boasted a café and was tucked into a narrow strip mall about halfway between Rose City and Portland, the kind of place you'd miss entirely if you weren't looking for it.

Inside, the air smelled faintly of cedar chips and hand sanitizer, undercut by the warm musk of too many cats—if there were such a thing—in one place. A long ledge circled the room just below the ceiling, a feline highway where sleek shapes padded from perch to perch.

In the front windows, little hammocks swayed lazily with the weight of napping tabbies, their tails flicking in slow, content arcs.

The rest of the space could best be described as a whiskered wonderland—cat trees erected like totem poles, cubbies stacked along the walls, little tunnels cut into the shelving so the cats could dart in and out like ghosts. Soft cushions and mismatched chairs dotted the floor, clearly meant for the humans who came to sit, sip coffee, and get covered in fur.

And then, there were the three women behind the coffee counter, all of them old enough to be my nana. Carolina had taken to calling them Flora, Fauna, and Merryweather because they reminded her of the three fairies from her favorite Disney film.

"There's our guy," one of them said, her face breaking into a grin. "Back again so soon?"

"Couldn't stay away," I said easily, slipping a check from my back pocket and sliding it across the counter. They didn't even blink, just smiled, already knowing what it was.

Beside me, Dani gawked. "You . . . come here a lot?"

I shrugged, guiding her deeper inside. A sleek black cat darted across the floor. "When I can."

"He's being modest," the tallest of the three women said. "Brooks is a certified Paws Pal, one of our biggest donors. He also subscribes to our monthly newsletter."

Dani's eyes lit up. "Oh, do tell."

"Uh, maybe later." I steered her toward the smaller room at the back, the one labeled with a sign that read *Kitten Kingdom*. "Dani, here, is in desperate need of some kitten cuddles, so if you wouldn't mind excusing us, ladies?"

"Have fun, you two."

Dani froze on the threshold, peeking through the glass. On the other side of the door, half a dozen kittens lounged across beanbags and perches, stretching lazily in the sunbeams.

"You brought me to cuddle kittens?" she asked, dazed.

"Damn right I did." I gave her a little push inside, watching her shoulders finally loosen as a ginger tabby padded straight up and pressed against her leg. "Told you I'd make you feel better."

The look she shot me—soft, disbelieving, already on the verge of a smile—was worth every mile of the drive.

The tabby wasted no time climbing straight into Dani's lap once she crouched, purring like a motor. She blinked down at it, stunned, then looked up at me.

"He just . . . picked me."

"Of course he did," I said, leaning against the doorframe with a grin. "They know who needs them most."

She shot me a look, half-exasperated, half-amused. "Have you been living some secret double life? Pro-baseball coach by day, cat whisperer by night?"

"It's not a secret," I said, crouching beside her. A calico padded over and butted its head against my hand, and without thinking, I scratched under its chin until it melted into a puddle of fur. "I just don't go out of my way to talk about it."

Dani arched a brow. "But like, they *know* you here."

I smirked. "I try to come in a few times a month, sometimes with Carolina, sometimes by myself. I've always had a thing for cats."

And one specific kitten, too. The irony wasn't lost on me.

Her face softened, fingers stroking absently through the ginger's fur. "Now that I think about it," she mused. "I can definitely see you having a cat. Like an old, one-eyed bitch named Bernice or something."

"You're not far off," I told her, stroking the calico as it rolled onto its back, batting at my hand. "My mom got me a cat right before she and my dad split. Said I needed something to keep me company when it was just the two of us, something to remind me I wasn't alone."

"What was her name?"

"Agnes," I said, grinning at the memory. "A sassy, old tortoiseshell with one hell of an attitude. She used to sleep on my head when I was a kid, and if I left my baseball glove lying around, she'd curl up inside like it was hers."

Dani laughed, the sound finally free of the sharp edge it had carried all day. "That explains so much. You're basically still that kid with his glove and his cat."

"I guess some things stick. Cats, baseball, bad hair days."

She gave me a watery smile, scratching behind the tabby's ears. "And now me."

That tugged hard at my chest, but I just tipped my head, grinning. "Yeah, kitten. Now you."

Another cat hopped up onto the back of her shoulders, and she squealed while I leaned back and chuckled. "Relax," I said, amused. "If he wanted to kill you, you'd already be dead."

"That's comforting," she deadpanned, but her laugh gave her away as she tried to coax the cat down.

I reached over, lifting the little daredevil off her and settling it against my chest. It curled there instantly, purring like a chainsaw.

Dani stared, wide-eyed.

"Seriously," she whispered. "You're a cat magnet. You didn't just bring me here to cuddle cats. You did it so I could watch you make out with them."

"Jealous?" I teased, kissing the top of the kitten's head. Cats had always smelled good to me—like clean laundry left drying on the line, simple and grounding in a way that made my chest ease.

She narrowed her eyes, lips twitching. "Of a furball that licks its own butt? Absolutely."

I chuckled, the sound rumbling in my chest. "Don't worry, you're still my favorite kitten."

A few hours later, after we'd gotten our fill of cat cuddles and even managed to knock a couple of things off our baby to-do list, I drove her back to her place.

She was quieter now, but in that content, post-laughter way, her head tipped against the passenger window, a faint smile curving her mouth. By the time I pulled into her driveway, the storm from earlier had dulled to nothing more than a drizzle in her eyes.

"You know," Dani said softly when I walked her to her door, a ginger hair or two still clinging to her sweatshirt. "That really did make me feel better. I know this probably wasn't on *your* list of things to do today."

"That's okay." I reached out, brushing a strand of hair behind her ear, letting my thumb linger against her cheek. "A few tears and hairballs sure beat the hell out of a trade meeting."

"Thank you."

She leaned into my touch, and for a second, I thought that was it—I'd tuck her in, say goodbye, and make an early night of it before tomorrow morning's flight at the ass crack of dawn. But when I started to pull away, her frown stopped me cold, like she was already bracing for the sound of the door closing behind me.

I bent down instead, my mouth brushing her ear. "Relax, kitten. I'm not going anywhere. We've still got one more thing to cross off your list tonight."

Her brows pinched, confusion flickering across her face until I let the grin curve my mouth.

"I told you I'd take care of everything, didn't I? Starting with those legs you swore you couldn't reach."

Dani

The steam rose in lazy curls, clouding the glass and what was left of my reason. I sat on the edge of the tub while the shower beat against the tile, already running hot, a steady hiss filling the room.

Clad in nothing but a white cotton bralette and matching underwear, I felt more exposed than if I'd been completely bare. "This is ridiculous," I said. "You seriously want to shave my legs?"

"I already am," he answered without missing a beat, pumping a squirt of shaving gel into his palm. "This will be easier if you stand."

"Brooks—"

"Into the shower, kitten." His gaze tracked over me, steady and unhurried. "Trust me. You *know* how good I am with my hands."

This shouldn't have affected me as much as it did. Brooks had already seen all of me—every tattoo, every scar, every inch—but sitting there, damp heat clinging to my skin, I felt stripped down in a different way. Naked, not just in body, but in the way his attention pressed into me, making it impossible to pretend I wasn't trembling on the inside.

I stepped into the tub, letting the shower spray soak my back.

Brooks stayed where he was, on his knees at the edge of the porcelain, the steam beading against the ink sprawled across his chest and arms. He'd stripped down to nothing but his boxer briefs, the fabric stretched tight over muscles in a way that should've been illegal—and had me wet for reasons that had nothing to do with the water.

The sight punched the air from my lungs—this hard, powerful man kneeling in front of me like I was something worth worshiping. It made my skin prickle, not just from the heat, but from the weight of being seen like a goddess.

"Quit looking at me like that," I muttered, cheeks burning hotter than the spray.

"Like what?"

My breath snagged when his palm wrapped around my calf, steadying me as if this weren't the most intimate thing in the universe, trusting him with a sharp blade against my skin.

I swallowed. "Like I'm your next meal."

His lips twitched, but his voice was soft, coaxing. "Best meal I've ever had, kitten."

I glanced down, unable to resist, and there it was—the outline of his thick, hard cock straining against his briefs. The sight made my mouth go dry.

My pulse stuttered as he crouched lower, razor in one hand, my leg balanced in the other like I was something fragile and precious. The first cool swipe of shaving cream across my shin sent goose bumps racing up my skin. He smoothed it with deliberate care, his fingers spreading it in long strokes that felt more like foreplay than personal hygiene.

My breath hitched, my eyes glued to the way his tattooed forearm flexed as he steadied me.

Then came the blade.

Slow, gliding strokes over my skin with practiced precision, each of them unhurried. His knuckles brushed lightly against me with every pass. It shouldn't have been so erotic, and yet my body hummed with it, every nerve stretched taut as I watched him work.

And still, it wasn't enough.

"This is . . ." My throat was dry. "Weirdly hot."

His eyes lifted, heavily-lidded, knowing. "It's about to get hotter, kitten. Time for your thigh."

He dragged the razor higher, thumb brushing dangerously close to where my thigh met the lace edge of my panties.

Heat licked through me, pooling low and heavy, until the words were on my tongue before I could stop them. "It might be easier if you take my panties off." My voice came out husky, breathless.

"You sure?"

My lips parted, the word no on the tip of my tongue, only it didn't feel like no. Not with him crouched there, looking at me like I was precious and breakable and something he wanted anyway. My pulse thrummed as I whispered, "Please. Take them off."

That was all the permission he needed.

He slid the cotton down my legs, slow and reverent, and I lifted my hips without thinking, heat rushing to my face. When his eyes found mine again, something bold slipped into my chest, chasing away the nerves.

"Careful, coach," I said, smirking to cover how wrecked I already felt. "You miss a spot, and I might post that photo of you scratching your balls in the dugout to the team's social media pages."

His grin was wicked, but his touch was anything but careless. Each stroke of the razor was torture, knuckles grazing higher and higher until I was squirming, biting back sounds that shouldn't belong to a woman getting her legs shaved. The air between us thickened until it was nearly impossible to breathe.

When he finally finished and rinsed me clean, I tested the smoothness with my toes poised on his chest. "Damn, you're really good at this."

"Smooth as silk." His gaze traveled up my body like a slow burn, pausing between my thighs. "Want me to keep going?"

The question stole the air from my lungs. My mouth opened, but no sound came out—just a shiver that raced down my spine and smacked me clean across the clit. Brooks waited, water slicking over the hard lines of his body, razor balanced in his hand like he had all the time in the world.

"You mean—"

His eyes dragged up to mine, patient but daring. "You know exactly what I mean, kitten."

My thighs clenched instinctively, betraying me. I could've said no. I could've laughed it off and made another joke about his ball-scratching photo, the one I had set as my phone's wallpaper—anything to break the spell he had me under. Instead, I felt my knees fall open another inch, giving him silent permission.

Brooks's grin was slow and devastating. "That's what I thought."

He set the razor aside for a moment, lathering his big hands with more cream. The sight alone had me trembling. Those hands smoothed the foam higher, over skin no one had ever touched like this. It wasn't crude or rushed, but rather reverent.

And as his thumb traced the tender crease of my thigh, edging my pussy lips, I realized I'd never been this exposed or undone.

I'd also never felt safer.

He lathered me again. The first stroke of the blade was steady, deliberate, skimming so close that my breath caught and held. Brooks's hand anchored me, his palm spread firm over my hip as he guided the razor with precision.

Every pass left me trembling, heat spiraling tighter inside me. His knuckles brushed against my mound, grazing too close, too teasing, until I was squirming on the slick porcelain, my breath coming in ragged bursts.

"Easy," he murmured, voice low and rough, his focus never wavering.

He tilted the razor just right, clearing another path, the cool drag of steel followed by the warmth of his thumb soothing the skin after. *Torturously slow.* Intimate in a way I had never experienced.

When he rinsed the blade under the spray, his fingers slipped back over me, spreading the gel lower this time. His touch wasn't an accident—not when his thumb brushed against my clit, light as a ghost. The jolt had me biting down on a whimper, my whole body arching without permission.

"Brooks," I breathed, desperate, trembling.

He glanced up through the rising steam, jaw tight. "Hold still, kitten. I don't want to miss a spot."

God help me.

His warning only made it hotter.

I could feel how close he was to losing control. His fingers slid over me again, spreading my folds open as the razor traced careful strokes along the softest parts of me. It was unbearable, the way I was laid bare for him, every inch on display.

By the time he rinsed the blade again, I was shaking, my body begging for more than careful strokes. And when his fingers lingered, rubbing foam away from my swollen clit with maddening gentleness, a choked sound tore from my throat.

"Christ," he muttered under his breath, his thumb circling once, slow and sure. "You're trembling, kitten."

And he was right. I was trembling all over, not from fear, but from the sheer, impossible ache of wanting him to drop the razor and stuff me full of his fingers. Or tongue, or cock—hell, my drawer full of toys was just down the hall.

"Dani," he asked, his voice thick with need. "Can I taste you?"

My whole body shuddered, nerves sparking hot under my skin. Fear and anticipation tangled in my chest, but my voice didn't falter. "*Please.*"

Without missing a beat, he spread my thighs wide, the water streaming over me as his head dipped. The first drag of his tongue through my cunt made me cry out, sharp and unrestrained, echoing against the tile. I slammed back into the wall, my fingers flying to his hair, clutching tight as the vibration of his groan shivered straight through my core.

His tongue circled my clit, slow, deliberate, and the sensation was so good it bordered on unbearable. When he sucked me into his mouth, the pressure building low in my belly went molten.

"*Fuck*," I gasped, grinding shamelessly against his face. "Right there."

He anchored me with his hands on my thighs, holding me open, owning every frantic movement. "Soak me with that cream, kitten," he rasped between licks, his mouth slick and hot against me. "Give me everything."

After that, he gave up all pretense of control.

His tongue worked me mercilessly, flicking and swirling, his beard rough against my skin in a way that made me writhing harder, chasing every jolt of pleasure. He sucked and licked like he hadn't eaten in days, like he wanted to devour me from the inside out. Nothing could muffle the frantic sounds spilling out of me—raw, desperate cries that didn't sound like my voice at all—not even the shower spray.

He pushed a thick finger inside me, slow at first, stretching me, then curling until sparks detonated behind my eyes. I swallowed my scream when he added another finger, thrusting deep, keeping pace as his tongue mercilessly circled my clit.

He moaned with every taste, every drop. "God, Brooks, don't you dare stop. *Please.*"

He didn't. If anything, he got rougher, hungrier, hammering into me with his tongue and fingers until my vision blurred.

The wave broke fast, tearing me apart. I screamed his name, thighs clamping tight around his head, drowning him in water and pussy juices as the orgasm ripped through me, sharp and devastating. He held me there, drinking me down until I was nothing but shaking limbs and shattered breath. It was too much and still not enough, and I never wanted it to end.

When he finally pulled back, his lips and beard glistened with me, and the sight nearly made me come undone all over again. He didn't look smug, didn't even look satisfied—he looked fucking ravenous. Like he'd barely gotten a taste and now he wanted the whole fucking meal.

"Holy shit." I gasped, chest heaving, legs trembling.

He rose to his feet in one smooth motion, towering over me, water dripping down the ridges of his body. And then his mouth was on mine, his tongue pushing between my lips so I could taste myself on him while his cock, hot and thick, pressed against my thigh.

Eventually, when we both came up for air, my eyes caught on something that broke me wide open in a completely different way. Brooks's glasses, crooked from our kisses, had completely fogged over, steam clouding the lenses. The laugh burst out of me before I could stop it.

He froze, confusion flickering across his face. "Huh, that's not usually the response I get."

I pointed, still giggling so hard my stomach ached. "Your glasses. You look like you just tried to run a marathon in a sauna."

He reached up, tugged them off, and squinted at me through the steam, one brow arched. And just as I slipped my hand down his body, tracing my fingers along his abs—

Bang. Bang. Bang.

"Five more minutes, Dani," Jared's voice bellowed through the bathroom door. "You're using up all the hot water."

I clapped a hand over my mouth, giggling helplessly while Brooks scowled in a way that only made me laugh harder.

"Fucking Christ." He groaned through gritted teeth.

I couldn't stop laughing, even as Brooks scrubbed a hand over his face like he was about to murder Pink through the door. He kissed my forehead instead, muttering a string of curses under his breath.

"Next time, my place," he grumbled, rinsing off the last of the shaving cream from my legs. "No roommates. No interruptions."

I winced, still smiling. "Sorry."

His hands slid down my calves one more time, slow and deliberate, like he couldn't quite stop touching me. "Don't apologize, kitten. I'm going to be tasting you on my lips for days."

I bit back another giggle, cheeks aching from how hard I was smiling. God, he was sulking like a thwarted caveman, all broad shoulders and scowl, and for some reason, that was stupidly hot.

We scrambled out of the shower, both of us laughing under our breaths like guilty teenagers caught making out under the bleachers. Brooks wrapped a towel around my shoulders and then grabbed another for himself.

"I should go, kitten. Early flight tomorrow."

The words deflated me, though I tried to hide it. "Okay."

"I'll text you when I land." He brushed his knuckles down my cheek, eyes warm despite the scowl still tugging at his mouth. "Or when I figure out how to save the sourdough. Whichever comes first."

Later that night, I lay staring at the ceiling fan spinning lazy circles above me. The bed felt too big, the silence too sharp. I reached for the other side of the mattress before I could stop myself, my fingers brushing cool fabric where Brooks's warmth should've been.

I hated how much I missed him already. Which was ridiculous because I'd always loved sleeping alone. Probably a byproduct of being an only child—my space was *my* space, and God help anyone who tried to share it. I used to roll my eyes at people who complained they couldn't sleep without their partner beside them. Needy, I'd thought. Codependent.

And now here I was, staring at the empty pillow next to me and wishing it were dented by his broad shoulders, his steady breathing filling the room. As it turned out, once I'd had Brooks's arms wrapped around me, his chest warm against my back, his low murmurs pulling me under, it was impossible to go back to empty sheets.

He left for Miami tomorrow. Normally, I traveled with the team, but this time around, Clarke was running the show while I stayed behind. It was a test run for when I went on parental leave in October. I should've been grateful for the break, but instead all it did was make me restless.

No sidelong glances across the dugout, no stolen kisses between stadium tunnels, no cuddling during the bus rides that typically made me nauseous, but which had become somewhat comforting when I spent them next to Brooks.

This time, it was just me, alone, wishing he were here.

I curled tighter under the covers, pressing my face into the bougie Tempur-Pedic pillow he kept at my place, breathing in what was left of him.

The team would be back in ten days, just in time for the big Father's Day game. And sure, that wasn't long, but tonight it stretched out ahead of me, endless and heavy. Lying there in the quiet, watching the fan blades turn, feeling that ache hollow out my chest, I realized something else that made my pulse trip.

I didn't want to keep us quiet anymore.

The team already knew. All of my friends did, too. Hell, anyone with eyes could probably figure it out pretty easily.

But I wanted more.

I wanted to be public.

To stand next to Brooks, not just behind him. To let the world see that he was mine and I was his, no shame, no hiding.

For the first time, I wasn't scared of that truth. I was ready to show Brooks that I was all in. The only question that kept me awake, long after the sheets cooled, was *how*.

Brooks

Roasters 45–32

T he roar of the stadium was a living thing, louder than any plane engine, steadier than any heartbeat.

It was Father's Day at the Roasters' ballpark, which meant dads and kids running the bases, special jersey giveaways, and sentimental jumbotron content nearly every inning. This year, the noise pressed harder against my ribs than usual. Partly because I was only a few months out from becoming a dad again, and also because I'd been running on nothing but falafel, hotel sheets, and late-night calls with Dani for the past week.

"Make it count, Matty!" Soren hollered from the bench, voice cracking over the noise.

Wes leaned over the rail, cupping his hands around his mouth. "Drive it deep!"

"That's what she said," Tucker added, earning him a gentle smack from the men on either side of him.

We were down by one in the sixth, which meant there was still a lot of game left to play. Matty adjusted his gloves at the plate and relaxed his grip, just the way he'd been coached. I caught his eye and touched my hand to my cap before giving the sign to take the first pitch. Their starter had been pounding the zone early all afternoon, and if he missed his spot now, Matty would be ready. He wasn't a heavy hitter, but he was a patient one.

I watched the pitcher wind up, my pulse ticking in rhythm with the ballgame, with the weight of a thousand small decisions that made the difference between winning and watching it slip away.

And we needed a win after a four-game losing streak.

Miami had been good to us, but our luck had dried up in Charleston with a three-game shutout. The guys were glad to be home, and frankly, I couldn't blame them—the humidity had nearly killed me, too. Ten days on the road had dragged like ten years, and by the time our plane had touched down last night, it had been well past midnight.

I'd walked through my front door and had dragged my ass straight to bed, when what I'd really wanted was to kick Dani's door open, throw her down, and eat her pussy until she was shaking apart under me.

Again.

The truth was, I'd jerked off more times than I cared to count, chasing the memory of Dani shattering on my tongue. Every night in some faceless hotel room, I'd fist my cock and picture her—head tipped back, body trembling, hands clawing at the shower tiles while I ate her pussy until she begged for mercy. I had stroked myself fucking raw replaying the way she'd come apart for me in her shower, every gasp and shudder burned into me so deep I couldn't get free of it.

The sharp crack of a bat snapped me back to reality, and the crowd came to life as the ball soared over the infield. I tracked it automatically, eyes on the arc, already calculating before the left fielder even broke into a sprint.

Routine fly. Out number three.

My guys grabbed their mitts and jogged back onto the field. I clapped the nearest shoulder as they passed, keeping my face steady even though I could feel the weight of the game tightening around us.

And still, my eyes strayed. I scanned the stands for the hundredth damn time that afternoon, restlessly searching for her face in the sea of fans. Nothing. Not a glimpse of her hair, not the curve of her smile. I told myself to focus on the game, but the truth was, I'd been looking for her since the anthem and hadn't spotted her once.

I missed her.

At some point in the past few months, my house had stopped feeling like mine and instead felt like ours.

She might not have been officially living with me—not yet anyway—but most of her things had migrated into my place. Half her shoes were stacked by the door, her favorite socks took up an entire drawer in my dresser, and her side of the bed always smelled like her shampoo. It was proof she belonged there, even if she hadn't said the words out loud.

And still, a part of me waited.

For a sign, a moment to show that she wanted this—she wanted *me*—for good. Because whether she knew it or not, I wasn't going anywhere. If she tried to run, I'd be right there behind her, steady and relentless. I'd let her go once before, and it had damn near gutted me. I wasn't willing to make that mistake again.

"Uh, coach?"

I turned at the sound of Pink's voice. He was slouched on the bench, a bag of ice strapped to his shoulder, chin jerking toward the outfield screen.

The jumbotron lit up, and my chest caved in.

There was Dani, glowing in the June sun, a little more pregnant than the last time I'd seen her, grinning like she'd been planning this all along. And in her hands—pressed lovingly against her bump—was a tiny white onesie with bold red lettering stretched across the center. *You call him coach, but I call him daddy.* The Roasters' logo sat neatly under the words like a goddamn exclamation point.

But it wasn't the onesie that made my blood pound.

It was my name stamped across her back.

My jersey was draped over her shoulders, the hem riding high above her cutoffs. And those socks. White with two red stripes that hugged her thighs.

Fucking perfect. Designed to undo me.

The crowd erupted, my team whooping and laughing from the field, but all I could think about was dragging the woman I loved down into the dugout, bending her over the bench, and fucking her until she couldn't stand. My cock was already hard, straining against my pants, and I had to force myself to keep my grip on the rail instead of storming up into the stands.

On second thought...

I didn't think. I couldn't.

Instead, I took off for the short wall separating the fans from the field, vaulting myself over the padded barrier like a man possessed. The crowd screamed louder when they realized what was happening, but I didn't give a damn.

Dani's mouth fell open when I reached her, cupping her cheeks in my hands and kissing her like she'd just handed me the world. Because she had.

The stadium melted away. The cameras, the noise, all of it—gone. There were only her soft lips, her trembling fingers clutching at my jersey, the sweet weight of her belly pressed against me.

When I finally pulled back, I leaned my forehead against hers and whispered, rough and certain, "You're mine, kitten. Always."

The kiss had barely ended before the announcer's voice boomed through the stadium speakers, his tone gleeful, milking the moment for every ounce of drama. "Looks like Coach Ward just scored the biggest win of the day."

The big screen replayed it instantly, our kiss blown up twenty feet tall, my hands cradling Dani's face like she was the only thing that mattered. Fans erupted into cheers, wolf whistles, and applause. Some even chanted my name. I didn't care about any of it.

I only cared about her.

About the fact that the entire city now knew what I had known for months—that Dani was mine, and I was hers.

This wasn't just some social media stadium stunt. It was a line in the sand. There was no going back from this, no hiding us or "keeping things casual." Not after forty-thousand people had watched me kiss Dani like she was oxygen.

It was terrifying and exhilarating all at once. It was everything.

And now, the whole goddamn city knew it, too.

The office door shut with a thud, and before she could take a step, I had her pinned against it, my mouth claiming hers in a kiss that was all teeth and tongue and the pent-up hunger I'd been sitting on since the seventh inning.

"Brooks." She panted against my lips, trying to laugh, trying to scold me, but her hands were already sliding under my shirt, nails dragging down my stomach.

"Don't start," I warned, spinning her around and nudging her toward the desk. "You knew exactly what you were doing out there."

Her ass bumped the edge of the desk, and I shoved her down onto it. The sight of her in my jersey and denim cutoffs that were borderline indecent, and those *fucking* socks, had me downright feral.

"What, claiming my man?" she teased. She smirked, breathless, tugging at my belt like she owned me. "Guess it worked."

"Worked too fucking well," I growled. Her lips curved into a knowing smile as I hooked my fingers into the waistband of her shorts and panties, yanking them both down her legs in one fell swoop. The smell of her hit me, hot and sweet, and my cock ached so bad I almost lost it right there.

I spread her knees wide and stepped between them, palms gripping the tops of those socks like handles. The hem of my jersey rose higher with the movement.

"Leave it on," I rasped, voice low and rough. "I've watched you walk around in these goddamn socks all day, so I deserve to get to fuck you in them."

Her smile said she knew exactly what kind of trouble she was in.

"*Yesss,*" she moaned. "I've missed you inside me, Brooks. I need your cock."

"Trust me, kitten, you're going to get all of me. But first, I'm going to taste you." I lowered myself to my knees and pushed the jersey up just enough to bare the wet heat between her thighs. "Been thinking about this all week," I growled before sealing my mouth over her.

The taste of her hit me like a drug.

I licked deep, slow at first, then harder, faster, until she was writhing against my desk, knocking various pens and knick-knacks to the floor. Her hands clawed for my shoulders, but I just anchored her with my grip on those socks, holding her open while I devoured her.

"Oh my god." She moaned, her head dropping back against the desk with a dull thud. Paper crinkled under her palms as her hips rocked back against my mouth.

"Mmm," I growled into her, the sound vibrating through her slick folds. "God's not the one eating your perfect pussy in my office, kitten."

Her answering whimper nearly undid me.

I wrapped one arm around her waist, holding her tight to my mouth, while the other slipped between her legs to press my fingers exactly where she needed them.

"Fuck, yes! Don't stop," she begged, grinding down onto my face.

She was close. I could feel it in the way her thighs trembled, hear it in the broken cries on her lips.

And that was when I stopped.

I pulled back, chin slick, breath ragged, and pressed a rough kiss to the inside of her knee. "Not yet," I growled, standing and unbuckling my belt in one fluid motion. My cock sprang free, thick and aching, already leaking from the torture of holding back.

Her eyes flew wide, desperate, pleading. "Brooks—"

"You want to tease me in front of forty-thousand people, kitten?" I bent low, lips brushing her ear. "Then you better be ready to take every fucking inch."

Her laugh broke into a gasp when I lined myself up, gripped the tops of those socks like reins, and slammed into her in one brutal thrust.

"Fuck," I snarled, the word tearing out of me as her heat clenched down hard. It had been too long since I'd had her, and I was already halfway gone. My hips pounded against her ass, every thrust rougher than the last.

Her breath hitched with every slap of skin, and she tried to push back against me, but I had her pinned, driving into her so deep she had nowhere to go. Her nails clawed at the desk, and all I could think about was how good she looked taking me in my jersey, my name stretched across her shoulders like a brand.

"You look so goddamn perfect like this," I rasped. "Those socks, that jersey, my baby inside of you. Fuck, Dani, I could lose my mind."

"Do it," she shot back, voice breathless but teasing. "Lose it for me, Brooks."

"You don't know what you're asking for, kitten."

Her answering moan was ragged, desperate. I couldn't get deep enough, couldn't get close enough.

I hooked an arm under her knee and then another, lifting, straightening both until they rested against my chest in a perfect ninety-degree angle. She yelped, the sound high and broken, and I braced her calves against my shoulders, holding her still as I pushed back into her.

Christ. The new angle had me buried so deep I saw stars.

I fucked her harder, my name tearing from her throat, nails clawing for purchase on the wood as she trembled beneath me.

"Unbutton the jersey," I growled. "I want to see your tits."

Her shaky fingers fumbled with the buttons, managing only two before I lost patience. I reached around her, tugging the fabric apart, dragging her bra down until her tits spilled free into my hands.

"That's it," I snarled, thumbs brushing over her hard nipples before I gave them a rough squeeze. "Want to watch them bounce while I fuck you."

I pulled back and drove into her again, harder this time, angling my thrusts so every snap of my hips had her tits jolting with the movement. The sight wrecked me—her head thrown back, jersey hanging open, her breasts bouncing in time with the brutal pace I set.

"Harder." She gasped, and I obliged, the sound of our bodies colliding filling the room. "I want more."

"Fuck, look at you, Dani. Begging for my cock."

Her tits bounced with every thrust, her moans climbing higher, sharper, until she was nothing but sound and heat under me. Sweat dripped down my spine, my cock throbbing inside her, and I knew I wasn't going to last much longer.

"I'm right there, kitten," I ground out. "Do you want me to fill you up? Make you walk out of my office dripping with my cum?"

She whimpered, clutching at me, her nails raking down my arms.

"Or . . ." I pulled almost all the way out, forcing a choked cry from her. ". . . I could pull out and cover you in it. Mark you up so every inch of you knows you're mine. Do you want that, kitten? Want me to come all over your pretty body?"

I slammed back in, hard enough to rattle the desk. "*Yes!* Fuck, yes, Brooks, I want it."

Works for me.

I snapped my hips harder, faster, until finally, she shattered beneath me, screaming my name, her whole body clamping down around me. The sound of her coming, wild and undone, ripped the last thread of control from me.

I yanked free at the last second, stroking once, twice before spilling across her rounded belly and tits, streaking the open jersey with my release. The sight destroyed me—my name on her back, my cum glistening on her skin.

It wasn't enough.

Still groaning, I shoved back inside her, burying myself to the hilt, desperate to feel every aftershock of her orgasm. Her cunt spasmed around me, hot and pulsing, milking me even as I emptied the last of myself deep inside her.

"Fuck, Dani, I swear to God, I'll never get enough of you."

She whimpered, soft and spent, and I gentled my pace, rocking into her instead of pounding, one hand smoothing down her hair, the other gripping her thigh possessively. I leaned forward, pressing my lips to hers, swallowing her breathless moans.

"Don't move," I rasped against her lips, my voice guttural. "Not until I'm good and ready to pull out of this sweet, little cunt."

She whimpered, half-laugh, half-sob, but didn't move an inch.

Because she knew I meant it.

She slumped back with a soft, breathless laugh. "Happy Father's Day, Brooks."

I kissed her again, still buried deep inside her. "Best fucking Father's Day of my life, kitten."

Dani

All-Star Break

The Roasters had a thousand ways of keeping themselves entertained, and ninety-nine percent of them involved some kind of bet. Trivia on long bus rides, who could plank the longest with somebody else on their back, whether Tucker could eat seven hot dogs in one sitting—spoiler alert, he couldn't, but that hadn't stopped him from trying.

This time, it was Matty who'd lost. Something about sinking the worst shot during a recent golf game.

And that was how the team's shortstop—all broad shoulders, strawberry blond hair, and southern drawl that could melt butter—ended up sitting two chairs down from me at a nail salon, his feet soaking in bubbles while a technician painted his fingernails neon green.

With glitter.

"I think that might be your color, Matty," June teased, snapping a picture with her phone.

Matty leaned back in the chair with exaggerated dignity, his voice dripping mock tragedy. "Don't lie. You know damn good and well that this color was not meant for a man of my complexion."

"What's the name of it?" June fired back.

"Sour Apple."

Beside me, Carolina squealed with delight at the sight of his nails, her own little toes already glowing purple. "You're so sparkly!" she said, pointing toward his fingers.

Matty winked at her. "Darlin', real men wear glitter."

"What about you, Benny boy?" June nodded toward his salmon-colored fingernails. "What bet did you lose?"

He shook his head. "I didn't. I usually keep them painted anyway to make the calls more visible."

"That's a good idea," Bella added, surprising the rest of us. She had been quietly flipping through her book for the past hour while a technician finished layering her toes with clear polish. It was a wonder we had gotten her in the pedicure chair at all, though I had a feeling that had more to do with Bennett than the allure of a spa day.

To her credit, his eyes had barely left her since we'd sat down.

I got it, though. Bennett wasn't flashy like Matty with his easy grin, or loud and boisterous like Tucker and Roman. No, he had a kind of quiet steadiness that felt . . . magnetic.

Hmm, sounds like somebody else I know.

Long brown hair tucked behind his ears, a trim goatee framing his mouth, bright blue eyes that crinkled at the corners when he smiled, he looked a little like Keanu Reeves, if Keanu had spent his life behind the plate—thick thighs, sun kissed skin, and forearms strong enough to hold the whole world steady.

Bella didn't blush, not exactly, but her fingers stilled on her book. And Bennett? He didn't grin or wink, didn't do anything to call attention to it. He just looked at her like her words mattered.

Like she mattered.

Something about it tugged at me. I knew what it felt like to have someone's attention hit that hard. To be seen and wanted at the same time. And god, if Bella felt even half of what I thought she might, she was in trouble.

Before I could linger on it, Matty nearly launched out of his chair, sloshing water all over the tile. "What the hell? That was a clean strike."

Our entire row turned toward the flat screen mounted above the polish racks, where the All-Star Game blared in high definition. The salon owner had looked at us sideways when we'd asked to put it on, but a little extra cash from Bennett had done the trick.

While the rest of the Roasters spent the break scattered across the greater Portland area—sleeping in, rehabbing sore muscles, or just breathing for the first time in months—three of our guys were on the clock. Pink, Roman, and Wes had all been tapped for this year's American League All-Star roster, a well-deserved honor that meant they'd spend the so-called "break" under brighter lights than ever.

The game was being played in Minneapolis this summer, and the broadcast showed a stadium packed to the rafters, a sea of navy, red, and white. Pink adjusted his cap on the mound and wound up with that smooth, easy delivery that somehow always looked casual even when he was throwing ninety-five miles per hour.

June smirked, sipping her mimosa. "Do you think the cameras will cut to Nessa in the stands?"

"I doubt it," I said, running a hand over my belly just as my little girl delivered a sharp kick. She was feisty already—just like her mom—always moving, reminding me she was there. Brooks and I had been tossing around names for weeks, but so far none of them had stuck. For now, I just called her BB—short for both *Baby Bernal* and *Baby Bailey-Ward*.

We hadn't even settled on her last name yet. And it wasn't because Brooks didn't support her taking mine; he'd told me, in no uncertain terms, that he would back me no matter what.

No, the indecision was all me.

I wasn't sure if I wanted to pass on *Bernal* with all the baggage that clung to it, all the memories tied up with my mother. Some days, I thought it was important to hang on to it, to keep that piece of myself alive through her. Other days, I wanted a clean slate, free of old ghosts.

Either way, BB kicked again, hard enough that I pressed my palm firmer against the swell. She didn't care what we decided—she already knew who she belonged to.

The salon erupted with cheers.

"Now that's what I'm talkin' about!" Matty shouted, nearly knocking over the bowl of cotton balls beside him.

The nail techs exchanged bewildered looks, muttering to each other under their breaths, but none of us cared. We were too busy cheering for our guys, glitter nails and all.

I bit back a smile. The whole thing felt ridiculous and sweet, like one of those sitcom episodes, "The One Where They All Go to the Spa," where everyone ended up in side-by-side massage chairs, except this was my life now.

And underneath it, I was still humming with the memory of lazy morning sex in Brooks's bed.

I squirmed in my chair, heat licking through me at the memory. My body still hadn't recovered from this past month's non-stop fuck-fest. He'd been starved for me after weeks apart—and to be fair, the feeling had been mutual—and once he'd had me again, he hadn't let up.

While the rest of my friends were busy cheering on their teammate, my body was remembering the way Brooks had bent me over my desk last week and fucked me so hard the wood had rattled. There was also the afternoon he'd found me stretched out, tanning in his backyard. He hadn't said a word, just knelt between my legs, tugged my bikini bottoms down, and buried his mouth in my pussy lips. I'd come with the sun blazing down on me, his tongue relentless, my moans echoing off the fence like I hadn't cared who heard.

And then, there'd been the dugout.

Holy fucking jinkies.

I'd snuck down there after a particularly grueling game, long after the last stadium worker had gone home for the night, straddled him on that long, narrow bench, and ridden him like my own personal hobby horse.

Every thrust of my hips had had the old wood creaking under us, splinters catching on the backs of my thighs, but I hadn't cared—I'd been too busy milking his cock.

"Fuck, kitten." He'd groaned, head tipping back against the cinderblock wall, eyes dark and hungry on me. His hands had gripped my ass hard, guiding me up and down. "Look at you, taking my cock like it was made for you."

"I love it." I'd gasped, bouncing on his lap, my nails clawing his shoulders. "God, Brooks, I want you to come in me. I want you to fill me up."

"Greedy little thing," he'd rasped, teeth scraping along my jaw as he'd thrust up again. "Take it all. I want you to feel me for days."

And then I was gone, falling apart on his cock, muffling my cries against his shoulder while he spilled inside me, holding me down on him like he'd never let me go. To this day, he was still pulling splinters out of his ass.

When I'd held up that onesie on the jumbotron—pregnant belly front and center, his name stitched across my back—I'd braced for impact. It was part of my job to think that way. As a social media manager, I'd spent my days perfecting angles, crafting captions, drafting responses before the comments had even begun to roll in. I knew how fast people made up their minds, how quickly an image or a moment could spiral into something bigger than you'd meant it to be. I must have written—and rewritten—every possible headline in my brain at least a dozen times before holding up that onesie.

All of them had gone away the second Brooks had kissed me.

Thankfully, the fans hadn't judged me for my grand gesture. They'd freaking loved it.

Within hours, the clip of our kiss had gone viral, set to every romantic ballad and pop anthem under the sun. We were a fucking GIF. People churned out fan art of me in his jersey, of Brooks cradling my belly, even one that looked suspiciously like a movie poster. They had even given us a couple hashtag—#*CoachKitten*—which somehow had managed to stick harder than anything else.

And then there was the fan fiction. *Jesus.* Some of it was swoony and sweet, painting our story like a fairy tale. But some of it was graphic enough that I'd officially been flagged by the Roasters' tech team for looking at "pornographic materials" during office hours.

Brooks ate that shit up. When I'd first told him about it, he'd simply laughed, lowered me to my bed, and ordered me to read one of the filthiest ones aloud while he made me come.

Reading was already sexy. Reading erotic fan fiction about me and my baby daddy while he fucked me with his tongue and my favorite vibrator was downright sinful.

And speaking of filthy fanfic—

I glanced down the row at Matty, who was currently trying to pose his glittery nails like they were part of a catalog shoot, eliciting squeals and giggles from Carolina. "You know," I said, unable to stop the grin spreading across my face, "I found some spicy fan fiction about you the other night."

Matty's brows shot up, his drawl thickening with amusement. "About me? How spicy are we talking?"

"The kind of spicy that could make big bucks in Nessa's bookstore," I said, savoring the way June immediately leaned in. "Whole novels' worth, too. Some between you and women . . . a lot between you and men. There's a particularly sticky situation between you, Mr. Clean, and one of the guys from *Supernatural.*"

He whistled. "You're gonna have to send me that one. Although, I've always been more of a Pedro Pascal kind of guy."

We all went still. The silence was sharp enough to hear the bubble jets fizzing at our feet. Bella looked up from her book, blinking like she was processing the words. June's mimosa froze halfway to her mouth. Bennett tilted his head, studying Matty like he was seeing a new angle of him for the first time.

And Carolina, wholly unbothered, piped up to say, "Mommy likes him, too. She says so all the time."

We all cracked up at that, even Bella letting out a small huff that might've been a laugh.

"So," I hedged. "You also dip you toes in both ponds?"

Matty's mouth twitched, and then, almost shyly, he said, "I guess I dip my toes in whatever pond I want to swim in that day. I like 'em all."

I smiled. "Good to know."

"What pond?" Carolina asked.

Before anyone else could stumble for the right words, Bella answered in a precise, even tone. "It means Matty likes boys and girls. Both." She quickly added, "And that's okay."

Carolina blinked, then nodded like Bella had just explained how rainbows worked. "Oh. Cool." She went back to admiring her glittery toes.

We all cracked up softly at that, the tension breaking. June reached over to pat Matty's arm. "See? Easiest explanation in the world."

Matty let out a short laugh, rubbing the back of his neck. "Yeah, well, I don't really like blasting my personal business everywhere. And truth be told, I'm still kinda figuring it out myself. Just . . . what feels right, you know?" He shrugged, shoulders rolling like he was trying to shake off the weight of the admission. "Maybe I shouldn't have said anything."

Finally, Bennett spoke, his voice low but carrying. "Your business is your business, man, but don't ever feel like you have to keep quiet around me. Or the guys." He tapped the armrest, meeting Matty's eyes squarely. "You've got my back on the field. I've got yours off it."

Matty finally looked up, and for a second the easy grin slipped, replaced by something raw and grateful. He gave Bennett a short nod, and Bennett returned it, simple and certain. The kind of exchange that meant more than a dozen speeches.

I smiled with them, warmth blooming in my chest. I knew what it felt like to hesitate, to wonder who you could tell and when, to weigh every word like it might tip the scales of how people saw you. For years, I'd tripped over the word bisexual in my own mouth, unsure of when to claim it or whether I even needed to. Hearing Matty just . . . say it like that—without over-explaining or apologizing—and watching Bella, of all people, hand down acceptance like it was the simplest truth in the world made something inside me loosen.

Maybe we were all braver together than we realized.

The moment hung there, warm and tender, until eventually, Bennett leaned back in his chair and deadpanned, "So where's *my* fanfiction, then? Seems like everybody's getting some but me."

The whole row cracked up. Even Bella's lips curved into the faintest smile, and Matty groaned, dragging a green, glittery hand down his face.

"Careful what you wish for," I warned him. "The internet is feral. You'll open your phone one day and find yourself in a fifty-chapter omegaverse with dragon shifters."

June choked on her mimosa. "Jesus, I hope somebody writes that."

That set us off again, laughter spilling through the salon so loud, even the nail techs started smiling at us.

Brooks

All-Star Break

When Soren had told me the team was meeting up at the stadium during the break, I'd figured it was for batting practice or maybe to get ahead on conditioning. What I hadn't expected was an ambush.

"Welcome to your dadchelor party," Tucker bellowed, nearly knocking me over with a clap on the back. "It's like a baby shower, but with more beer."

"*Way* more beer," Roman added, fisting a bottle in each hand.

"I can see that," I muttered, unable to fight the grin tugging at my mouth.

The infield had been transformed into some kind of outlandish carnival—cornhole boards painted with pacifiers, a stack of oversized baby blocks was stacked up at home plate, and a suspiciously small kiddie pool had been laid out at second base, filled with ice and what I assumed were at least a dozen cases of beers. A highchair—one that looked suspiciously like the overpriced monster from Dani's registry—sat parked at the pitcher's mound like a throne, and beyond the outfield, deep in the bleachers behind left-center, balloons in the shapes of rattles and rubber duckies bobbed in the wind.

And looming above everything, the scoreboard was lit up in big, block letters. CONGRATS, COACH DADDY—complete with a cartoon stork hauling a screaming baby with my face slapped on it.

It looked like a county fair and a frat party had both lost a bet, and the stadium was where they'd come to settle it.

"You've got to be kidding me," I said, looking around.

"Nope." Soren grinned, tossing me a burp cloth like it was a towel. "You've got a whole afternoon of festivities, coach."

"Starting with baby bottle chugging," Pink announced, stepping out from behind the dugout, his six-pack abs on full display, warpaint streaked across his cheeks, and a red bandana tied Rambo-style around his forehead. He held a baby bottle filled with beer in each hand like they were weapons. "Rules are simple—the first one to finish their bottle and run the bases wins."

A chorus of cheers went up. The guys raced to claim their bottles, eager to show each other up.

My attention caught on the diaper station at third base, which had life-sized baby dolls laid out side by side, some already leaking suspiciously yellow liquid.

"Diaper changing relay," Wes explained proudly. "After that is the baby toss, diaper pong, and finally 'ice ice baby.' But that one is really just who can stay in an ice bath the longest."

"While solving a puzzle about nursery rhymes," Matty added.

I shook my head, but damn if my chest didn't ache a little at the sight. These grown men—loud, messy, impossible—had built me a baby shower in the middle of a ballpark.

Scratch that, a dadchelor party.

By the time the first game kicked off, half of the guys were already well beyond buzzed. Roman cheated immediately, unscrewing the top of his baby bottle and pouring it straight down his throat before taking off around the bases. Pink was the next to finish, chasing after him while shouting something about violating the sacred "dadchelor code."

I laughed so hard, I nearly spit out my beer.

When I slipped into the dugout to catch my breath, still chuckling, Brock was already there, leaning over the fence with a bottle of cider in hand, watching the chaos unfold.

"Your man's out there committing war crimes," I said, jerking my chin toward the mess.

Tucker was hauling himself out of the kiddie pool after Diaz had tackled him straight into it, both of them shrieking like kids at summer camp. He still clutched his beer bottle triumphantly, water and foam streaming off him as he climbed out like some kind of half-drunk Poseidon.

Brock snorted. "Yeah, well. I knew what I was signing up for. He doesn't exactly do things halfway."

His eyes lit up as he tracked the water sluicing down Tucker's burly arms and chest.

Yup, my friend was head over heels.

We stood there for a moment, the noise of the guys echoing through the empty stadium, laughter bouncing off steel and concrete.

Finally, Brock said, softer, "The crazy thing is, I used to think my life was already full. Good job, great friends, a steady routine. And then Tucker came barreling in, and suddenly everything felt . . . more. Like someone turned on the lights."

I felt something pull in my chest because I totally got it. "Yeah, I know what you mean."

Before Dani, I'd thought my life was set. Coaching, raising Carolina, keeping my head down—that had been enough. At least, that was what I'd told myself. But then she'd crashed into my world, all sharp wit, softer edges, and fucking socks, and suddenly everything looked different. Lighter, brighter. Like I'd been living in black and white and she'd handed me a box of crayons. She made home feel like more than just four walls.

"I didn't even realize some of the shit I had been carrying around until Dani came along," I told him. "She just . . . makes me better."

Brock smiled into his beer, eyes still on the field where Tucker was now flexing like a WWE star. "Guess we're both lucky bastards."

"The luckiest," I agreed, tipping my beer toward him.

We clinked our bottles together, a quiet moment between two men surrounded by pandemonium, bonded by the people who'd cracked our hearts open and let light in.

And love. Because there wasn't a doubt in my mind that I loved Dani Bernal.

Even if I hadn't told her yet.

Out on the field, the guys were already moving into the next phase of chaos—the diaper changing relay, which looked more like a demolition derby. Pink and Roman, the designated captains of the relay teams, shouted instructions like drill sergeants, pacing the foul line with all the seriousness of a playoff game.

"Tabs first, *then* wipe!" Pink barked, pointing at Wes, who looked like he was trying to hogtie the baby doll instead of diaper it.

Roman was no better. "Tuck and fold, fuckers!" he shouted like he'd been studying swaddling tutorials all week.

For all I knew, he might have.

The dolls littered the infield like casualties, diapers dangling, wipes fluttering in the breeze. At least a few of them were already missing limbs, and one had lost its head completely. Tucker managed to get his doll into a diaper—backwards, but still. He hoisted it into the air like Simba on Pride Rock, making Bennett double over with a laugh so powerful, his implants might've shorted out from the noise.

"Time," Wes yelled, blowing a whistle he'd stolen from the bullpen.

The guys collapsed in a heap of laughter, no one entirely sure who had won—they were all too drunk to care. I shook my head, biting back a laugh of my own.

"Lord help us all if any of these idiots ever have real children."

"Coach," Pink called out, pointing a dripping finger in my direction. "You're up next. No excuses."

I shook my head immediately. "I'm good. Somebody's got to supervise before one of you breaks an ankle."

"Bullshit," Roman scoffed.

"Yeah, that's what Hell is for," Tuck added, pointing toward his boyfriend. He traced the outline of a heart across his chest like something out of a cheesy music video. "Besides, this is *your* dadchelor party. We put this together for you."

"Yeah," Soren added, grinning like a wolf. "Can't be a dad-chelor if the dad won't play."

Pink stepped forward, separating himself from the herd. "Besides, Dani told us we have to get photos of you."

I arched my brow.

Of course she had. I should've known the guys couldn't have pulled this whole circus off without some help. Giant, inflatable babies, bottles full of beer, diaper races in the infield—this had Dani's fingerprints all over it.

The woman didn't want a baby shower for herself, but she was more than happy to throw me a dadchelor party. She was always thinking of me, of us. Always finding ways to make sure I didn't just shoulder the weight, but felt the joy, too.

Hell, she knew me better than I knew myself.

Left to my own devices, I'd have spent the break in my office, reviewing tape. But Dani? She wanted me out here laughing my ass off, drunk and ridiculous, surrounded by the people who had, much to my reluctance, become something like family.

And damn if I didn't love her more for it.

I huffed, shaking my head, but the truth was . . . I kinda wanted to. Just this once. "Fuck it," I said, twisting the cap off another beer. "Let's do it." A chorus of cheers went up from the team, their voices echoing through the stadium.

I held up my hand. "But if any pictures end up on social media, it's one-thousand burpees for all of you."

Within minutes, I was lined up with the rest of them for Roman's cursed invention—baby food beer pong. Red Solo cups lined the dugout bench, half filled with pale ale, half with suspicious jars of various pureed vegetables.

Way to ruin carrots for me.

Somewhere around my third round of bottle chugging, the stadium started to spin. The guys were a blur of laughter, shouts, and smeared eye black, and for once, I wasn't the steady one in the center of it. I was just Brooks, drunk off my ass in an empty stadium, letting the men I trusted most take care of me for a change.

And god, it felt good.

"Coach, you're fuckin' wasted," Matty howled, doubling over as I tried to Velcro a diaper onto the baby doll in my hands.

"Am not," I slurred, jabbing a finger in his direction. "I am perfectly capable of diapering a baby."

"Headfirst?" Bennett teased.

Fuck. Maybe I am wasted.

I turned, squinting until my eyes landed on Pink. He wasn't chanting—just sitting on the third base line, a small smile tugging at his mouth.

I staggered over, dropped down beside him, and grabbed his shoulder with all the solemnity in the world. "Listen to me, kid," I slurred. "I love her. She might be your friend, but she's my whole damn life. I wake up thinking about her. I fall asleep thinking about her. That woman is *it* for me. Forever."

Pink blinked at me, caught between laughing and rolling his eyes, but his grin softened. "Yeah, coach. I know. She loves you, too."

I thumped my chest with the heel of my hand. "No, but you don't understand. I would do anything for her. And our baby. *Anything.*"

Pink's grin shifted, something sparking behind his eyes—mischief, sure, but also that protective streak he carried for Dani. He leaned in, voice low. "*Anything?*"

The next few hours blurred together—being half-carried up the tunnel to somebody's SUV, a few of the guys bribing a tattoo artist with seats behind home plate, the delicious burn of a needle scraping across my chest. It wasn't until I got out of bed the next morning, head pounding like drums at a Killers concert, that the full weight of it hit me.

I stumbled into the bathroom, blinking against the sunlight streaming through the window, and froze.

There it was.

A kitten.

Holy shit.

Inked in clean black-and-gray lines, small but sure, sitting right above my heart. My skin was still raw around the edges, the red tenderness only making it look more permanent.

I braced my hands on the sink, staring at it while its inspiration slept not six feet away, and despite the hangover trying to split my skull, a grin crept across my mouth.

I could still hear the guys chanting, their playful gibes, Dani's laugh when I rolled into bed around two in the morning. And now? I had a kitten over my heart, her nickname etched into me forever, exactly where it belonged.

Dani

"**Y**our dagger misses," Nessa announced, smirking behind her Dungeon Master screen. "Bounces, actually—*plink*—clean off the ogre's breastplate." She mimed the motion with both hands, complete with sound effects.

"Rude," I said, leaning forward in my chair to adjust the maternity bike shorts that were riding up my ass. Ogres were one thing, but going through my third trimester in the middle of summer was a level of hell I hadn't been prepared for. "Okay, who wants to help me with this wedgie?"

June snorted. "Girl, you have a bearded bear of a man at home for that."

"I can't just tote him around with me everywhere I go."

"Something tells me that Brooks wouldn't have a problem with that," Clarke said around a devilish grin.

I smoothed a hand over the swell of my stomach, which looked more like a beach ball each day. In fact, just last week, during Carolina's back-to-school field day, one of the parent volunteers had pulled me into the face-painting station and decided my belly was fair game. Ten minutes later, I'd been wandering around the blacktop with bright stripes painted across my bump, officially transformed into a fleshy beach ball.

Carolina had howled with laughter. Brooks had taken a page out of my book and pulled out his phone to snap some photos. It had been a good day—one of those rare ones where everything felt easy and carefree, made easier by Brooks clasping my left hand and Carolina's sticky, snow cone-covered fingers gently squeezing the other.

Allie had handed me sunscreen without me asking, and her fiancé, Mitchell, had made sure I got the shady chair when my feet had started to swell. It hadn't been perfect, but we were all learning how to belong to Carolina together, each in our own way. And the fact that they had welcomed me into their orbit so easily had hit me harder than I'd expected.

"Settle down, BB," I whispered to my belly. "Your mama is trying to avenge the villagers."

Clarke pushed a curl out of her eyes. "Mama is going to have to roll a lot better than a four to even have a chance."

Jo laughed, the kind of deep laugh that made his shoulders shake under his T-shirt. "Careful, *mami*. With your luck, she'll pop out a *bruja* instead of a baby."

I didn't even bother rising to the bait—just reached for my sweating glass of iced tea, too hot and too pregnant to waste energy on comebacks.

The five of us were all tucked into the back room at Thorn Tavern, the one with the *good* air conditioning, arguably the most magical part of our entire campaign. Outside, Portland simmered in ninety-plus-degree August heat, the sidewalks glowing like stove burners—hot enough to fry an egg. Inside, we were cocooned in coolness, surrounded by the faint smell of fried food and spilled hops.

Nero had taken pity on us the second I'd waddled in, plying us with endless pitchers of iced tea and baskets of his famous "Totchos." Between the air conditioning, the food, and cushy club chairs, it was basically heaven.

"Okay, but for real," June cut in, stretching her long legs out under the table. "How are you feeling? Like, body-wise. You're what, thirty weeks?"

"Thirty-three," I said with a groan. "Baby girl is the size of a bunch of celery, which feels very wrong because I've been eating *a lot* of celery lately. Like, am I committing some kind of prenatal cannibalism? Is this how my horror movie starts?"

Nessa snorted into her tea. "Relax, Hannibal. She's fine."

"Yeah," Jo added. "If anything, you're just training her to like ranch dressing."

"Aside from that, my feet hate me, my back hates me, I peed myself when I sneezed yesterday, and apparently, my ankles have gone on sabbatical without telling me."

"Hot," June said dryly.

"You asked." I pointed my pencil in her direction. "Be nice before I cast an eldritch hex on you."

The table broke into laughter, but underneath it, I felt that same warmth I always had with these people, like no matter how messy or terrifying this whole becoming-a-parent thing felt, I wasn't alone.

Eventually, their laughter quieted, and Clarke took her turn with the dice. I let myself lean back, one hand resting on my belly which had become second nature.

Seven months in, I still didn't know if I would be a good mom, but I did know one thing for sure. I was in love with Brooks—madly, stupidly, terrifyingly in love. Coach Daddy was all mine.

And it wasn't just because he smacked my ass whenever he slid past me in the kitchen or whispered filthy things against my neck with his hand spread over this belly. Don't get me wrong, those things still had the power to make my pulse race even after all these months.

No, it was the quieter moments that stuck with me. The everyday, ordinary parts of him that made life feel steady, even when mine had always been anything but. I saw it in the way he braided Carolina's hair in the mornings, his big hands clumsy but careful, tongue caught between his teeth in concentration. And the way his glasses fogged up when he leaned over a sink full of dirty dishes, muttering about the water temperature like it had personally betrayed him.

Lately, he had taken to reading bedtime stories—or box scores or *Below Deck* weekly recaps, whatever really—to our baby girl. And every time, something in me lit up right alongside him. The sound of his voice, low and steady, with his hand spread across my stomach—it made me feel like our daughter already belonged here, folded seamlessly into the rhythm of us.

And it made me fall for him all over again, in a way I hadn't known was possible. That knowledge grounded me more than anything else. No matter how swollen, exhausted, or unprepared I felt, I knew I wasn't doing this alone. And I didn't just mean the whole parenthood thing.

I meant life. *Love.*

"Alright," Nessa said suddenly, clapping her hands together. "Before we continue the ogre massacre, we have something else to do first."

My brow furrowed as Jo disappeared into the tavern's kitchen and returned a minute later carrying a cake box with the Would Smell as Sweet logo stamped on top. Nero followed, carrying a stack of small plates, forks, and napkins shaped like . . . witch hats?

"What is this?" I asked, suspicion rising.

"You said you didn't want a baby shower," Nessa said with a small smile. "But you said nothing about a cake."

"Or presents." Clarke pulled a gift bag from beneath her seat.

Jo set the cake on the table and flipped open the lid to reveal a gorgeous, white-frosted thing with piped vines and tiny sugar dragons marching across the top. The words *Welcome, Tiny Goblin* had been scrolled across the center in curling pink and purple script.

"Oh my god." My throat tightened. "Jo—"

"Don't cry yet," he said, wagging a finger. "Not until you taste it. And I promise, it's not celery flavored."

I laughed, even as my eyes burned. Clarke handed me the bag, insisting I tear into it right away. Inside were a series of small, thoughtful gifts—a soft swaddle covered in tiny bats and moons, a picture book of queer fairy tales that Nessa had hunted down, a pack of onesies Jo had embroidered with sarcastic phrases like *Future Dungeon Master* and *Critical Hit on Poop Saves*.

Even Nero had slipped in a pair of teeny-tiny baby Converse—black, of course—tied together with a ribbon. "She's gonna need good footwear to keep up with the two of you," he said with a shrug, like it wasn't the most gut-punching thing I'd ever seen.

At the very bottom of the bag was a small velvet pouch. I untied it to find a set of rainbow-colored dice, glitter catching in the low light of the tavern. Nessa smirked. "For when the goblin is old enough to play with us. Gotta start 'em young."

That did me in. Tears spilled hot down my cheeks, and for once, I didn't bother trying to wipe them away.

It wasn't big or fancy or a Pinterest nightmare of bows and games like matching a baby's name to their celebrity parent. It was even better.

"Okay," I managed, voice breaking. "This is perfect."

"Good," June said smugly, raising her glass of tea, which was likely spiked, in a toast. "We love you, Dani Bernal. You and your tiny potato."

The words wrapped around me like armor, warm and indestructible. There wasn't a doubt in my mind that with friends like mine, my little potato goblin was going to be the luckiest adventurer in the realm.

Later that night, the smell of fresh paint hit me the second I walked in the house. Technically, it was Brooks's, but at some point in the past few months, it had started to look more like *ours*.

I hadn't stayed at the townhouse for weeks. The baby stuff from my registry and his ridiculous dadchelor party was piled up high in the corner of the living room, my shampoo now lived in the shower right next to his, and most of my shoes and clothes had sneaked their way into his closets, little pops of black tees and denim wedged between his endless rotation of athletic gear.

I was the Hot Topic to his DICK's Sporting Goods.

Best of all, there were no roommates to accidentally run into in the hallway after a midnight fuck or bang on the bathroom door when I was sucking Brooks's dick.

"Brooks?" I called out, dropping my loot from today's Dungeons & Dragons session-turned-baby shower by the door.

"Upstairs, kitten."

I smiled as I started up the stairs, my hand brushing the banister. Just the thought of him waiting at home for me was enough to make my chest ache. And then, of course, my brain served up the memory of the little souvenir he'd come home with after his so-called dadchelor party—my name forever tied to him in the form of a tiny kitten tattoo, inked right above his heart.

The image still made me melt. Every time I saw it, I couldn't decide if I wanted to tease him or climb into his lap and kiss him senseless. Usually, I did both.

Upstairs, I padded down the hall, tugging my hair out of its braid, already rehearsing how I was going to tell him about the absurdly adorable wand-shaped rattle Nessa had insisted the baby needed. But the second I crossed the threshold to the spare room at the back of the house, every thought in my head evaporated.

It wasn't a spare room anymore; it was a nursery.

The changing table we'd purchased months ago stood against the wall, white wood gleaming like it had just come out of the box. A soft rug spread across the floor, patterned with tiny clouds and furry critters in airplanes. The walls were still bare, save for the yellow paint and a single framed print he must've hung while I'd been gone—an abstract splash of colors that somehow looked like both a heart and a baseball in motion.

And Brooks, my impossibly stubborn and incredibly caring man, was crouched beside an antique, wooden crib, tightening a screw with the kind of concentration he usually reserved for pitch counts. When he looked up, his grin was boyish, proud.

"Don't worry, it's sturdy. Passed my stress test." He gave the crib rail a firm shake for emphasis.

My throat closed. "Brooks . . ."

He wiped his hands on his sweats before circling them around my waist, resting them at the base of spine in that way I loved.

"I didn't want to do too much without you," he said. "But I figured I could get a jumpstart on the heavy lifting. We can pick out the rest together—the paint, the toys, whatever ridiculous, little decals you want on the walls."

I blinked. "You did all this in the span of a few hours?"

These days, it took ten minutes just to get my shoes on.

A rare flicker of nerves crossed his face. "And if you'd rather have the nursery at your place . . ." His jaw flexed, like the words physically pained him. "That's fine, too. Just so long as you know that I'll be there every night by your side."

The weight of his words sank into my chest, heavy and light all at once. I glanced at the crib, at the space already carved out for a future I wasn't sure I deserved, and felt my eyes sting.

Brooks exhaled, steady but firm. "I'd be lying, though, if I said I didn't want you—*both* of you—living here with me."

I caught the faint edge of nerves in his movements, the way his thumb tapped against his thigh, the way he looked at me like he was bracing for impact. This wasn't the first time we'd circled the idea of our post-birth living situation, but it was the first time he'd cut straight to the chase, no hedging, no half-jokes. Just raw truth.

I swallowed hard, then forced a smile. "I guess I could get on board with that."

His laugh came out soft, full of relief, like he'd been holding his breath for months and finally let it go. He cupped the back of my neck, pressing his forehead to mine.

"Kitten," he murmured, voice thick. "You have no idea what that means to me."

I did, though. Because it meant just as much to me.

His words echoed off the butter-colored walls, warm and steady, but I needed to move, to do something with the rush of emotion swelling in my chest. My gaze landed on the new glider in the corner, the cushions still stiff and smelling faintly of fresh fabric. I lowered myself into it, rocking experimentally. The chair gave a soft squeak as it moved beneath me.

I glanced up at him, lips twitching. "Damn, this thing is dangerously comfortable. You might lose me to it."

Brooks huffed a laugh, one corner of his mouth lifting. "Pretty sure it's for the baby, kitten."

"She can fight me for it," I said, giving the chair another gentle rock.

He shook his head, still smiling.

God, he looked good like his—sweatpants slung low on his hips, a worn T-shirt stretched across his chest, lids heavy as he watched me from under dark lashes. And fuck, the outline of his cock was right there, thick against the soft gray fabric, just out of reach.

Gameday Brooks was hot, but slightly mussed, sweatpants Brooks was downright lethal. Unguarded, relaxed, and so fucking tempting, I could barely breathe.

"Tell me something," I murmured, letting my eyes rake over him. "You said you stress-tested the crib, but what about this chair?"

For half a beat, he blinked at me, brow furrowing like he hadn't caught on. I curled my fingers into the waistband of his sweats and tugged him closer, the fabric stretching as I pulled until his hips brushed the edge of the glider. My hand slid lower, pressing against the thick outline of his cock.

"Jesus, kitten," he rasped, bracing a hand on the armrest as the chair rocked beneath us.

"Mm," I hummed, curling my hand firmer against him. "Feels like you're holding up just fine. So . . ."

I eased his pants down just enough, the elastic snapping against his hips when his cock sprang free, thick and flushed and already leaking for me.

". . . let's see about the chair."

Brooks

I didn't think anything in this room could undo me. Not the crib I'd wrestled with for two hours, nor the tiny stack of clothes I'd folded with hands too damn big for the job. Not even the glider, which I was convinced NASA engineers couldn't have put together more by the book.

But Dani sitting in that chair now, thighs spread, belly round under her stretchy shorts and tank top, face lined up perfectly with the cock jutting out of the top of my sweatpants?

That fucking undid me.

Her green eyes were locked on mine like I was the only thing in the world worth looking at, and fuck if I didn't believe her. One hand stroked lazily along my length, teasing, as the chair rocked beneath her in a slow, steady rhythm that made my head spin.

"Kitten," I rasped, curling my hand around the armrest just to keep from grabbing her hair and shoving myself deeper into her touch. "You don't have to—"

She cut me off with a look that made my cock weep. "I want to."

And then she proved it, leaning forward and wrapping her mouth around the head of me in one slow, devastating stroke. Heat and wet and tongue—filthy perfection. My hips jerked before I could stop them, and she hummed like she liked it, like she was asking for more.

"Christ, Dani."

My hands left the armrest and sank into her hair, tangling in the soft strands as if I could anchor myself there. She let me, lashes fluttering, and fuck if that wasn't the hottest thing I'd ever seen.

The chair creaked softly beneath us, rocking in time with every shaky breath I pulled in. My grip tightened in her hair as she dragged her tongue along the underside of me before sucking harder, swallowing me deep. Deep enough to make my vision blur at the edges.

"Easy," I choked, though my grip contradicted the word. "You're gonna kill me, kitten."

It was goddamn torture trying not to come right there.

The glider rocked beneath her, back and forth, steady and obscene. She set the pace, lips dragging up, tongue circling, then sinking down again until her nose nudged the wiry hairs at the base of my cock. Every hot drag of her mouth, every wet swirl of her tongue made my whole body tighten like a bowstring. But what really took it up a notch was the way she looked at me while she did it. Like she was giving me something I didn't deserve but would kill to keep.

"Fuck." It was getting harder and harder—pun intended—not to lose control. On second thought, maybe that was what she wanted. "You want more?"

She dug her nails into my thighs in answer, daring me.

"Hold still," I ground out, my hands tightening in her hair. She moaned around me and my hips jerked, the wet sound of her throat taking me only adding to the madness. Tears welled in the corners of her eyes when I pushed deeper, and the sight nearly broke me in half.

Raw, messy, *fucking* beautiful. Just the way I loved her.

"That's a good girl," I rasped, holding her in place while I buried my cock down her throat. "You take me so fucking good."

She gagged softly, her nails digging crescents into my thighs, and I felt her hum against me.

"Cup my balls," I ordered, my voice breaking on the words. She obeyed instantly, one small hand sliding underneath to cradle me while I held her head steady, filling her mouth. The added pressure tore another curse from my throat. "Fuck, that's good."

Saliva pooled at the corners of her lips, glistening as it dripped down her chin, coating my balls. My cock throbbed against her tongue, and the sight of her, wrecked, obedient, *swallowing me whole*, was enough to unravel every last thread of control I had left.

Tenderness snapped like a rubber band. I pulled back, her lips dragging along my length until just the tip rested against her swollen mouth. She barely had a second to gasp in a breath before I drove back in, the wet heat of her throat swallowing me down again.

I fucked into her mouth in short, ruthless thrusts, one hand tangled tight in her hair, the other gripping the armrest so hard I swore I'd snap the wood. Her throat clenched around me, tears streaming now, and the sight of it was enough to drag a snarl from my chest.

"Look at you," I growled, my hips slamming forward again. "Taking me like you're made for it. You love this, don't you?"

You love me, don't you?

The chair rocked beneath her in rhythm with my thrusts, squeaking like it was protesting, but I couldn't stop. Not when she was gagging softly, drool dripping down to coat my balls, and looking up at me like she'd let me ruin her this way forever.

And she wasn't just taking it.

She was grinding against the seat, her hips shifting restlessly, chasing her own relief even with her mouth stretched wide around my cock. The sight of her rubbing that sweet cunt against the cushion while I fucked her throat just about killed me.

"Jesus, kitten." I groaned, my cock pulsing so hard I had to grit my teeth. "You gonna make yourself come like this? While I'm in your mouth?"

She hummed low in her throat, and the vibration shot straight up my spine.

I forced myself to ease up, thumb swiping away a tear even as my cock twitched against her tongue. "Breathe, baby. I've got you."

But she pushed my hand away, stubborn as ever—I wouldn't have her any other way—and sank back down on me with a hunger that made me shiver. I couldn't decide if I wanted to worship her or ruin her throat completely, so I did both—stroking her hair back from her damp face even as I fucked her face, each thrust claiming her a little more.

"Mine, Dani." I groaned. "Every part of you is mine."

Fuck, I need more.

I yanked her up and out of the glider, cock slipping from her swollen mouth with a wet pop. She gasped, lips glossy, chin wet, eyes glassy with tears. Christ, I could have come just looking at her.

"Why did you stop?" she started, breathless. "I wanted you—"

"Not in your mouth," I growled, dragging her up against me, my cock pressing hard against her stomach through the thin fabric of her clothes. "I need to be inside you, kitten. Now."

"But—"

I cut her off with a kiss, my tongue tangling with hers. "Trust me," I rasped against her lips. "You have the rest of our lives to suck me off. Right now, I need to feel you coming around me."

Her whole body shuddered, and she didn't fight me when my hands slid to the hem of her tank, yanking it over her head in one rough pull. She was bare underneath, soft curves and flushed skin, and fuck if my chest didn't ache at the sight of her like that—in *our* house, on the floor of *our* baby's room, offering me everything.

After we removed the rest of our clothes, I spun her, helping her down to the floor until she was braced on the arm of the glider, knees sinking into the rug. Her back arched, ass high, slick and swollen and ready for me. My hand came down hard on one cheek, the sound sharp in the quiet room. She moaned, pushing back against me, eager for more.

"That's it," I said hoarsely, lining myself up behind her. "Just like that, kitten. Let me take care of you."

"Brooks—"

She broke off on a scream. I sank into her in one long, relentless thrust that had both of us cursing loud enough to wake the whole damn neighborhood.

"Fuck," she cried, clutching the chair for balance.

"Jesus Christ, kitten," I snarled, hips snapping forward again, the wet slap of our bodies filling the nursery. "I'll never get enough of this tight cunt. So wet. Gripping me like you don't ever want to let me go."

"I don't." She whimpered, rocking back to meet me.

My hands branded her hips as I drove into her again, the chair rattling against the wall with every thrust, her swollen cunt clenching around me so tight it nearly made me see stars.

"You're fucking perfect." I groaned, my gaze devouring every inch of her—the curve of her ass, her rounded hips, the way her tits bounced with each snap of my hips. She had always been beautiful, but all filled out like this, thick with my baby, she was downright irresistible.

Her moans pitched higher, raw and desperate, and I felt it, the slick heat of her juices coating my cock, spilling down my length with every thrust. Each time I pulled out, I watched myself glisten with her, only to bury it right back inside where I belonged.

"Christ, kitten. You're drenching me."

"Yes," she cried, bracing harder against the chair, hips rocking back to meet me stroke for stroke.

"You like taking my cock on your knees in our baby's room?"

"*Yes.* More, Brooks! *Please.*"

Who was I to deny her?

I slid an arm around her middle and hauled her upright, her back flush against my chest. She gasped, clutching the arm of the glider for balance as I adjusted my stance, bracing my feet against the rug. My other hand clamped down on her hip, holding her still as I drove into her again. Slower now, deeper, every inch of me stretching her wide.

"That's it." I groaned into her ear, lips brushing the damp edge of her hairline. "All the way in, kitten. Right where I belong."

"Yes—*fuck*—yes." She gasped, knuckles white as she clutched the chair.

Sweat slicked my skin, dripping down her spine as I bent over her, chest to her back, my hips pounding into her with bruising force. Her body tightened around me like a vise as I drove us both closer to the edge.

I slid one hand down between her thighs, rubbing her clit in rough, insistent circles that had her whole body jolting. She was close. I could feel it in the way her pussy clenched around me, milking me tighter with every thrust.

Growling low in my throat, I pressed her forward again, bending her over the seat of the glider to open her up for me. My hand slid down the curve of her ass, spreading her wider, my thumb tracing the puckered rim of her asshole.

Her breath hitched. "Brooks—"

"Shh," I rasped, pressing forward until the tip of my finger breached her tight ring. "Relax for me, kitten. Let me give you everything."

"Oh my god." She moaned, trembling hard as I eased inside.

"That's it." I groaned, working her open slowly, shallow thrusts of my thumb matching the rhythm of my hips pounding into her. "One day, you're gonna take me here."

She whimpered at that, broken and wanting, and the sound just about destroyed me.

I kept fucking her hard, my thumb working in sync with my cock, every thrust deeper and rougher, until her body shook like she couldn't hold it together another second. The sight of her like that—pussy dripping down my length, asshole stretched around my thumb, trembling under my touch—nearly broke me in half.

"Don't stop," she sobbed, her whole body shaking now. "I'm gonna come."

I pinched her clit, pressed deeper with my thumb, and slammed my hips into hers. She came undone with a scream, her body convulsing around me, pussy clamping down so hard I nearly lost it right then.

"*Fuck*. Dani—"

I broke off, driving into her through the pulsing waves of her orgasm before burying myself to the hilt and spilling inside her with a guttural roar. Hot pulses of cum filled her, my thumb still lodged in her ass, keeping her open and shaking while I gave her everything I had.

We collapsed together, both of us panting, bodies trembling, the smell of sex heavy in the air of our baby's nursery. I stayed buried inside her, refusing to let her go.

"My girl," I rasped against her damp skin, kissing the back of her neck. "My perfect, filthy girl."

The tremors in her thighs slowly eased, her body softening under me as the last aftershocks rippled through. I kissed along her spine before finally easing out of her, murmuring quiet praises against her skin. She leaned forward, resting her cheek on the glider, her cheeks flushed, hair wild.

"Oh my god," she said, half-laughing, half-mortified. "We've officially ruined the baby's chair."

I grinned, tilting her chin back so I could kiss her swollen lips. "I'll buy another one."

"Deal." She huffed out a laugh, still trying to catch her breath. "We can put this one in our room."

Our room.

The word lodged in my chest, sharp and sweet, and I knew I'd be holding onto it long after tonight. "I like the sound of that."

Her lashes fluttered, but she nodded, brushing her thumb across my jaw. "Me, too."

I kissed her again, slower this time, even though my cock twitched at the thought of everything we'd just done. At the thought of doing it again.

I pulled back just enough to catch her gaze, my mouth curving. "Next time, I'm going to sit back, let you get on top and ride me hard, until you can't move without feeling me for days."

Her laugh came out shaky, her eyes glinting like she was already imagining it. "I'm going to hold you to that, coach."

You fucking better, kitten.

Dani

B y the time summer melted into September, my travel days with the Roasters were officially over—doctor's orders. Between the swollen ankles, the occasional dizzy spell, and my elevated blood pressure, Dr. Kong had strongly recommended ceasing all jet-setting for the rest of my pregnancy.

Brooks had agreed, of course. Overprotective papa bear that he was, he would've kept me laid out, naked, on a pillowy throne all day if he thought for even a second, I might be okay with it.

Not that I didn't appreciate it. His fussing made me feel loved, even when it drove me a little nuts. He'd stopped trying to talk me into "taking it easy" at work after I'd reminded him that my job wasn't exactly a full-contact sport. That didn't stop him from having lunch delivered to me every day, though. Both of our offices now had mini nurseries tucked into the corners, complete with bassinets, baby bouncers, and baskets of diapers and wipes stacked neatly, like we were staging a photoshoot. This kid was going to have more nurseries than she knew what to do with.

"Look, Dani!" Carolina gasped, darting toward a ginger tabby sprawled upside down, all belly and whiskers. "He's smiling at me."

Bella trailed behind her, clutching a slim paperback like it was armor. She cast a skeptical glance around the café, taking in the communal tables, the bulletin board of information about adopting and fostering, and the cats padding across every surface.

"That's just how cat mouths look," she corrected.

"Bella," Nessa scolded gently, though I caught the twitch of a smile she tried to hide.

Carolina mulled over this information, eyes bouncing between the cats splayed out around the room. "Then, all cats are smiling."

Touché.

Bella blinked, quietly processing Carolina's response. For a second, it looked like she wanted to counter—her lips parted, a thought poised on the edge—but instead, she just gave a small nod. "I'm going to grab a tea."

She excused herself to the café counter without another word.

This had become somewhat of a routine the past couple of weeks. While the guys ground through back-to-back road series in Chicago and Kansas City, I visited Pawsitive Vibes, soaking up the scent of coffee and catnip, sometimes while I got some backend paperwork done. It had become my go-to office away from the office. The kitten-induced serotonin boost didn't hurt either.

Even better, I had befriended "Flora, Fauna, and Merryweather," aka Sherri, Celia, and Nancy, the trio of septuagenarians who owned and operated Pawsitive Vibes like some kind of modern-day *Golden Girls*. Talk about friendship goals.

I was currently working with them to coordinate a Roasters sponsored adoption event at the stadium, one where the fans could cuddle and, hopefully, take home their next furry friend. It wouldn't be the first time the team had partnered with a local animal shelter—just last month, we had orchestrated a jersey auction with paw prints smeared across the fabric courtesy of some rescue dogs—but the idea of filling the concourse with cats and kittens, especially from an organization so dear to the man I loved, felt like something special.

And then, there was the calendar.

I had taken Nessa up on her suggestion. The Roasters were getting a calendar—a sexy one, with rescue animals—just in time for next year's holiday season. *Merry fucking Christmas, baseball fans.*

Now I just needed to talk Brooks into posing for it.

"I should get a cat for Smutty Buddies," Nessa said, sweeping her hand across the back of black furball. "And name him something romance-y, like Axel. Or Wyatt."

"Sebastian," I offered. "There's always a Sebastian."

"It's like the universal romance hero fuckboy name." She sank into one of the café's mismatched chairs. "Even though I've never met a Sebastain in my life."

I pressed a hand over my bump and eased into the chair opposite her with a sigh of relief. Pregnancy had turned sitting down into an Olympic event.

Nessa's grin sharpened. "Speaking of romance heroes, I was thinking about something the other day that I wanted to run by you."

"And how much nudity is involved in this one?"

"Minimal, at best."

I laughed so hard, my bump jiggled. "Hit me with it."

"Okay, imagine this . . . A baseball romance signing event at the stadium during the off-season. Authors, merch tables, and maybe a few photo ops with the guys."

I tilted my head, already spinning through the logistics. This was the part of my job I loved most—taking a half-formed idea and figuring out how to make it sing, how to connect it with the fans, the brand, the bigger picture. My brain immediately started sifting through dates, sponsorship tie-ins, and at least half a dozen ways we could market the hell out of an event like this.

"That could work," I told her. "Off-season, we'd have the space and staff available. Authors would get exposure to a whole new audience, fans would get an excuse to come back into the park, and the team could promote it as a community crossover event. Sponsors would eat it up."

Nessa leaned back, smug as hell. "I knew you'd see the vision."

I took another sip of chai, fingers drumming against my bump as the idea solidified. "We would need to frame it right. Something playful but accessible. Not just for romance readers, but also baseball fans who might get curious. It would help if we could tie in a charity, too. Maybe a portion of the ticket sales could go to a literacy program or library?"

"Damn, Dani."

I arched my brow. "What?"

"You make my harebrained ideas sound like marketing gold."

I shrugged, but inside I was already drafting the pitch in my head—just one more thing to add to my "before birth" to-do list.

We batted around ideas for another ten minutes or so, sketching out possible author panels and merch tie-ins until eventually, the scrape of a chair signaled Bella's return. She sat down across from us with her tea balanced in one hand, her book in the other. The title—*Beekeeping Basics: From Hive to Honey*—was printed in bold yellow letters across the cover.

Carolina moseyed over to our table with a kitten cradled in her arms like a baby. "Can we take him home, Dani? *Please.*"

"Not today, sweetie."

Carolina shot me a pout that looked suspiciously like Brooks's game-day scowl.

God help me, I'm in trouble.

"But he purrs like a motorboat," she announced proudly.

"Fun fact," Bella said without looking up from her book. "Cats can purr both when they inhale and exhale. It's one of the only sounds they can make continuously."

Carolina's eyes went wide. "Like a superpower."

Nessa shot me a grin before turning casually toward Bella. "You know, Belles, now that Dani is moving in with Brooks, a room is opening up at our place. Bennett was interested in maybe moving in."

Bella blinked, finally glancing up. "That sounds nice."

I hid my smile behind my drink.

"Although, if he's going to live with you and Jared, you both should probably consider learning some ASL," she quickly added. Her brows furrowed like she was trying to solve an advanced equation. "He signs a little different when he's excited. His movements are sharper and faster. And he pushes his hair back behind his ear when he's thinking about what to say."

Nessa's brows shot up, but Bella had already gone back to reading.

"I have a few books on sign language, though," she added matter-of-factly, flipping a page. "You can borrow them if you want."

I bit back a smile, warmth blooming in my chest. Bella wasn't the type to gush or daydream out loud, not like Clarke or, hell, me. But the way she had catalogued those tiny details said plenty. I knew what it meant to notice someone like that. To want to learn their language . . . literally.

Still, neither of us were about to push her. Bella might've been blunt as hell, but her heart was softer than she let on. She didn't need us meddling. What she needed was space to figure it out herself.

So, I just sipped my latte and filed away the information like any good pseudo-older sister would. Besides, if Bennett had half a brain in that handsome head of his, he'd catch on eventually.

I shifted in my chair, wincing as something—well, someone—pressed against my ribs. "Oh, for the love of—" I set my chai latte down and rubbed a hand across my belly. "BB's doing gymnastics again."

Carolina's head snapped up from where she'd been coaxing the ginger tabby onto her lap. "Can I feel her?"

"Of course." I leaned back a little, tugging my shirt tighter across the swell of my stomach. Carolina's small palm pressed against me, tentative but eager, and a second later, the baby rolled again, right under her hand.

Her face lit up, pure wonder. "She's saying hi to me."

I laughed, even as my eyes stung. "Guess she is."

It wasn't the first time—Carolina had asked to feel the baby almost every day since I'd started showing—but each time hit me harder.

Every morning, after she stayed the night with Brooks and me, she'd sit next to me on the couch, hand glued to my stomach, whispering secrets to the bump as if the baby could understand. Watching her now, brown eyes wide and solemn, hand spread over my belly like she was guarding it, I couldn't help but think about how lucky and loved this kid was already. Not just by me and Brooks, but by Carolina, too.

Her grin went lopsided, a little shy. "I can't wait to meet her."

"It won't be long now," I said, covering her hand with mine and smiling. "You're going to be the best big sister."

"I know."

My chest ached, but in the best way.

This was it, the life I hadn't realized I'd been craving. A circle that kept widening, making room for me in ways I hadn't known possible.

Brooks and Carolina. Pink, the brother I had always wanted. Nessa, with her books and loud opinions. Clarke, June, and the rest of my chaos crew. They weren't just friends or coworkers anymore; they were family. The kind I'd always secretly wanted, the kind I was finally building.

A soft *meow* pulled my gaze down.

The ginger tabby I'd seen earlier hopped up onto the empty chair beside me, her tail curling neatly around her paws as if she'd chosen her seat with purpose. Wide amber eyes blinked up at me, unbothered, patient. Like she knew something I didn't.

"Hiya, pretty girl."

I reached out and scratched gently under her chin. She leaned into it without hesitation, purring loud enough to rattle her whole body.

"Yeah," I whispered, smiling despite myself. "I get it."

Brooks

The house was dark when I slipped the key into the lock, quiet except for the low hum of the fridge. My bag slid off my shoulder with a dull thud, and for the first time all week, I let myself breathe.

Road series were always a grind, but being away while Dani was this far along in her pregnancy felt different, especially since she was under strict instruction not to travel anymore. I hated leaving her. Hated knowing she was counting the days until I came home, same as I was.

The funny thing was, I even missed the parts I used to groan about. Like the way she somehow always managed to rope me into those ridiculous social media trends with the rest of the team, insisting that as the coach, it was necessary for me to "lead by example."

One week, it had been a TikTok dance challenge with Roman and Pink flailing around like idiots while I'd stood stiff as a board in the back, looking like someone's pissed-off dad. Another time, she'd strapped her phone to my chest in one of those harnesses during batting practice. I'd spent the entire time trying not to swear like a fucking sailor. And then there was the "finish the lyric" challenge she'd filmed during warm-ups one day—me deadpan, muttering lyrics from some boy band Carolina loved while the bullpen had belted them off-key like it was karaoke night.

And sure, I rolled my eyes and grumbled, but the truth was, I loved it. I loved her laugh when I messed up the moves, loved knowing she was the one holding the camera, spinning her magic out of our chaos.

Without her, the days felt too quiet. The wins were flatter. Even the losses didn't sting the same. They just felt . . . empty.

The only thing that gave me comfort was knowing that she was waiting for me at home, in bed. *Our* bed.

I padded into the living room and froze.

Apparently, I had spoken too soon. She hadn't even made it to bed tonight.

Dani was out cold on the couch, curled into the corner with her tiny tank top rucked up over her belly, and even tinier shorts bunched up around her hips. Carolina was tucked into her side, cheek pressed to Dani's belly, her arm thrown over it like she was already hugging her baby sister.

Both of my girls. Together.

All three of them really.

My throat went tight. *Christ.* The sight hit me square in the chest—I hadn't realized how much I needed it until just now.

I crouched beside them, brushing a hand gently over Dani's hair. The vibrant blue she usually kept streaked through it had faded in the summer sun, softening now into a silvery pastel that glowed against the dark strands.

"Kitten," I murmured softly, not wanting to startle her. "I'm home."

Her lashes fluttered before her eyes blinked open, hazy with sleep. When they focused on me, a slow, sleepy smile curved across her face. "Hey, coach," she whispered, her voice rough with exhaustion but warm enough to melt me straight through.

Something stirred low in my gut at the sight of her like that—soft, undone, eyes heavy-lidded in the dim glow of the lamp. It was the same look she got after I'd fucked her slow and deep, sated and wrecked in the best way. The kind of look that made me want to scoop her up and never let her go.

I bent down and kissed her forehead, lingering there for a moment just to breathe her in. She smelled like her shampoo and faintly of Carolina's strawberry-vanilla bubble bath, the kind of mix I never wanted to wash away.

Carolina stirred against her side, shifting but not waking. Dani glanced down at her then back up at me, her smile soft but tired. I understood without her saying a word.

Carefully, I slid my arms under Carolina, lifting her small body against my chest. She murmured something unintelligible before burrowing into my shoulder, still fast asleep. Dani eased herself up with a quiet groan, adjusting the blanket around her shoulders before trailing after me up the stairs.

We moved together in silence, the kind born from knowing each other's rhythms. I laid Carolina down in her bed, pulling the covers up around her and brushing a kiss over her temple. Dani smoothed her hair back with one gentle hand, eyes lingering on her like she could stay there forever.

When she straightened, she caught my hand and tugged me back down the hall. "Come on," she whispered. "I have a present for you."

I arched a brow, keeping my voice low. "Mm, that sounds promising. But I probably need a shower first."

She smirked, lips quirking as she laced her fingers through mine. "Not everything's about your dick."

"But most things are," I muttered, tugging her close enough that her hip brushed mine as we walked down the hall. She squeezed my hand, eyes sparkling with interest despite the exhaustion still clinging to her features.

"Take a load off, coach," she said, closing the bedroom door behind us. A nervous smile tugged at her lips when she handed me a wrapped book before settling onto the bed beside me.

When I opened it, I damn near forgot how to breathe.

It wasn't just a photo album. It was *our* story, pieced together in her hands.

The first page was the sonogram photo—the one we'd nearly lost to my shortstop's demon dog—its corners still smudged and torn. It was now pressed flat and safe behind plastic, surrounded by stickers—baby bottles, baseballs, and a jar of pickles—as well as a small, handwritten note in Dani's loopy scrawl: *16 weeks, the size of an avocado.*

I kept turning pages, each one punching a hole straight through me. Dani with her bump framed between the dugout rails, her shirt riding up as she leaned on the bench like she owned the whole damn stadium. Dani laughing with her friends at Thorn Tavern, one hand on her belly like she was already protecting what was ours. A series of pregnancy progress shots she must've taken every few weeks—her growing stomach framed by the same bathroom mirror, the same cocky tilt to her mouth, like she was daring me not to fall harder.

Each picture came with a message, sticky notes with silly little captions only she could've written. *I went to field day and all I got was this beachball belly* under the shot of her stomach painted in stripes, or *The biggest wiener: Coach Daddy* next to a particularly incriminating photo from my dadchelor party.

Every page was layered like that—photos, stickers, scraps of our lives woven together like she was building us a scrapbook in real time. It wasn't neat or polished, like something you might buy in a store. Instead, it was messy and funny and so perfectly *her*, and it felt so much more like *us* because of it.

"Dani." I choked. "I—"

My chest ached, full to bursting as I flipped another page, then another, each one anchoring me deeper to her, to this life we were building. The sonogram, the painted belly, her laughter, my smile—it was all here, proof that we'd lived it, that I hadn't dreamed her up.

I closed the book gently, laying it on the bed between us. "This is the best thing anyone's ever given me," I finally managed, my voice shredded with everything I couldn't say. I cupped her face between my hands. "You—fuck, Dani—*you're* the best thing that's ever happened to me."

Her lashes fluttered, her hands curling into my shirt, and for a long, quiet beat, it was just the two of us breathing the same air.

"I just thought one day, our little girl might want to see it all. What it looked like before she was here. And—"

She bit her lip, suddenly shy, like she hadn't just destroyed me with the most beautiful gift I'd ever been handed.

"—how her mama fell in love with her daddy."

Her voice was quiet, but it hit me like a fastball to the gut. For a second, I forgot how to breathe.

My head snapped up, eyes locking on hers. She just sat there, staring at me like she'd ripped her chest open and handed me everything inside it.

She loved me. Dani Bernal fucking loved me.

A slow, certain smile pulled at my mouth—no smirk, no front, nothing but the raw truth burning through me. "Say it again," I rasped, my voice so wrecked I barely recognized it.

"I love you," she repeated, stronger this time, like she knew I needed to hear it twice just to believe it. "I love you, Brooks."

That was it. I was gone.

I pulled her over my thighs until she straddled my lap, bracketed her face with my hands, and kissed her like she'd just handed me the greatest victory of my life. Hell, maybe she had. I kissed her until my lips ached, until she was clinging to me like I was the only thing keeping us both upright.

When I finally tore my mouth from hers, I pressed my forehead to hers, breath ragged.

"Kitten," I growled, rougher than I'd meant to. "You don't get it. I've *been* in love with you. Since before the baby. Since before all this shit. You just beat me to saying it out loud."

Her eyes shimmered. "You mean it?"

I barked out a sharp laugh, the kind that sounded more like disbelief than humor. "Mean it? Dani, I'd etch it into my skin if that's what it took to make you believe me."

Her hand slid over my chest, her fingertip finding the spot where, beneath the thin cotton of my shirt, the tattooed kitten marked my heart. She looked up at me through her lashes, a small smile tugging at her mouth. "I think you already did."

The way she looked at me then—wild and wanting and mine—nearly leveled me. Heat surged through me, a sting pressing behind my eyes, and I couldn't stop myself. I kissed her again, rough and greedy.

"By the way," she muttered against my lips. "You missed a few pages."

"I'll look at them tomorrow," I said between kisses, not about to break the spell of her body pressed against mine. Nothing was more important than this, *us* right now.

Her mouth curved against mine slyly. "Oh, I think you're going to want to see them."

That made me pause. Reluctantly, I pulled back just enough to glance at the album lying abandoned on the bed. Every part of me wanted to stay buried in her kiss, but the look in her eyes—mischief and nerves tangled together—had me reaching for it.

I thumbed to the back pages and—

Holy. Shit.

My cock twitched instantly.

There she was. Dani, stretched out on a set of white, rumpled sheets. Naked. One shot had her lying on her side, hand draped low, her tattoos framing the curve of her stomach like art. Another—*fuck*—had her on her back, thighs parted just enough, belly front and center, nipples tight and dark as if daring me to look away.

I couldn't.

"Holy fuck, kitten," I breathed, my voice ragged. My thumb hovered over the image, not touching, just tracing the shape of her like it could burn into me. "God, you're perfect. Do you know what this does to me?"

Her teeth caught her lip, a flush blooming across her cheeks. She didn't answer, and she didn't need to.

"I have a pretty good idea," she teased, rocking against the erection tenting my sweats. "But you're welcome to show me your appreciation."

And just like that, reverence gave way to need.

She gave a startled laugh as I shifted, guiding her back until she was stretched across the mattress. The album slid to the floor with a soft thump, forgotten, while I braced myself over her.

God, she was beautiful like this—hair fanned wild against the pillow, belly round and proud between us, lips swollen from my kisses.

"Look at you," I muttered, my mouth dragging down her throat. "My perfect girl. My perfect mama."

Her fingers tangled in my shirt, tugging, urging me closer. I shoved it over my head and ground against her, groaning at the heat radiating through her thin sleep shorts. She arched beneath me, gasping when my hands slid under her top to cup her tits, thumbs brushing over her sensitive nipples.

"Brooks," she moaned, her hips rocking up, hungry. "God, I need you."

And just when I was ready to tear those shorts down her legs and bury myself inside her, a sharp sound cut through the room.

"Mrrrow."

I lifted my head, blinking toward the closet door. A small orange tabby sat there like she owned the place, tail flicking, green eyes fixed on us with pointed disapproval.

"Umm, Dani?" I muttered, half out of my mind with lust.

Dani bit her lip like she'd been caught red-handed. "Oh, yeah," she said, her eyes dancing. "Funny story—"

"I can't wait to hear it," I said, my voice low, already caving even with my hands still full of her tits.

She pushed at my chest just enough to sit up on her elbows, cheeks flushed and hair mussed, looking equally guilty and smug. "So, I've been spending a lot of time at Pawsitive Vibes since I'm not allowed to travel anymore. Which, I get—doctor's orders and all that—but a girl has to find a serotonin boost wherever she can. And the cats have basically become my support group. And this beautiful girl—"

She nodded toward the tabby, who was now licking her paw like we weren't the rudest interruption in the world.

"—was abandoned by her owners. Just left behind when they moved. Can you believe that? And she's sweet, Brooks. Well, sweet in that prickly, I-only-like-you kind of way. She follows me around the café, sits in my lap while I work on social posts. She even headbutted me once, which I've realized is basically a feline declaration of love."

The cat meowed again, as if to back her up. Great, they were already double-teaming me.

Dani's voice softened. "I just . . . I couldn't leave her. Not when she'd already been tossed aside once."

Something in my chest just cracked wide open. Of course, Dani had done this. Of course, she'd taken one look at something abandoned, something unwanted, and had decided to make it hers. To make it family.

My throat went tight, my hands still cupping her breasts because I couldn't seem to let go. "Kitten, you're gonna make me fall in love with you all over again."

Her smile was small and knowing, the kind that told me she already understood. My mouth brushed her cheek, my voice dropping low, filthy. "But don't think this gets you out of what I promised. Once we get her—"

"Velma," she cut in, grinning.

I pulled back just enough to give her a look. "Seriously?"

She laughed, wicked and unrepentant. "Don't act surprised, coach. You knew what you were signing up for."

I smirked and slid my hand lower, over the curve of her belly, teasing the waistband of her shorts. My voice turned rough again. "Once we get *Velma* settled for the night, I'm still gonna lay you back and eat your pussy until you scream my name loud enough to wake the neighbors."

Her breath hitched, her pupils blown wide as her nails dug into my shoulders. "Deal."

Dani

Roasters 92–70

I'd once written a paper during my first master's program about the validity of athletic rituals, seemingly silly things that players believed in like wearing a particular brand of briefs on gameday or drawing in the dirt before each at bat. And much like the sports psychologists who had come before me, I had concluded that these superstitions were, more than anything, a way to help a player feel grounded and focused.

I respected them, even found them fascinating to study, but I'd never really felt the pull of them myself. My brain leaned more toward facts and explanations, hence my obsession with true crime documentaries and horror films, my comfort watches.

Pink had even gotten me a book of children's ghost stories, which I had taken to reading aloud to my belly at night. Brooks hadn't exactly been thrilled about me introducing our baby to tales of haunted lighthouses and vengeful spirits before she was even born, but he put up with it, grumbling every time before settling in beside me anyway . . . so long as he could follow up whatever story I read with one of his own, lighter in tone.

I had never been the superstitious type myself. Not until Brooks had made *me* his pregame ritual.

"That's it," he growled, breath hot against my ear. "Fuck me back, kitten."

My palms were flat against the glass wall of my office, hours before the first pitch, the empty field stretched out in front of me. Rows of seats waiting to be filled, bases gleaming in the afternoon sun—none of it mattered. Not when Brooks's body caged mine in, his naked, sweaty chest pressed to my back, his cock driving into me with enough force to make the window shudder under my hands.

"God, kitten, you're soaked," he rasped. "Like you've been waiting for this all fucking day."

I had. And he knew it.

I moaned, forehead tipping against the cool glass as he filled me again and again, each stroke deeper than the last. My breasts bounced with every slam of his hips, nipples pebbling in the chilled air. He reached around, his calloused fingers closing over one tight peak, rolling it between his fingers until I gasped and arched into him.

The shock of pleasure tore through me, raw and sharp, making my pussy clench around him like I couldn't bear to let him go.

Brooks groaned low, like he couldn't get close enough, couldn't get deep enough. "Look out there," he ordered, voice wrecked, his breath hot against the side of my neck. "Empty seats, empty field. And you're mine. Before anyone else gets a piece of me tonight, I'm getting all of you."

I couldn't even remember when it had started. Maybe that first home game after I'd shown up in his jersey on the jumbotron. Or maybe when he'd started sneaking into my office between batting practice and first pitch. But at some point, it had become routine, unshakable as a lineup card.

Fine by me.

If Brooks needed to fuck me on every surface of the stadium to keep his wits—and hopefully get the win—who was I to complain?

"Look at you," he ground out, voice rough against my ear. "Tits bouncing, pussy dripping all over me."

"*Yessss,*" I choked out, my hips grinding back against him shamelessly, desperate for more. I could feel him everywhere, thick and heavy, filling me until my legs shook. "Harder, Brooks."

His hand slid up, covering mine against the glass, pinning me in place while the other curved around my front, finding my clit and working me in rough, perfect circles. My cry bounced back at me in the empty office, loud and broken.

"Perfect, kitten," he growled in my ear. "You're my favorite goddamn lucky charm."

My laugh broke into a gasp as he thrust harder, deeper, stealing every ounce of air I had left. "Pretty sure this is more for you than the team."

His teeth scraped my shoulder. "Win-win."

He bent me deeper, chest pressed to my back, hips pounding into me so hard my knees nearly buckled. His rhythm turned merciless, grunts punctuating every slap of skin. The pleasure was brutal, overwhelming, curling sharp and hot through my body until I was gasping, teetering right on the edge.

"Come for me, Dani," he commanded, rubbing my clit harder, faster. "Let the whole damn world know who you belong to."

If you insist . . .

I shattered around him, crying out as my orgasm tore through me, pleasure detonating so hard my vision went white. My walls clamped down on him, milking his cock, and his low, guttural groan was pure sin. He kept thrusting through it, chasing his own release, until he buried himself to the hilt and spilled inside me with a ragged curse.

The glass cooled under my forehead as my body went limp. *Holy fuck.* Who needed spicy foods or long walks? This man was going to send me into labor any day now with the power of his perfect fucking penis. That would be a fun one to explain to our daughter one day.

When my legs finally gave out, Brooks caught me, humming low and steady against my hair as he eased me back. He straightened my maternity bra back into place and smoothed my shirt down with those big, careful hands, his touch suddenly gentle where moments before it had been rough and raw. He crouched to tug my leggings back up, pressing a kiss against my hip like an apology and a promise all at once.

And then, he dropped to his knees in front of me, palms sliding over the curve of my belly. He pressed his forehead to it, voice soft but certain. "Listen up, baby B. It's our last game before the playoffs, and Daddy's gonna go out there and win for you," he told our daughter. "But the truth is, you're the real prize. You and your mama."

The words hit me harder than any orgasm ever could.

I looked down at him, all six-plus feet of tattooed, muscle-bound Coach Daddy folded onto the office carpet like it was an altar. His big hands cradled my belly with reverence that made my chest ache. He'd just fucked me against the glass like I was his dirty little secret—even though we both knew I was anything but—and now here he was, talking to our baby like she was the most sacred thing he'd ever known.

The contrast was dizzying. And devastating.

I pressed a hand to the back of his head, threading my fingers through his hair, watching him soften in a way I hadn't thought possible. He wasn't doing this because he thought he had to or because it looked good. Brooks meant every word. I could feel it radiating off him, grounding me even as the emotions swelled too big in my chest.

Lately, as the weeks ticked down, closing in on my due date, I'd been thinking about my mom more than usual. Not because I'd suddenly forgiven her, but because I couldn't help seeing the gaps. The ache of what she'd never had.

She'd never had this.

All those nights she'd worked doubles, stringing us together with grit and exhaustion, she hadn't had a partner kneeling at her feet, holding her steady. No one to kiss her swollen belly like it was the most sacred thing in the world, no anchor, no quiet strength to lean on. Just her alone, carrying it all.

And maybe some part of me had always assumed that would be my story too.

But Brooks was rewriting it.

I blinked hard, my throat tight. God, I was lucky, so fucking lucky that he was the one. That this messy, imperfect, beautiful man was the father of my baby. My partner. *My love.*

He stayed there for another minute or so, murmuring low against my belly, his lips brushing over the curve of me like he was telling our daughter secrets. I didn't even need to hear the words to know what they were: promises. Fierce and steady vows, the kind he'd keep no matter what.

I glanced at the clock on the wall, the red digits blinking back at me, and sighed. "Okay, *Daddy*," I teased, sliding my hands over his to pull his attention up. I gave him a flirty, little look over the swell of my belly. "You have a game to go get ready for. And *Mama* needs to clean up the mess you made in her c-u-n-t."

His head snapped up, eyes blazing, and for a second, I thought he really might say screw the game. His hands tightened on my hips, his cock already hardening again against my thigh. "*Kitten*," he groaned, the word rough enough to scrape over my skin. "You can't just say shit like that when I have somewhere to be."

"Consider it motivation," I said sweetly, though my grin gave me away.

He cursed under his breath, kissing me like he wanted to drag me right back down to the floor. And god, what I wouldn't give to get lost in him all over again. But just then, my stomach tightened, a low cramp rolling through me that had me sucking in a sharp breath.

Brooks froze instantly. "What was that?"

"Nothing," I said quickly, straightening, forcing a smile. "Just one of those Braxton Hicks things. Practice runs. Dr. Kong warned me they'd get stronger the closer we get to the big day."

His jaw worked, worry flickering across his face even as he searched mine.

I kissed his chin, softer this time. "Go. I promise, if it turns into something, you'll be the first to know, but right now? You've got a game to win."

He didn't move. Not right away, at least. It looked like he was trying to decide whether to believe me or whisk me away to the emergency room. Finally, he exhaled through his nose and pressed his forehead to mine. "You scare the hell out of me, kitten," he murmured.

"Good," I whispered back, brushing my lips to his. "Means you'll come running."

"Always."

By the top of the seventh inning, I knew I was in labor.

I'd been telling myself it was nothing for the past hour, just stronger Braxton Hicks, my body gearing up for the real thing that was still two weeks out. The truth hit me with every wave that rolled through my belly, sharp enough to steal my breath.

I clenched my tablet a little harder, forcing my focus on the half-finished caption glowing back at me. *Just a few more innings, BB.* I smoothed a hand over my stomach, willing my baby girl to be patient, a fruitless endeavor considering who her mother was.

"Are you okay?" Clarke asked, her eyes bouncing between me and the field. The game was tied at three, and the entire stadium was on edge because of it. "You're breathing kind of weird."

"I'm fine," I lied, though my nails dug crescents into my thigh. Another contraction gripped me, hot and merciless, and this time I had to fold forward with a muffled groan.

Clarke gasped. "Oh, my stars! You're in labor."

"No, I'm—" A curse tore out of me, startling a kid in a Roasters jersey at the end of a nearby row. "Okay, fine. I'm in labor."

Clarke went pale, fumbling for her phone. "I'm calling Brooks."

"He's not going to answer," I snapped, forcing myself upright. "He doesn't keep his phone on him during games."

"Why would he do that?" she shot back. "You're having a baby!"

"Clarke." I panted, a cramp knocking the air out of me. "I can wait. Just . . . let him finish. I can manage another inning or two."

She stared at me like I'd lost my mind. And maybe I had because another contraction ripped through me, sharper than the last, and I yelped, clutching my belly.

This was not how this was supposed to go. Brooks and I had a plan—a hospital bag packed to the gills, a carefully mapped route, the "Push it" labor playlist loaded onto my phone that we'd argued over for hours because Brooks refused to accept that he had horrendous taste in music. And yet, here I was, doubled over between Clarke and section 112, my birth plan unraveling like cheap twine.

But I would be damned if this baby was born six feet from the cotton candy cart.

"Fuck this," Clarke said, already yanking me to my feet. "We're not waiting."

Even through the pain, a startled laugh tore out of me. Clarke hardly ever swore. She was all sweet tea and Southern manners, the kind of woman who said *shoot* instead of *shit*. Hearing her drop an F-bomb was almost enough to distract me from the fire ripping through my belly.

We hobbled down the stairs, me half-bent over her arm, both of us weaving through the narrow tunnel. The dugout wasn't far, but the bullpen was closer. And Clarke was single-minded, dragging me along like her life depended on it.

"Hang on, Dani." My legs shook, sweat dampening the back of my neck. "We're almost there."

By the time we stumbled into the bullpen, the guys sitting there shot to their feet, eyes wide. And right in the middle of them—Jared Pink.

He took one look at me doubled over, one arm wrapped tight around my belly, and his face went white. "Holy shit. Dani? Are you—"

"In labor," Clarke snapped, practically shoving me into the nearest chair. "And we need Brooks. Now."

Pink froze, mouth opening and closing like he'd just been asked to solve advanced calculus. "Wait, like *labor* labor? The baby is coming?"

"Yes, Jared!" Clarke barked. "Get Brooks on the line now."

That shook him out of it. "Oh, fuck. Right, phone!"

He skidded to the wall, grabbing the bullpen receiver like it might explode in his hands. His long legs tangled in the cord as he fumbled, nearly tripping over his own cleats. "Coach? Uh, yeah, don't freak out, but also, you might actually freak out—"

"Give me the phone, Sir Pink-a-lot." I panted, staggering up enough to snatch the receiver right out of his hand.

Pink yelped and threw his arms up. "Oh, thank God."

I pressed the phone hard to my ear, another contraction gripping me so tight it felt like my spine might snap in half. My voice came out raw, uneven. "Brooks?"

There was a pause, the crackle of dugout noise bleeding through the line, and then his voice, low and edged with alarm. "Kitten, what's wrong? Where are you—"

My free hand lifted, weak but certain, and I waved toward the dugout.

Across the diamond, I saw him. Brooks stood at the very edge of the dugout steps, the bullpen phone pressed to his ear, his other hand braced hard against the rail. Our eyes locked across the field—him in his jersey, me doubled over in the bullpen—and the noise of the game, the crowd, everything fell away.

My eyes squeezed shut. "It's time."

The line went dead.

Brooks

"Well, that was fun," Dani rasped, her voice wrecked but wry. "But I'd rather not do it again."

Her head lolled back against the hospital pillow, her hair damp with sweat. In her arms was the tiniest, most perfect girl I had ever laid eyes on—well, tied for first. Pink cheeks, green eyes, and a head full of dark hair already escaping her custom, knitted Roasters hat.

Our baby.

I huffed a laugh, my chest too full to manage anything more. "You were incredible, kitten," I said, leaning down to press a kiss to her temple. "Absolutely fucking incredible."

She tilted her head enough to meet my eyes. "I had a lot of help."

I swallowed hard, brushing a thumb down her cheek. Truth was, I hadn't done a damn thing compared to her. Sure, I'd held her hand, barked at a few nurses, whispered every encouragement I could think of. But the real work? That had been all her. Nine plus hours of sweat, pain, and grit as she pushed our girl into the world. And she'd done it with a strength that made me fall in love with her all over again.

"Help?" I said, shaking my head. "Dani, I just sat there like a useless fool while you did the impossible. You carried her. You brought her here. That was all you."

Her lips curved, tired but sharp as ever. "Uh-huh. And now you're stuck loving me even after seeing my vagina turn into a crime scene."

I barked out a laugh, startled and hoarse. "Jesus, kitten."

"You are still gonna love it, right? Even after . . . all that?"

My chest tightened, and I bent closer, letting my lips graze her ear. "Kitten, I'd build a shrine to your pussy if I thought the hospital would let me."

Her tired laugh caught, broke, then melted into a grin that hit me harder than any foul ball.

The sound quieted, leaving just the steady beep of the monitors and the soft squeak of the baby shifting in her arms. I let my forehead rest against Dani's, reminding myself for the umpteenth time today that she was safe, our baby was safe, and I was the luckiest bastard in the world.

"She's beautiful," Dani whispered, her voice cracking on the word.

My throat closed as I looked at her. I'd bet my left nut that every parent thought their kid was the most beautiful baby in the world. The difference was, they were all wrong. Because this one, our girl with her scrunched-up nose and perfect little fists, she was the real deal. And she'd gotten it all from her mama.

I brushed a kiss across Dani's damp temple, my voice rough with conviction. "Sorry, but it's official. Every other parent's been lying to themselves. Ours is the reigning champ."

Dani huffed a soft, watery laugh. "Coach, you can't just turn our daughter into a competition."

"Can and did," I said, grinning down at her like she'd just clinched the World Series. "She's already my MVP."

"I can't believe she's really ours."

I slid an arm around her shoulders, pulling her against me so I could look too, our daughter nestled between us like the missing piece we hadn't even known we'd been waiting for. My chest squeezed so hard it almost hurt. "Yeah," I said, my voice wrecked. "Ours."

For a long while, neither of us spoke. We just stared at her, counting every finger, every breath, letting the quiet wrap around us like something sacred. And in that silence, I knew without a doubt—no game, no win, no championship ring could ever come close to this.

Finally, Dani dragged her gaze up to me, eyes still shining with exhaustion. "So . . . ," she whispered, a hint of a smirk tugging at her lips. "Did we win?"

"Doesn't matter," I replied, leaning in to kiss her again. "I already won."

For a minute, I just breathed her in—her sweat, her shampoo, the faint antiseptic of the hospital room—and then, like a replay on the jumbotron, flashes of how we'd gotten here rolled through me.

Pink's panicked voice on the bullpen phone. Dani's voice, raw and uneven, telling me it was time. The way my chest had split wide open when I'd glanced across the field and seen her, doubled over, waving at me from left field while I'd stood frozen at the dugout rail. I didn't even remember dropping the phone. Just running, barreling through the tunnel, ignoring every shout behind me.

The ten-minute car ride to the hospital had felt like an hour—me gripping the wheel like I was a character out of *The Fast and the Furious*, Clarke in the back seat, trying to coach Dani through her breathing, Dani cursing me and my "incredible cock" for getting her into this mess.

And then came the hospital. Doctors barking orders. Me at her side, holding her hand so tight my knuckles cracked, kissing sweat from her forehead while she bore down through hours of pain I couldn't shoulder for her.

And somehow, she'd done it. My fierce, stubborn, impossible woman had brought our daughter into the world.

"You still with me, coach?" she asked softly.

I blinked back to the present, my vision blurring when I looked at her again. "Always," I said, my voice breaking.

Her lips curved, tired but teasing. Then she looked down at the tiny bundle in her arms, brushing a fingertip over our daughter's downy hair. "Want to hold her again?"

"Yeah," I rasped, already reaching before the word was out of my mouth.

Dani shifted carefully, easing our little girl into my arms. My throat went tight because somehow, she was both fragile and indestructible, everything I'd never known I needed until she was here.

I rocked her gently, brushing a thumb over the softness of her cheek. "You know, at some point we're going to have to give her name. Unless you want to stick with BB?"

Dani's voice came quiet, tentative. "I was thinking about Bailey."

My gaze flicked to hers. "Bailey?"

She nodded, smoothing a silvery-blue strand of hair back from her damp forehead. "Bailey Bernal. I know you wanted her to have your name . . . and I do, too. This way, she gets a little piece of both of us."

For a moment, I couldn't speak. Couldn't breathe. Just looked from Dani, glowing and spent in the hospital bed, to the tiny miracle in my arms.

Bailey Bernal. Our girl. *Ours.*

My chest squeezed, a laugh catching in my throat. "Kitten, that's perfect." I bent, kissing our daughter's forehead, my heart hammering. "Bailey Bernal."

The name settled in my bones, steady and sure, like it had always been hers. Like it had been waiting for us, for this moment. I traced a finger along the curve of her tiny ear, marveling at how something so small could tilt my entire world on its axis. She was only a few hours old, but already she had me wrapped around her itty-bitty finger.

"Bailey," I repeated.

A soft knock pulled me from my thoughts. Dani's brows lifted in surprise as the door eased open. Allie stepped inside, her hand resting lightly on Carolina's shoulder. She looked tired, because who wouldn't be after shepherding a six-year-old through the longest night of their little life? Nonetheless, her smile was warm and genuine.

"Congratulations," she said softly, her gaze flicking between Dani and me before settling on the bundle in my arms.

"Thank you," I managed, my voice thick. "You didn't have to stay so late."

"Somebody insisted she meet her little sister."

Carolina practically vibrated with energy, bouncing on her toes as her eyes went wide. "Can I see her? Is she here?"

Dani's smile spread, luminous even in her exhaustion. "Of course you can, sweetheart. Come meet Bailey."

Allie gave Carolina's shoulder a gentle squeeze and then stepped back, letting her daughter dart toward us, her excitement filling the room like sunlight. Carolina's eyes went as round as saucers when she reached the bedside. She climbed carefully onto the chair beside me, her knees tucked under her, and peered down at the tiny bundle in my arms.

"She's so small," she whispered, awe written all over her face. Then, after a long pause, her little brow furrowed. "She looks like one of my dolls."

Dani let out a tired laugh, brushing her hand through Carolina's hair. "She's real, I promise."

Carolina studied her sister another beat, then grinned, showing off the small gap where her tooth used to be. The tooth fairy had visited twice in the past month. "And she poops, right? Because my dolls don't do that."

The room filled with laughter. But when Carolina leaned closer, pressing one tiny finger to Bailey's palm and gasping when her sister's fist curled tight around it, her smile softened.

"She likes me," she whispered, her voice reverent. Then she wrinkled her nose thoughtfully, leaning closer to sniff. "She smells kind of like sugar cookies."

Dani blinked, amused. "Sugar cookies, huh?"

Carolina nodded seriously, her eyes never leaving Bailey. "Mm-hmm, warm and buttery. I guess that means she's gonna be the sweetest sister ever."

Silence fell for a moment, thick and fragile, and I thought my chest might split open right there.

I pressed a kiss to the top of Carolina's head, my voice like gravel. "That's exactly right, sweetheart."

Dani's breath hitched, and then the tears came fast, hot, and unstoppable. She pressed a trembling hand over her mouth, laughing through the sob that broke free. "Oh my god," she choked. "You can't just say things like that."

From the doorway, Allie smiled softly before slipping out, closing the door with the kind of quiet grace that made me grateful all over again for how we'd learned to move forward. And then it was just us.

The *four* of us.

I settled Bailey back into Dani's arms and helped Carolina curl up beside them. Within minutes, both of my little girls were asleep, their breaths syncing like some unspoken lullaby. Dani's lashes fluttered closed and then opened again. It was a losing battle, trying to fight off the exhaustion. I had a feeling that any second now, she'd be out like a light, too.

Now, though, the hospital room was still. Just me, half sprawled in a chair with my arm draped across the bed so I could keep a hand on Dani, my little girl warm in the crook of her arm, Carolina's soft hair tickling my wrist.

My whole damn world, right there in one frame.

Dani shifted, her tired eyes finding mine. "You okay, coach?" she whispered.

I huffed a laugh, leaning closer, careful not to wake the girls. "Better than okay." My throat worked as I looked at her, at them, at everything I never thought I'd get to have again. "Would this be an inappropriate time to ask you to marry me?"

Her eyes went wide, then narrowed in disbelief, her mouth curving like she couldn't decide whether to laugh or cry.

"Extremely inappropriate," she whispered back. "You're running on no sleep and hospital Jell-O, and I'm rocking the world's least sexy adult diaper. Try again later, Coach Daddy."

I smirked, brushing a thumb over her knuckles where my hand rested in hers. "Noted. I told you once, kitten, I'm playing the long game."

Her lips twitched, that sharp, knowing grin flashing for just a second before exhaustion pulled at her again. "Good," she murmured. Her lashes fluttered, her voice already thick with sleep. "And just so you know, when I *do* say yes, I won't be wearing some white, frilly dress."

I huffed a low laugh, leaning in to brush my mouth over her temple. "Kitten, I don't give a damn what color you wear—black, red, neon green. The only thing that matters is that I get to take it off you after we say 'I do.'"

Even half-asleep, she smirked. "Pervert."

"Yours," I murmured back, watching her finally drift into sleep.

I leaned down, pressing a kiss to her temple, then to the baby's downy head, then finally to Carolina's crown where she slept curled between us.

My girls. My family. The rest could wait.

For now, this was the only victory I needed.

Dani's breathing evened out, soft and steady, leaving me in the quiet hum of the hospital room. I shifted, careful not to wake either of them, and cradled Bailey closer against me. Her eyes blinked open, a flash of bright green so much like her mama's it nearly undid me.

"Hey, sweet girl," I greeted her, my voice low, meant just for her. "Do you want Daddy to tell you a story? It's about how your mama and I fell in love. And funnily enough, it started with these blue donut socks . . ."

Thank You

Thank you so much for reading *Addicted to Glove*.

I never thought I would see the day where I wrote a surprise pregnancy romance—childfree by choice girly, here—and yet, somehow I knew that that would be the only way to write Dani and Brooks' story.

This book is for every woman who's been told that motherhood should define her, and for every mother who's quietly wondered if she's "allowed" to still be her own person. *You are.* You always have been. Dani's journey is about what it means to become a mother without erasing the rest of yourself, to hold space for ambition, desire, fear, and joy—sometimes, all at once.

It's fucking terrifying to imagine bringing life into the world right now, but it's also brave. Brave to choose yourself, to question expectations, and to live fully in your truth, whatever that might look like. Thank you for spending time with this story. I hope it made you feel seen, or at the very least, a little less alone.

Stay tuned for the next book in the series, Bella and Bennett's story, coming in April 2026.

If you liked this book, please let me know and share with others by leaving a review on **Amazon** or **Goodreads :)**

Acknowledgements

I might not be a parent—nor do I have ambitions to be one—but I look at every one of my books as if they were my babies. Each one arrives into the world after a long, messy, and often miraculous process, and none of them could have come to life without the support and encouragement of a whole community of people. This one is no exception.

Mamasita, you've always been my number one reader, and for that, I will always be grateful. And even though I know you will probably *never* read my books, Papa Bear—which is probably for the best for all of us—you still deserve big praise for answering all of my random questions about baseball.

To my amazing editor, Norma. Thank you for your notes and more importantly, your flexibility. You always put up with me no matter how many times I send you "just one more set of pages" during crunch time.

As always, shoutout to my found family, aka the chat groups that keep me sane and entertained. The Ladies, not to be confused with The Gal$—two separate groups. The Real Housewives of Alameda, Thursday night writing club, the WhatsApp Bookish Girl Squad—you all know who you are and how much you mean to me. Thank you for the hours of input, memes, incessant questions (mine, not yours) and TikTok videos.

To the baristas at my new favorite coffee spot, The Great North, in Portland, Oregon, thank you for the coffee and writing space. And let's not forget about the Portland Pickles and

Hillsboro Hops, my local baseball squads. Your games never fail to provide . . . inspiration.

Finally, to the romance readers, and every person who has supported Boobies & Noobies over the years, thank you for welcoming me into your community. Every day, I am more and more thankful I picked up that copy of *I'm in No Mood for Love* by Rachel Gibson back in 2009. Who knows where I'd be or what I'd be doing today if I hadn't. Above all else, Boobies & Noobies has always been a podcast about exploring readers and writers' unique romance reading journeys. Thank you all for being a part of *my* romance reading and writing journey.

And as I say in every one of my newsletters...

Be feral. Stay dangerous.

About the Author

By day, Kelly Reynolds works primarily as a creative writing/screenwriting professor and author's assistant. By night, she hosts the comedic romance related podcast, Boobies & Noobies. She currently lives in Portland, Oregon. When she isn't writing, you can often find Kelly eating her way through hole-in-the-wall restaurants, tending to her side porch veggie garden, or binge watching old episodes of *Top Chef* or *Dateline*.

Keep up with Kelly on social media @authorkellyrey (Instagram and Threads) and @realkellyrey (Tiktok). You can also join her Facebook group, Kelly's Book Baddies, and subscribe to her Substack.

Keep up with Boobies & Noobies on social media @boobiespodcast, and listen wherever you stream your podcasts.

Books by Kelly Reynolds

Holidays in L.A.
Meet Me in Los Feliz
Venice Actually
Santa Monica Baby

Rose City Roasters
Hit it and Quit it
Pitches be Crazy
All Bats Are Off
Addicted to Glove

www.ingramcontent.com/pod-product-compliance
Lightning Source LLC
Chambersburg PA
CBHW020359110726
47899CB00006B/1778